Anne

A novel

Zarina Macha

Cover and back illustration by oliviaprodesign:
fiverr.com/oliviaprodesign

ISBN 978-1-9161326-0-3

www.zarinamacha.co.uk

Also by Zarina Macha:

Every Last Psycho: A Collection of Two Novellas

Art is a Waste of Time: Poetry Collection

For my wonderful mum and dad, with love and gratitude xxx

With special thanks to Jacqueline Wilson, my childhood role model. Your stories will always have a special place carved out in my heart.

Youth is wasted on the young.

— George Bernard Shaw

We will not regret the past nor wish to shut the door on it.

— From the Alcoholics Anonymous Step 9
Promises

Prologue

Picture this. A room with two cosy armchairs and a brown wooden table resting between them holding a small clock, tissues, and minuscule pieces of *Celebrations* chocolate. The temperature was not cold, and not hot, but that perfect warmth you get from adjusting both the window and radiator heating. In one of the armchairs sat a middle-aged man, bespectacled, foreign — German, perhaps — with a balding patch on his head and weight around his middle. A kind smile spread across his face, his head tilted, garnering the same curiosity as an inquisitive child. In the other chair sat a girl. Fourteen, black hair cane-rolled on top and pulled up into a tight bun. Black hands, black duffel coat, black shoes, black tights. All that shed a silver lining — or a blue one — were the sapphire-crystal earrings hanging from her ears.

The girl was me.

The foreign man peered at the clock. He and the girl had been sitting in the room for forty minutes, the slight utterance of monosyllabic dialogue passing between the two. The girl was staring at the floor, her face expressionless. With only twenty minutes left, the man took his cue to pick up the bowl holding the chocolate and offered one to her. She refused.

"I do like *Celebrations*," said the man. "Always a succulent choice." He was definitely German. "They really melt in the mouth. Maltesers are my personal favourite, though. They're the most popular, aren't they?"

I grunted in response. He sighed; not in exasperation, merely in concern. "I know this is only our second session, but it would be nice to hear a little bit from you."

I uncrossed my legs. It was amazing how interesting your shoes became when you had nothing to say.

"I'm not trying to force you," he said gently. "I know this has been difficult for you. You have had a lot to deal with recently, and in the past. But that is why I want you to know we are here for you. When somebody close to you dies, it's the most horrible thing in the world. That's why we want to help you get through this challenging time."

I closed my eyes, raising my head to the ceiling.

"How are you feeling right now?" he asked.

I shrugged.

"Anne, you are more than welcome to take your time, but remember, in here, you are safe. No one can hurt you. What we say is confidential, and you can say whatever you like."

He was right. And yet, the clenching in my stomach wouldn't stop. It was a reminder that no matter how awful things became, you were still left with the scars.

I spent the remaining twenty minutes in silence. So much had happened in my fourteen years of existence, I was unsure of how to form the words.

That week, I mulled over my previous two sessions and decided I was tired of being a prisoner of my past. I no longer saw the point of keeping myself closed off. Help had been offered to me, so surely now was the time to take it. I could keep the ghosts chained to me, or I could let them be released, freeing myself in the process.

When I returned to Henry — he said I could call him by his first name — that following Tuesday, I was ready to begin telling him everything.

Chapter One: Mummy and Daddy

I was born on the 7th of September 2000 at West Middlesex University Hospital. Mum was only twenty. My dad was in his mid-thirties; a self-made man.

They had met in 1998 at a club. She had been with a group of friends, dancing, slightly tipsy, wearing tight trousers, high-heels, and a crop top, unaware of the looming gentleman watching her. He softly tapped her on the shoulder, offering to buy her a drink. He had come from nowhere, shrouded in a sharp black suit and trilby hat. His gaze was intense as his razor-shaven face regarded her, carrying a self-assured coolness lacking in the boys she'd been dating.

He took her to musicals, fine restaurants, weekend visits to Paris and New York. He was a man of principle — a regular church-goer, always dressed in crisp suits. A year on, he proposed, and she said yes. They moved to Richmond, and the following year, had me. He swept her from her old life, wiping her old friends and mother away as if they were drawings on a chalkboard. She and her own mother never got on, and her father had died years prior to that. They'd lived in Clapton, miles from Richmond. Black people didn't live in Richmond. *White* people could barely afford to live in Richmond or Ealing or Harrow.

In the space of two years, she had gone from the Murder Mile to Palace de la Special, a tiny two-bedroomed flat to a vast residence. Long gaping corridors and soaring ceilings decorated our house. Not a trace of dust garnished the window ledges or Egyptian ornaments. The garden was filled with acid green hedges sharply pruned by the gardener and blood orange poppies fearfully peeping out of their stems.

My dad owned Mason's Units, a furniture company. They sold sofas, chairs, desks, wardrobes — everything you needed — to large branded stores and warehouses in Britain and internationally. He always said he was born a natural entrepreneur, buying sweets and magazines and selling them at twice the price to his friends in the school playground. By sixteen, he was working at a stall in Brixton Market selling hats and T-shirts. He went on to study business management at university, graduating with first-class honours. His first business was selling tie-dye clothes back in the '80s—

"When Thatcher's Britain was booming and London was brimming with opportunity. A black man has got to make his own way in London," he would say. "And times were different back then. It wasn't all nicey-nice like it is now. There were areas we couldn't go down, where we got chased out of. Brixton was rough as hell."

His own father had left when he was barely a toddler, and his mother was a poor Grenadian working migrant. He had sought to help his two younger brothers and sister, dreaming of days when he would no longer have to struggle.

We attended church every Sunday. I was baptised shortly after my birth, as were my father's wishes. Everyone in the church loved my dad and talked about what a respected and adored member of the community he was. This old lady would bend down and tell me I was the luckiest girl in the world.

"You've got it all, you have. Your daddy's rich and your mummy's good looking," she chortled. "What's not to like?"

I was supposed to attend school in September 2005, when I turned five. Mum insisted I start Deer Park School, or The

Vineyard Primary School, or St. Stephen's CE Primary School — all in our catchment area. My father had scoffed.

"No child of mine is going to some comprehensive," he said. "We have the money to send Anne to private education and give her the chances we never had."

"But a comprehensive will give her an all-rounded education, both socially and academically," Mum retorted. "Why should she hang around with posh snobs when she's only a child?"

"Excuse me!" That had annoyed my father. "Martinique, you can't just assume everyone who attends private education is a posh snob. Sure, you have a few gits, but they exist everywhere. Private school students are all pushed to achieve the highest grades. You don't have any of this 'equality' nonsense about all students being treated the same. And as it's funded by the parents, we know we're paying for teachers to equip our children with lifelong skills." He nodded, feeling triumphant. My mum shook her head, her hands on her hips.

"I don't know, John. I don't want Anne to feel complacent, to feel like having a head start in life makes her better than everyone else."

Dad had laughed, then slowly walked up to her while she swallowed. He gently placed his palm against her face. I was standing in the landing, watching them.

"Now, Martinique," he said softly. "I only want what's best for our daughter. She's a bright girl, spends all day with her head in those books. What do I work so hard for, if not to provide the best chances for my family? Wouldn't you agree?"

She nodded, biting her lip and turning away from him. He kissed her on the cheek, then grasped a chunk of her thick curly hair in his hand. She pressed her lips together, a scream barely escaping from her mouth. My heart thumped.

"You *agree I* know what's best for our family, right, darling?" He hadn't been shouting, but his tone had been iron-strong. She nodded, tears streaming down her cheeks.

"Tell me you agree."

"I agree, John," she gasped, the words a raspy knife against her throat. "I agree, you know best."

He relaxed his grip. She grabbed her head, deeply breathing in and out and almost keeling over. He smiled at her and kissed her forehead.

"Good girl. Now, I have to go to the office. There are some meetings I must organise dealing with our exports within the European market. Hopefully Blair and his pals up in parliament have our back on this." He clasped his hands with glee. "New Labour isn't turning out as terribly as I thought they would be. Let's hope they stay that way."

He'd walked out of the living room and through the door, slamming it as he left. My mum sank to the living room floor, her head in her hands. I ran to her.

"Are you okay, Mummy?" I asked. She gazed up at me, tears streaming down her face. She wiped her eyes with her hands. "Mmm, yes, I'm fine."

"Did Daddy hurt you again?" My hands quivered. She pulled me close in a warm embrace, avoiding my eyes. "Everything's fine, hon. Sometimes, Mummies and Daddies fight, and that's normal. What matters is we both love you." She stroked the top of my fluffy hair.

"Would you like me to plait your hair for you?"

"Yes, please, Mummy. And will you read *Dimble Goes to the Moon* to me?"

"Have you already finished *Dimble Goes to Australia*?" she asked, with a touch of surprise. I nodded. She murmured under her breath. "He's right, you are a bright one. Hmmm, maybe...I don't know. Come along then."

My father returned from work later that night. The following day, my mother told him she would compromise. She had a suggestion, and that suggestion was I be home-schooled. Taught by a suitable curriculum planned and supervised by my parents, I would learn and progress in the comfort of my home and have private tuition on a weekly basis.

"That way, we can monitor how well she's doing and push her and help her achieve," my mum said, biting her lip and blinking rapidly. He faced me, his arms folded. And then, he smiled. "Sounds like a great idea. We can hire the best tutors for English and math, though I'm sure you'll have no problem with English, will you, Anne? We can take her out to museums and art galleries...well, you can do that, Martinique, as I'll be busy working. Yes, this is fantastic. A most excellent idea. I'm proud of you."

I remember the way my mum had beamed, her shoulders sagging and fists unclenching.

We spent our days in parks, aquatic arenas, museums, galleries, cinemas, cafés, concerts, watching West End musicals. London was her haven. She adored the hustle and bustle, the chaos and colours. I did too. She would take my hand and make us dance along Southbank, our feet springing to the steps of the Steel Pans and guitar players. Coins would spill from her hands as she paraded around Covent Garden, smiling at the street performers and mime artists.

"Dance with me, Anne," she would say, twirling me around.

My dad didn't let her have her own bank account, but he gave her a generous weekly allowance. She would take me shopping in the West End, in all the big department stores like Zara and H&M and New Look. I had a wardrobe filled with colourful outfits: pink dresses, red scarves, glittery purple jeans, sky blue T-shirts, paisley leggings. She was also dressed so: tight jeans clinging to her athletic legs, short skirts, bandeau tops, little black and white leather jackets. Men would turn their heads, whistling as she walked past. She never minded, smiling and playing up to the attention.

"Don't you tell your dad about this. It's all just a bit of fun. I'm allowed to have fun, aren't I?"

Chapter Two: Trouble in Paradise

When I was six, my mother fell pregnant again. I was overjoyed. I had always longed for a brother or sister, someone to share the time with. Books were great, but a conversation or a game with a person was priceless.

Mum had a miscarriage. I heard her weeping, leaning against the kitchen counter. My dad walked in, smacking his lips together after polishing off a can of beer. She told him what had happened, and he shook his head.

"So, this is it," he said. "Now I don't have anyone to inherit my business. Such a shame."

"What about Anne?" Mum said, wiping her eyes. "Or we can try again—"

He seized her arm, twisting it behind her back. She cried out in pain. He began to laugh, leering at her, while I watched from the landing.

"Anne has her head in the clouds most of the time," he said. "There's no use trying to explain this to her." He wiped his hand across her face. "Nice lipstick. Have you been out again, Martinique?"

"No, of course not. I've been here all day. I cooked se—"

"Shush." His grip tightened. She cowered in front of him, a rabbit against a hungry tiger. "I know you're lying to me. I know you went out the other night with your stupid friends. While I've been out working hard, giving you money to spend on clothes and jewellery, paying for Clarence and Paula to teach our daughter ABCs and Numeracy." He yanked her necklace off, bits of jewels spilling onto the ground.

She shook her head. "Please…I didn't. You said I couldn't because we couldn't find a babysitter—"

"That's *right*." He let her go and she fell back against the counter, stumbling in her silk nightie and heels. He walked to the cupboard and took out a bottle of whiskey, slogging it back.

"Hmmm…" He wiped his mouth. "Funny, honey. I've had people tell me they've seen you here and around…seen *you*. Woman I married, betraying me behind my back in the eyes of the Lord. Did God not teach us to love and honour our spouses? Hmmm? To *honour* them? Do you know what that means — do you?"

She shook her head, trying to edge away from him. He started undoing his belt from his trousers. "I know you've been out seeing other men behind my back. Purging yourself and your unholy soul. And now, you've rid me of my heir. You're a useless, selfish whore."

Tears ran down her face. "John…John, please. I'm so sorry. I don't know what you're talking about. Please, don't hit me—"

I ran up to my room as the harsh leather lashed against my mother's soft flesh. Slamming my bedroom door, I grabbed a pillow and screamed into it. Then I picked up my colouring book and pens and started to draw a fat red circle, round and round, until it stabbed through the page, blinking hot tears from my eyes. I wished I could disappear into the paper, sinking through the empty red void.

Later, the door slammed. I ran downstairs to my mum. She was lying on the kitchen floor, bruises all over her body. I reached for the bowl under the sink and filled it with warm water. The flannel was in my hand already. I begged her to call the police or the hospital, but she shook her head and insisted she couldn't, that she would be fine. He loved her…this was just a misunderstanding…

There were days when I had to call A&E, especially as the years progressed and Dad's drinking got worse. She always said the same things. She fell in her heels. She tripped. She walked into a lamppost and banged her head. Not once did she say a word against my father or tell anyone what was happening. She was a butterfly trapped in his cocoon.

The same year my mother had the miscarriage, a family moved in next door. They had two children: a four-year-old boy named Thomas, and a chubby girl my age named Lucy. She wore glasses and had her hair in bunches. My mum sent me to give them a box of chocolates as a welcoming present. I smiled politely at Lucy's mother as she answered the door, pleased and grateful for the gift. I peered behind her and saw Lucy standing in the doorway. She gave me a little wave. I waved back. She smiled at me.

Mum took me to the park the following day, and we saw Lucy with her parents and brother. Her brother was running around the sandpit, laughing with the other boys. Lucy was sitting on a bench, reading.

"Shall we go say hello?" my mum asked. She walked us over. Her parents were astonished she was my mum, saying she looked more like my older sister. She laughed and said everyone said that. They began chatting, and I sat next to Lucy, both of us shyly acknowledging each other.

"What are you reading?" I asked.

"*Rainbow Magic*." She showed me the cover, *Pearl the Cloud Fairy*, and I gasped.

"I love the *Rainbow Magic* books!" They were about two best friends, Kirsty Tate and Rachel Walker, who had all these magical fairy friends. "You're on the *Weather Fairies*? I'm still reading the *Rainbow Fairies*. Which one is your favourite?"

"I love Fern the Green Fairy. She's funny," said Lucy. We started talking about them, discussing how much fun it would be to live on Rainspell Island, and how horrid Jack Frost was. I asked her if she went to school. She said she went to Deer Park Primary, one of the comprehensives my dad hadn't wanted to send me to. "Do you like it there?"

"Yeah, it's good. The teachers are nice. Literacy is my favourite subject."

"It's mine too," I said. "I'm home-schooled. My mummy and daddy couldn't decide what kind of school to send me to."

"What's being home-schooled like?"

"It's okay. I learn a lot. I have Literacy and Numeracy tutors come every week, and I also might be getting piano lessons soon. We have a big piano at home."

"Oh, so do we! I can't play it, but my mum can. Hopefully, I'll get to learn violin next year."

"That sounds nice. My dad can play the piano, though I haven't heard him play in a while."

Mum told me he used to play for her, back when they were first dating. He would play Debussy, Chopin, Mozart, and Jazz too — Ray Charles, Thelonious Monk, Herbie Hancock. Sometimes, they would sing together, having their own private concert in his living room, complete with wine.

Lucy and I began to see each other regularly. We would go to the park after school and talk or swap books. We made up this secret game where we were both queens of this magic land called Pachidale. All the girls were fairies and all the boys were leprechauns. It was sunny and snowy at the same time, and no one ever felt cold. Everyone would skate around on the ice and build snowmen and snowwomen, and music played all day long. We lived in a giant ice palace with our own pet snow leopards and mountain lions, and no one could hurt us.

But then, Lucy started saying if we were queens, we needed kings, or a handsome prince. I said we didn't because we had each other, but Lucy wanted to create a prince who adored her and could reign the castle with her. She called him Prince Philip, like in Sleeping Beauty.

I said Prince Philip smuggled an evil potion into her chamber one day to try to poison her so he could take over for himself and lock her away in a tower and not let her have any friends.

"What? That's *mean,* Anne. Prince Philip isn't bad. He's a nice prince with his own unicorn, and he wants to help keep the peace between our land and his."

I shook my head. "I don't trust him."

She pondered. "Maybe Prince Philip has a brother, Prince Patrick, and you two can get married?"

"I don't *want* to get married," I said.

"You'll have to get married someday."

"Okay. I don't want to get married to a boy."

"What?" She giggled. "You want to get married to a girl?"

"Maybe."

She burst out laughing. "That's silly, Anne. Only boys and girls can get married. Well…men and women. You can only get married when you grow up."

"I don't like boys." They were messy and scruffy and ran around a lot. Lucy said boys always chased the girls and tried to kiss them on the playground at school.

"There's nothing wrong with boys," said Lucy. "I love my brother. He can be a bit silly, but he'll grow out of it. My mummy said girls grow up faster than boys anyway. And if you don't like boys, that means you don't like your dad. And you have to like your dad. He helped make you."

"My dad is mean to my mum." It slipped out. Lucy's lip quivered. "What do you mean he's mean to your mum?"

"He...he yells at her, and he gets very drunk and calls her horrible names. And at times he...he hits her."

Lucy clamped her hand over her mouth, and I glanced down at the ground. I hadn't meant to say it.

"That's really bad. My dad would never hit my mum."

"You can't tell them," I said. "Please don't tell them, Lucy. I'll be in so much trouble, and then my dad might hit my mum even harder." I burst into tears. Lucy put her arms around me, giving me a big hug. "It's okay, Anne. I won't tell them."

"Pinky promise?" I stuck out my little finger. She wrapped hers around mine. "Pinky promise. I won't tell my parents."

"Mummy, why does the girl always have to marry a prince at the end?" I asked one evening while we were watching *Cinderella*. I examined her. She was gazing out the window, her face blank and barely watching. She shifted her gaze to me. "Sorry, love?"

"In fairy stories, why does the girl always marry a prince?"

"Why indeed," she muttered. "To give you kids a non-realistic image of life."

I shuffled uncomfortably on the sofa. "What?"

"Ignore me, love. The girl marries a prince because that's what supposed to happen. When we grow up, we get married and live in a...nice house."

"Do princesses ever marry each other?"

That made her laugh. "Not normally. Well, it does happen. They don't get married as such, but may live together, in the same way a prince and princess might live together."

"What about princes? Does the same thing happen to them?"

She was really laughing now. "Yes, love, the same thing can happen. Again, it's not common, but it does happen."

The Bible said marriage was between a man and woman, and it was sinful for a man and a man to be together. It didn't say it was wrong for two women to be together. I was just being curious. I poured over the Disney Princesses, captivated by their beauty. Belle was my favourite. She was a bookworm like me, and I loved her gold dress, brown hair, and creamy skin. Some nights, I would whisper to her, pretending she was lying next to me; my special secret friend.

Chapter Three: Eruption

When sober, my dad was very calm. He was a dormant volcano waiting for enough movement to shake his lava fury.

In church, he sang the psalms with pride, his heart full of joy. The preacher told us about Jesus giving his life for humanity, shepherds going out to herd their sheep, and King Solomon sparing the life of the baby. I let the stories run over my head, my mother would bite the skin of her thumb, but my father's eyes shone. He listened to the preacher's words as if he really were speaking for God and placed his hand humbly on his heart when he said the Lord's Prayer. After service, he always shook everyone's hand, then helped serve tea and biscuits. My mum hung behind him, smiling and nodding, always putting on a brave face.

In 2010, the year I was nine-going-on-ten, the Liberal Democrats broke the trust of their voters and formed a coalition with the Conservatives. Lucy also broke her promise to me. We were best friends, but the few times she came to our house instead of me going to hers, she was jumpy and anxious, expecting to see cans of beer or smudges of blood. The shouting and slapping was becoming unbearable. Lucy told her parents, and they called the police. The police came to our door.

Mum was in the living room, weeping. I was by her side, as I always was. Dad answered the door. Mr. Charm was switched on, from Hyde to Jekyll. I don't know what he told them, but it was enough to get rid of them. He brought my mum to the door, and she put on that same brave face and said nothing was wrong. How could it be? All was fine and calm, they were just arguing, all couples argued.

Shortly after that, Lucy and her parents put their house up for sale. I said goodbye to her. She told me repeatedly she was sorry. I forgave her. It wasn't her fault. She gave me a big hug and told me we would always be friends, and then she was gone.

My mum continued to sneak out, though by dad had forbidden it. He said she was not allowed to leave Richmond and if he caught her anywhere near Central London without his permission, there would be trouble. She said what if she and I were going somewhere. We had been to every haunt in London — the London Eye, the London Aquarium, the London Dungeons — where we screamed and laughed like crazy.

He said if she went somewhere with me, she would have to call him every hour because he didn't trust her, and if he didn't answer, she had to leave a message on his phone. She said what about every two hours. He slapped her. She said every hour was a little excessive. How were she and I supposed to relax and enjoy ourselves? He reluctantly agreed on every hour and a half.

This was how Mum ended up taking me out on her "trips." Things were okay for the next couple years. I drew the beautiful land of Pachidale, envisioning this fantasy world I could lose myself in. I believed holding on to my imagination kept me sane all those years, and still had today.

2012 was the year everything went wrong again. That was the year London hosted the Olympic Games. Mum had been taking me up to Stratford for trips to Westfield Stratford City, the shopping centre that had opened in 2011. The city was raving with Olympic fever. We had tickets, Mum, Dad, and I, to watch Usain Bolt in the 100m race. We drove down in my dad's BMW, Diana Ross blaring. I was colouring the drawing I had done of an evil demon called Javawok, inspired by Lewis Caroll's *Jabberwocky*, who invaded Pachidale and shattered all the ice and kidnapped one of the queens, so she was sent away forever and couldn't return.

It was the worst possible timing. The three of us were walking into the seating bays. A steward paused to check our tickets. Dad started talking to him, making jokes and saying Bolt was the best role model for young black men since Obama. The steward smiled at Mum, then stared hard.

"Martinique, is that you?" he asked her. She was wearing a silver mink coat and heels, her face all made up. She blinked at him. "It's me, Cameron." The man had light brown skin and black curly hair, handsome even in his yellow hi-vis jacket. He must have been around my mother's age.

Dad peered from the man to my mum, his eyes twitching. Mum gave him a delicate smile and hello, taking my hand. Her palm was sweating. Cameron smiled at her. "Remember, we were like thirteen! You were the first girl I ever kissed." He shook his head and nodded to my dad. "Aren't you a lucky man, married to such a beautiful lady. My first girlfriend. Did she tell you?"

"She didn't," said Dad, forcing a smile. "First girlfriend, eh?"

"She was a real heartbreaker back in school. All my mates were so jealous of me," he continued. He peered down at me. "This is your daughter? Hello, darling."

I nodded, then backed away, leaning against my mother, who put her arm around me. Cameron beamed at us all. "What a lovely family. Guess you turned out all right! Are you still singing? She's got a great voice." He nudged my dad, who was staring at Cameron like he wanted to rip bits of his hair off his head.

Usain Bolt had been dubbed the fastest man in the world. His sprints couldn't have surpassed the speed of my heart as I sat next to my mum, who was gnawing away at her thumb. Dad put his arm around her shoulder, lightly asking about Cameron and whatever other men she hadn't mentioned. She said they had been children and she'd barely remembered the guy.

We drove back in silence.

"Anne, I think you should go upstairs for a bit," said my dad when we returned home. The house seemed larger and emptier than normal, waiting to swallow us up.

"Your mother and I have things we need to talk about."

I looked at my mum. I didn't know what was in my expression, but my eyes were pleading. *Please. Please.* She cast glances from my dad to me. "Yes, Anne, go upstairs."

"But—"

"Now." My dad was firm. "Go upstairs now. Like your mother said, we have things to discuss."

I didn't argue. I got up and walked halfway up the stairs before sitting down. I listened.

"Well, Martinique." I heard the rip-back metallic clank of beer cans ready to be poured down his throat. "I suspect you haven't been totally honest with me. All those times you've been going out, waiting for me to be away? I guess I underestimated you." His rubber-souled shoes paced the living room floorboards.

"I haven't seen him in years, I swear!" she cried. "Please, can't we just have a normal evening? I'll cook chicken casserole. I'm so sorry we ran into him. I had no idea—"

"*Be. Quiet.*" Down when the beer. "Shut your mouth, you filthy whore. How is it you continue to humiliate me like this?"

"John, I'm sorry, I really am. I know things haven't been perfect, but please listen! You don't know how hard it's been for me here. You're never around, Anne is growing up, she has hardly anyone her own age to talk to, and neither do I—"

"Selfish cunt." A harsh smack of hand to skin. She screamed. "All this time, you've been out seeing all these other men behind my back, continuing to humiliate me after I gave you everything. I pulled you out from the ghetto, gave you a child despite your womb being so broken you couldn't give me another—"

"*Please, please stop it!*" she shrieked, tears raining down her skin. "I can't live like this anymore. I can't. I've made so many sacrifices for you—"

"*Sacrifices?* What do you know about sacrifices, Martinique?"

"I haven't talked to Mum in years, I have no friends, this house isn't a home — I'm a prisoner in my own life! The one good thing in my life is Anne, and I won't let you destroy her with your bullshit, John — I won't!"

Silence. A gasp. My dad walked into the kitchen, presumably taking another bottle.

"I think I need to give you a reminder, sweetheart," he said. I knew the belt was unfastening. I knew I should have ran to my room and thrown the covers over my head, but I couldn't. Her weeping continued. "I'm so sorry, I didn't mean that—"

"Shut your mouth and listen to me." The belt was in his hand. "No woman who is married should be disloyal. *A wife of noble character is her husband's crown, but a disgraceful wife is like decay in his bones."* Slap of leather against flesh. *"Wives, submit yourselves to your husbands as you do to the Lord. As the church submits to Christ, so also wives should submit to their husbands in everything."* Another slap. Another scream. A beg for mercy. *"The wife does not have authority over her own body, but yields it to her husband."*

"JOHN, PLEASE, PLEASE STOP!" she screamed, trying to pull herself up, but the beatings came, raining down one after another. Then, the door swung, giving way to sounds of the rain outside, before slamming. I ran downstairs. Through the window, I saw my dad dragging Mum into the car. They drove off. I wanted to run outside, but my feet were rooted to the ground. I sat on the stairs, waiting, wondering if they would ever return.

Eventually, Dad did. I had dozed off on the sofa and heard the door open around four or five in the morning. His face bore a strange mixture of fear, disgust, sadness, and relief. He ran his hand down his face and walked past me as if he didn't see me there. He walked into the kitchen, taking out a bottle of whisky and opening the top. I followed him in there.

He cleared his throat, not meeting my face. "Anne, as you know, your mother and I have had some...disagreements, for many years. Things haven't been the best. She's never appreciated me, all the things I've done for her..." He coughed loudly and took a swig of whiskey. "Anyway, unfortunate as it sounds, I'm afraid your mother has left us."

I blinked at him. "Left?"

"She's gone, Anne. I'm very sorry. I guess it all got to be too much for her."

I didn't know what to say. Did he expect me to believe she would just up and leave me? I was the thing she loved most in the world.

"Do you know where she's gone?" I asked. He shook his head.

"No, I don't know where she is. I don't know where she's gone or what she's doing. All I know is it's unlikely you'll ever see her again."

Chapter Four: Pieces of a Man

I sank into my bed, face buried under the pillow while the covers pulled me under. Later, I turned on my back, staring at the ceiling as it twisted and turned in a spiral of white, sucking me out of existence into a different plane.

As I drifted to sleep, images of my mother flashed up and down my dreams. Her happy, holding my hand, dancing with me as we strolled by the River Thames and waved at mime artists. Images of my dad holding an axe, battering her to death, woke me up. I did not scream. I studied the dark room. Called for my mother. Got out of bed. Walked across the landing. A light was on. Half asleep and delirious, I crept downstairs. He was sitting down in the dining room, an empty bottle of whiskey next to him. He appeared faraway again. I stood in the doorway, waiting for him to notice me, waiting for something. His eyes turned to me.

"Are you okay?" he asked, sounding genuinely concerned. "I know it's a lot to take in. But remember this, she cared far more about herself than she cared about us. She was a selfish woman, Anne. I hope to the dear sweet Lord you don't turn out like her." He shook his head. "Such a pity."

I fainted. When I woke up, I was in my bed again. The whole thing was a dream. I had been having a nightmare, and Mum had put me to bed. I peeled off the bedclothes, seeing the same blue dress I had worn to the Olympic park.

So many questions. Did he kill her? Did he make her run away? Was she alive? Was she dead? I felt very numb, somewhere between life and death. Non-existing. Floating in a transparent zone with no chance of escape.

For the next eight months, my father and I lived in a home of solitude. I spent the days alone, often wandering the streets. I began to wear and buy all black, my wardrobe resembling an abyss. At night, the sounds of my mother's screams sang through my dreams.

I often came home to find my dad passed out on the sofa, bottles and cans lying by his feet. He would stir, and then hiccup, sitting up, his eyes bloodshot. He would call to me, and I would rush wordlessly with the dustbin or a bowl or something for him to be sick in. One day, I came back to find him playing piano. I heard the sound, the soft keys pattering against strings and wood. It was "Pieces of a Man" by Gil Scott Heron. He played beautifully, the pedals amplifying the mood and tone of the song. Beer after beer went down his throat. He must have drank dozens a day, or bottles of whiskey. He was constantly coughing and clearing his throat. I began to cook for myself, flicking through cookbooks to learn how to make simple meals. My dad disappeared for days at a time. I never found out if he was seeing other women or just out drinking.

In January of 2013, my dad decided I couldn't stay with him anymore. Something in his head flipped a switch. I had no idea what made him change his mind. Could have been the whole "New Year's resolution" thing, or maybe I reminded him too much of Mum. Whatever the reason, he posed the question to me.

"Would you like to go stay with your auntie? Aunt Colette."

I had never met any of my dad's siblings. Aunt Colette was the only one who lived nearby. His brothers both lived abroad, one in America and the other back in Grenada. I was sitting in the living room, colouring, thinking about nothing.

"Where does she live?"

"It's a small town just outside London called Copperwood. She lives with Uncle Brian and their three children. I can drive you there."

I was calculating this in my head. My father was suggesting I leave where I was and live with other people — family members, but strangers.

Leave him.

A whole new start.

A whole new situation.

I blinked, then realised I was colouring a fat orange over and over. My hand was shaking. I didn't ask why, or how he had come to that decision. I simply got up, nodded my head, and said, "Of course. That would be lovely."

I didn't ask for how long. I walked into the kitchen, got a glass of water, then went upstairs to pack my suitcase. It lay like a ghost at the back of my room. I moved, flinging all my possessions in. I had a way out of this living nightmare.

I checked the hallway, then scurried into my parents' room. I opened my mother's suitcase, still home to the same belongings it had when we had re-arrived. I took out a couple dresses, some scarves, and perfume. I dug deeper and found something at the bottom. It was an envelope. I opened it, my hands trembling. Glossy, unspoilt photographs were cradled inside, colourful and well-developed. Me as a baby. My mother and I on the London Eye. Us at the zoo. Us sitting in her room. They were all pictures of us together. I turned over photo after smiling photo, my palms sweating. She had never shown me these. I wondered why, wishing she had. They all had dates sprawled on the back. I closed my eyes, clutching them to my chest. Tears began to fall down my cheeks. I hadn't cried in a long time, but now, I did.

An hour later, I lugged my suitcase and two bags down the stairs. My father was in the living room, polishing off a bottle of Jack Daniels. He smiled when he saw me. It had been ages since I had seen him smile. He had shaved and wore a freshly ironed shirt.

"Let me get that for you, darling." Walking over to me, he picked up the suitcase. "I've already spoken to your aunt and uncle. It's all been arranged. They're looking forward to seeing you." He got my belongings into his car, and we drove away from Richmond, out of London, out of this life.

Chapter Five: Extended Family

Twelve years old, dressed in a black duffel coat and armed with luggage, I stood on the doorstep of my aunt's house. My dad gave my aunt a huge hug, and they talked about how it had been years and she had always longed to meet me and she was so happy I was there and *would you like to stay for a drink, John? No? Okay. No problem. Well, it was lovely seeing you, oh okay.*

Sad bewilderment brushed across her face as she watched my dad rush off, not even an inch of curiosity to meet his niece and nephews, that suspicious linger of whiskey on his breath. Aunt Colette was short and buxom with braids hanging down her back. She was dressed in a long-sleeved red and gold dress and maroon sandals. Ducking my head, I stepped into this new house, feeling like the Pevensie children from Narnia when they went to stay with Mrs. Macready. It was big like ours, but with glossy brown wooden floors rather than carpet. They had a massive garden and long hallways and stairs that curled downwards. I stared at it, marvelling at the gorgeous design.

"So, I understand you were home-schooled?" said my aunt cheerily. "Patrice, my eldest, goes to boarding school. It's called Lakeland Boarding School, for eleven to eighteen. It's in Lake District Town, about an hour drive." She shook her head when she saw my confusion. "Not the Lake District up in Cumbria, this is a Greater London county near Bletchfield and Highwood. Just west of Aylesbury," she said, waving her arms like she was conjuring up a map of South-East England.

"Oh, okay." I tried to hide my awkwardness, tapping my foot on their polished floor.

"Marcus and Zoe go to the local day school, though Marcus was home-schooled for a bit. We put him back in education last year."

"H-How old are they all?" I clenched my fists, trying to stop them from trembling. I'd never stuttered before.

"Patrice is sixteen, Marcus is fifteen, and Zoe is twelve." My aunt smiled. "Zoe will be delighted when she sees she has someone her age to hang out with! We were all so excited when we heard you were coming to stay with us. My brother's always been a bit reclusive." She shook her head. "Sorry, I probably shouldn't say that in front of you. He's your dad, after all. He said your mum left?"

My tone was static. "That's right."

"I'm terribly sorry. What an awful shame." She sighed. "Before your mother, John was married to another woman named Eliza, but things didn't work out so well either. Such a pity. He was devastated when she left him. I had met her. Nice lady. I always wanted to meet your mum, but we didn't keep in much contact after his second marriage."

I wasn't sure what to say, so I took to admiring my aunt's paintings. "Oh, that's nice." It was a lake with a canal boat and a man with a pair of binoculars watching while another man held out a fishing rod. She nodded. "Those are all Brian's, your uncle. He does love his artwork. He's got all surrealist pictures in another room. Frida Kahlo and Salvador Dali. I don't suppose you're familiar with them?"

"Not really. Well, I've s-sort of heard of Frida K-Kahlo. I think my mum and I watched a d-documentary about her y-years ago." I'd thought it awfully sad she'd spent her entire life in pain, with prosthetic legs, yet amazing she still managed to paint and do what she loved. I'd also thought her incredibly beautiful, monobrow and all.

"Yeah, it's a bit of a hobby of his. He's an architect, so he's really into design and what not. I'm a university lecturer. I teach politics at the University of Bedfordshire."

I was taken aback by this. Not so much by their professions, but that they *had* professions. These were real people — *my family* — who I'd barely heard about.

"Your uncle is at work. He'll be back this evening. Patrice won't be home until half-term, and Marcus and Zoe should be back shortly." She blew a *whew* noise up into the air. "Sorry if this all seems a bit rushed. Your dad only rang us a few days ago to say you were coming."

I nodded, swallowing. She gave me a kind smile. "He said he's going to be away for six months on an important business trip and doesn't want you left alone." She tapped the ground with her sandal. Her tone was light and casual, but she was chewing on her lip and not meeting my eyes, as if there was something she didn't want me to know.

"I know it all seems a bit sudden, and if you want to leave at any time, you can. You could perhaps stay with some of your mum's relatives?"

I'd met my grandma once, when I was much younger, although I didn't remember her. She and my dad had had a massive argument, and then we never saw her again.

"I'd love to stay here."

"Excellent! You can stay in the spare bedroom next to Zoe's. I can take your suitcase up now for you."

"Erm, no t-that's fine," I said, stumbling over my words. I pulled my suitcase protectively towards me. "I can take it."

"Oh, all right. Would you like a drink of anything? Water, juice, tea?"

"Water, p-please."

"No problem." She went into the kitchen whilst I lugged my suitcase and bags up the stairs. There were paintings everywhere, some of landscapes, some of angels, some of the stars and seas and people walking across the sand barefoot, gazing into the horizon.

I stared across the upstairs landing. The floor was polished and clear. I peered into one of the rooms, the door ajar. There were some posters of cats and puppies and dolphins and smiley boys with floppy hair. I heard footsteps behind me and jumped. It was only my aunt, carrying a glass of water.

"Sorry, I should have shown you the spare room. That one's Zoe's." She nodded, and I stepped back, then edged into the room that was mine. It was medium-sized, with a giant painting of a red daisy on the wall, a bed, wardrobe, and chest of drawers—all the things I would need. I pulled my suitcase inside, along with my bags, insisting my aunt needn't do it. I opened the empty wardrobe, picturing all my clothes hanging up, and took in the image of my aunt and I in the mirror. The room was reflected behind me, clean and fresh and untouched. My new home.

"Would you like any help unpacking?"

I shook my head. "No, I'm f-fine, really." She looked a bit disappointed, but I was used to being left alone. "Okay…well, dinner will be ready in a couple hours. Agatha, our cook, is making risotto. Just let me know if you need anything." I nodded, then closed the door. Laying back on the bed, I stared up at the white ceiling. I was going to live here. Away from my dad. My fingers stroked the crisp white sheets, the daisy patterned duvet. I took in the matching painting of the red daisy. And then, I burst into tears.

After I washed and changed and mulled around, I went downstairs, following the sound of voices calling out. My cousins. The hairs on the back of my neck pricked. Gulping, I peered over the stairs. A boy and a girl, presumably Zoe and Marcus, were chatting to my aunt. They sounded loud and jovial and happy-go-lucky, as if nothing in the world could faze them. I stepped farther down.

"Anne! There you are, dear!" said Aunt Colette. "Here, come down, don't be shy." Zoe and Marcus both smiled at me. Marcus held out his hand and cleared his throat. "Hey, I'm Marcus. Nice to meet you!" He shook my hand vigorously. Zoe giggled, putting her hands to her mouth. "Sorry about him, he's so awkward with people."

"I'm not frickin' awkward!" he said.

"Language, please," my aunt said, tutting and rolling her eyes. She smiled at me. Zoe reached forward with her arms out, and I stepped back, unsure. I held out my hand instead. She seemed slightly hurt, but I tried to smile at her to show I was friendly.

"I'm Zoe. And you're Anne, right?"

I nodded. I was startled by how striking they both were. Light brown skin. Big, dark eyes. Zoe had gorgeous curly brown hair and wore glasses, and Marcus had short darker hair curling on top of his head and shaved at the sides. He was a bit taller than Zoe. Both were thin and dressed in the same red school uniform: blazers, white shirts, Zoe in a skirt and Marcus in trousers.

"Mum, can I play my PS3 before dinner?" asked Marcus. Aunt Colette tutted. "Get changed out of your uniform first. Dinner will be ready in about forty minutes."

"Yay!" He tossed his arms up in the air, then ran upstairs, his school bag on his back. Zoe chortled. "I swear, I never understand why boys are so obsessed with video games. All they do is shoot random zombies and aliens and soldiers and act like it's the coolest thing in the world. *I* think they're boring."

"You're boring!" Marcus yelled from the top of the stairs. Zoe and Aunt Colette laughed. "Right. Well, I'll leave you two alone for a bit. Your dad will be back just in time for dinner," she said to Zoe, who nodded eagerly, beckoning me to come upstairs.

"I'm so happy you're staying with us," she said. "It's going to be so much fun having another girl round here. And our house is huge. There's so much space. We can do whatever we want. My parents are pretty chill." She opened the door to her room. I stepped inside, now getting a full view of it. I was re-introduced to all the posters and photos plastered around her wall of Zoe smiling with a bunch of other girls, pulling faces.

"Those are all my friends," she said. "Most of us went to the same primary school, and now we all go to Copperwood Secondary." She pointed them out to me, naming them. I forgot their names as soon as she said them. I peered at Zoe, wondering what it would be like to grow up with so many friends in a warm and loving household.

I felt I should say something. "I-Is, erm…is your dad white?"

"Yeah. He's from Scotland originally. Moved here when he was a bit younger. He doesn't really have an accent, but it comes out sometimes when he's pissed or whatever. And Mum's from Grenada, same as your dad." She giggled. "Isn't it, like, weird we're cousins? I mean, I know that's such a dumb thing to say, but we're *related.* Like, it's so cool! I barely even knew you existed. Apparently, my mum and your dad don't talk."

"Really?" I wasn't surprised.

"Like, I dunno, my mum doesn't mention your dad much. In fact, I haven't really met much family from mum's side. We go to Scotland once a year to see my dad's family. He has two sisters. They live there with their families...and yeah, it's nice. Marcus wore a kilt! He looked so silly in it." She giggled again. "Yeah, it's fun."

We sat down on her pink-patterned bed. "So, w-what has your mum told you...I mean, has she, like, s-said anything ab-bout...my dad?"

Zoe shook her head. "Not really. Just that your mum left you and your dad had to work for a while, so you have to stay here. She was really happy, but also kind of shocked. I dunno. I think my parents had a bit of a...not *argument,* but disagreement about it. If you know what I mean." She sighed. "I mean, they won't really tell us anything. I bet they told Patrice, even though he barely lives here anymore. He's at boarding school, so he only comes down on the holidays." She lay back on her bed. "It's all a bit weird, but you know how grownups are, they never tell us shit. They think we're too young or too stupid or whatever. But tell me, what actually happened between your parents?"

I must have appeared terrible because Zoe's cheerful expression turned worrisome. "Are you okay? You don't have to say if you don't want to. I bet it sucks, your parents splitting up like that. One of my friend's parents split up, and she was so depressed."

I nodded. "I don't really want to talk about it."

She patted my shoulder. "No probs. Another time, maybe. Hey, look, lemme show you my magazines!" She jumped up. I turned around, then noticed a big glossy poster of a topless man with black hair. Puzzled, I examined it. "Who's that?"

She gasped. "*Who?* Oh my God, it's only Taylor Lautner!" She ran up to the poster, drooling all over his six pack. "He's beautiful. He's basically my dream guy. Like, I have this plan, right. When I'm seventeen, I'm going to meet him. Me and my friends have it all figured out. We're going to go off to Los Angeles for a weekend, sneak into Hollywood, and he's going to take each of us out on a date. I haven't told the others yet, but I'm going to get in there first. I have so many dreams about him, *eurgh*, you wouldn't *begin* to imagine." She laughed guiltily. "Sorry, I must sound really weird to you right now."

"No, not at all." I swallowed. "I h-have dreams too."

"Cool! Anyway, here are my mags." She jumped over to a fat stack of magazines. Her room was a bit messy, with clothes and magazines and lip-gloss scattered around the white carpet. She scooped up a handful, tossing them to me. "These are literally my life savers. I don't know what I'd do without them! Here, let me read you one of these embarrassing stories." She flicked open the pink and purple pages. Beaming, she came to a page with lots of colourful illustrations. "This one's called 'Farting Fright.' It's about this girl who farts loudly in front of her crush." She read it out loud, and I laughed. It was a funny story, and a bit sad. She read some more, and I listened, observing all the posters of grinning boys and animals.

Aunt Colette called us down for dinner. Zoe sighed, tossing her magazines across the carpeted floor. "We'd better go down. Oh crap, I haven't changed. Mum always gets annoyed if we don't change out of our uniform. She says we'll get it all spoilt. Plus, school is kind of strict about presentation, and, you know, all that other crap." She was flinging her clothes off as she spoke. I turned away, staring at the fluffy white carpet.

"Like, they always moan about the length of our skirts, but seriously, no one gives a *shit.* Some girls just walk into school with their knickers practically showing, and I'm here like okay, what are you trying to say? Have some class *please,* this isn't the slut walks. And they say stuff like 'you're in year seven now, you're not little kids anymore, you must be role models for primary school pupils, blah, blah, blah.'" She tugged on a pair of white jeans and a baby blue T-shirt. She peered down at her chest, sighing. "It's so embarrassing. I don't even wear a bra yet. My life is so sad. I have to wear a stupid vest like a baby."

"Oh, really?" We started going downstairs. "You're probably, erm...j-just a late bloomer." That's the kind of thing my mum would have said. I was hit with nostalgia. Zoe didn't seem to notice.

"Yeah, maybe. But I hope they appear *soon.* My friend Meg has these big balloons on her chest and all the boys whistle when she walks by. She complains about it, but at least she's *got* something there for boys to notice." She rolled her eyes. "Some people just don't know how good they have it."

Chapter Six: Cliques and Cups

Dinner was a cheerful affair. We all sat down at the table together. My uncle Brian had joined us, a bald man with a broad grin. When he saw me, he peered across the table as if he had no idea who I was.

"I-I'm Anne, your...n-niece?"

"Anne?" He scratched his head. "I have a niece called *Anne?* No, I'm sorry, you're terribly mistaken." He shook his head. "I have no idea who that is. You must have the wrong house." He tutted at his wife. "Really, Colette, what did I tell you about bringing stray kids from the street into our house? She did this last week as well. Right, Anne, I'm sorry, but you'll have to go. Come on then." He gestured his head out of the room. I hung back, uncertain, while Marcus and Zoe were in silent stitches.

"I don't know what you two are laughing at. We can barely afford to keep your greedy backsides, let alone have another mouth to feed."

"Brian, please." Aunt Colette slapped her palm to her forehead. "Just ignore him, Anne."

"Ignore him! I'm telling you; she says this every time. Always with the bloody human rights nonsense. If it was up to her, she'd turn our house into a homeless shelter. I'm sorry, Anne, but you'll have to go."

"*Dad!*" Zoe was laughing her head off. "Come on, Dad, leave her alone."

He sighed. "All right, all right, you got me. My apologies, dear. It's this hair, you see, it worms its way into my skull and makes me forgetful. That's another way of saying I'm getting old."

"You don't have any hair," said Marcus. Uncle Brian tutted. "That's what *you* think, but really, I have this invisible wig on my head no one but me can see, and every time I look in the mirror, I see a full, thick head of hair."

"In your dreams," said Zoe, pouring a glass of orange juice. My uncle frowned. "My hair is way nicer than yours. You think your hair's great? Mine's the greatest."

"Everyone is always trying to touch and grab my hair at school," said Zoe, shaking her head. Her ringlets bounced as she did. "You'd think they'd never seen a mixed-raced person before. It's so annoying."

"You see?" My uncle nodded at me. "Where do you think she gets it from? Your mother? Nope. Underneath this shiny melon, I've got a beautiful shock of curls, I do. They're way nicer than Zoe's."

She stuck her tongue out at him. I tried to imagine sticking my tongue out at my own dad. Uncle Brian drank too, a giant pint of Guinness, but only one, and he sipped it. Aunt Colette poured herself a glass of red wine.

"Mum, can I have some wine please?" asked Zoe. My aunt shook her head. "Zoe, you know you can't until you're eighteen."

"But that's not fair! Just a little tiny sip? Or even some in my juice?"

"Now, Zoe, you know drinking is for adults only," said Uncle Brian. "If kids drink alcohol, you know what happens to them? Their ears fall off and their mouths disappear."

Zoe snorted. "That's stupid! That doesn't happen! Oh, Mum, please." Her mum shook her head. "But Marcus does, with his friends — OW, MY LEG!" She bent down to rub her calf, glaring at her grinning brother.

"That's not true. It was just the one time," said Marcus. "And I barely had anything."

"I don't like alcohol," I said. Aunt Colette nodded. "You see, you could learn from your cousin. She's sensible."

Zoe moaned. "I bet she's only saying that to sound good! But whatever." She shrugged it off, scooping up her risotto with her fork.

I settled into my aunt and uncle's house quickly, getting used to my uncle's sense of humour in the process. He and Aunt Colette had friends over all the time, usually on the weekend, for drinks and dinner. Marcus would invite his friends over too, and they played on his PlayStation in his bedroom.

Zoe had her friends all round one evening for a sleepover party. "I can't wait for you to meet them all!" she declared, clapping her hands. They arrived at separate times. Jessica was first, a skinny girl with ginger hair and a laugh that sounded like a duck quacking. Shortly after her was Emily, a brunette who brought a couple DVDs along.

We had all gotten changed into our pyjamas and were lounging on a bunch of pillows on Zoe's carpet, surrounded by crisps and coke and skittles. "I'll get my laptop set up so we can watch a DVD," said Zoe, opening it up on the carpet. Jessica took some crisps and peered at me. "So, you're Zoe's cousin?"

"Yep."

"Well, then, that makes you our friend!" She and Emily threw thrilled glances at one another. "You should totally start our school in September, that would be so cool," said Emily. "We can help you get all settled in."

"I'll th-think about it," I said, ducking my head and helping myself to skittles.

Then Zoe's phone buzzed. "Oh, Meg's here."

"Why didn't she just ring the doorbell?" asked Emily, while Jessica scurried downstairs. Zoe rolled her eyes. "Duh, it's easier to text than ring the doorbell."

Emily shook her head at me. "This one's such a lazy idiot."

I smiled politely. Jessica returned, accompanied by a beautiful girl with long blonde hair and large breasts. She was wearing an orange tank top underneath her coat and blue jogging bottoms, and she had a big smile on her face. I stared at her. I couldn't help it. I stared and I stared.

"Oh, Anne, this is Meg," said Zoe. I didn't respond. She waved her hand in front of my face. The room had gone quiet. They were all gaping at me. I blinked. "Sorry, just…erm, z-z-zoned out..."

Zoe rolled her eyes, laughing. "I'm not surprised. All that reading conks your brain out!"

Meg settled herself down onto a cushion, waving at me. "Hey, nice to meet you." She took off her coat. I swallowed. Something inside me wasn't right. I fought hard to ignore it. No one else seemed to have noticed. They were all burbling and chatting amongst themselves.

"Have any of you guys done Miss Palmer's homework yet? I don't even know how to start it."

"Oh, it's dead easy. I did it like last week."

"Yeah, isn't it due tomorrow?"

"Oh my God, I gained a *stone*. I look disgusting."

"Can you believe Kim Kardashian is pregnant?"

"I hate her. She's so hot and perfect. It's annoying. Her body is amazing."

"Who do you think's better looking out of her and Beyoncé?"

"Oh, Beyoncé *definitely*. She's like, the definition of a modern goddess."

Agatha came and brought up some freshly made pizza. It tasted delicious. Emily jumped up and flashed one of her DVDs at Zoe, saying we should watch it. She and Jessica had seen it, but the rest of us hadn't. It was called *The Clique* and had an image of four fashionably dressed pre-teen girls and a fifth one standing slightly behind them on the cover. We all leaned forward, swathed in pillows and blankets, pizza and drinks in our hands. It was fun, though I was too shy to say much. Also, I couldn't get Meg out of my head, and was terrified of saying something stupid in front of her. I realised my hands were sweating.

Emily and Jessica kept talking through the movie, and Zoe kept shushing them to be quiet while Meg giggled and commented on the characters.

"Alicia is so pretty. She's definitely the hottest of them all."

"No way!" said Emily. "Massie is. And her clothes are so cool."

Meg rolled her eyes. "Yeah, but Massie's a bitch, and no one dresses like that in real life. Except in America."

"Yeah, who wears clothes like that at the age of twelve? Can you imagine if we turned up to school in a full vintage outfit and that weird hat? We'd get sent home for sure."

"It's called a trilby hat," I offered. "Similar to a fedora, though not quite the same. My dad used to wear them a lot. Apparently, they were once known as 'the rich man's hat.'" I laughed, then stopped as they all blinked and stared at me.

Except Zoe. "Can you guys shut up and watch the film please?" she said, sounding really annoyed. I was grateful for her carefree naivety. She rolled her eyes at me. "They always do this. They always have to talk throughout the entire film, and then I have no idea what's even going on."

Emily held up her hands. "Loser, loser, double loser, whatever, as if, get the picture, *duh.*" She chanted in time with the girls on the screen. Jessica laughed. Zoe made an *argh* noise. She got up, getting herself another cup of coke.

"Would you rather be a friendless loser or a person with tons of friends who secretly hate you?" Emily said in time with the girls on the screen, who were at a sleepover at Massie's house and being deliberately hostile to Claire.

"I think I'd rather be a friendless loser," said Jessica. "Cos then you know who your friends are, and you know they can't be fake. That's basically what happens to Massie anyway."

"Can you *shut up*!" snapped Zoe. "Now you've just spoilt that bit for me!"

"Yeah, but it happens, like, soon anyway. And Massie deserves it."

"They're all just really mean and bitchy," said Jessica. "Except Claire. And Layne; she's the coolest character."

"Her brother is so ugly." Emily shuddered. "Why are they all obsessed with him?"

"Chris Abeley isn't *that* bad looking."

"Layne dresses like a goth, though." Meg frowned. Jessica shrugged. "So? What's wrong with goths and emos? People can dress however they want."

Steam was practically leaking out of Zoe's ears. "Guys, for the last time, I swear—"

Someone's phone buzzed. It was Meg's. She picked it up, her arm squashing against her bosom. My insides weakened. I had been trying hard to just concentrate on the movie, though it wasn't easy with Zoe's friends talking over it.

"Linda's here."

"Oooh!" said Zoe. "I thought she said she wasn't coming?"

Meg shrugged. Zoe grinned. "Who's gonna answer the door?"

"It's your house," said Emily. Zoe scoffed. "Can I be bothered, though?"

"Oh, I will," said Meg, flouncing up. I instantly felt more relaxed when she left the room. We all turned back to the film. Moments later, Meg re-entered with another blonde girl, her hair tied up in a messy bun.

"What you guys watching?" asked Linda.

"*The Clique*," said Zoe. "Or at least *some* of us are trying to."

Linda sat down on the cushions next to us. She stole an apprehensive glance at me, then continued talking to the others. Zoe shook her head. "Sorry, I forgot to mention, this is my cousin, Anne."

We said hello and nodded at each other. Linda smiled at all of us. "You guys want to see something more interesting?"

Zoe groaned. "Can we *please* finish watching this first? There's not that much left."

Everyone piped down for the last part of the movie. When the credits started rolling, Linda clasped her hands together. "Okay, who wants to see something *mad*?"

"What, like a vine of a kid crying because they missed the ice-cream van?" said Emily. Linda shook her head. "No, better. Who wants to watch *Two Girls One Cup?*"

Zoe instantly groaned, shaking her head. "Oh God no, no way. Marcus made me watch that, like, a few weeks ago, and no, oh God no. Please, never again."

"Didn't that come out years ago?" said Jessica. She typed it into her phone. "It said it came out in 2007."

"Yeah, but we were like seven. No one needs a childhood *that* messed up." Linda patted her hair. "You know how everyone went on about it when it came out? Well, I think we might as well watch it now."

"Oh, I've h-heard about that," I lied. "Is that the one where those two girls start fighting over a golden cup?"

They all roared with laughter. My stomach crumbled and my cheeks burned, making me grateful for my dark skin tone. "Anne, *Two Girls One Cup* is a porno," said Zoe, giggling and patting my arm. "Marcus wanted to film my reaction and put it on YouTube, and I was like, no, there is no way I am ever speaking of this again. No, please, I have buried it in the back of my head."

"I think you got it mixed up with golden showers," said Linda, still laughing and nudging Emily. I blinked at them, then Meg ran her hand through her hair with her chest stuck out, and I became distracted. "Is it really disgusting?" she said, pouting her lips. "I'm kind of curious."

"*No,* you are not!" said Zoe. "Trust me, you don't want to watch that. It is the most awful, horrible, just purely fucked up thing in the world. Just no! *Eurgh.*"

Grinning, Linda had already placed herself in front of Zoe's laptop. Zoe left the room, insisting she would rather walk on hot coals than sit through that video again. She said just thinking about it made her want to throw up. "That kind of thing doesn't leave you. Don't say I didn't warn you."

We sat around Zoe's laptop, all of us intrigued. Linda clicked on the video. "God, check them getting it on." Jessica and Emily giggled. Two women were kissing and sucking on each other's body parts. A sizzle of hot energy rippled through me, and I wiped my hands on my pyjama trousers. I glanced at the other girls, then back at the computer screen, and my mouth fell open.

"Ew!" cried Emily as the women began to urinate into each other's mouths. Meg made a gagging noise. "What the actual fuck."

"Oh, good god…" Linda's voice trailed off as we saw them squeeze something else into their mouths. "FUCK!"

"What the hell!" Emily got up and ran out of the room.

"Please tell me that is chocolate…oh, what the fuck." Jessica clapped her hands over her mouth. I backed away from the laptop like it was a venomous scorpion coming to bite us all.

"Oh god, STOP! What is she DOING!" Meg screamed. Linda leaped forward and slammed down the laptop. I rubbed my stomach, hoping the crisps and coke from earlier wouldn't spill from my mouth.

Zoe walked back into the room, laughing. "I *told* you guys not to watch that."

"I can never eat ice-cream again," said Emily, scowling at Zoe. "You've ruined that for me."

"Blame Linda, watching it was her idea," said Jessica. Meg slapped Linda. "Why did you make us watch that! That was the most disgusting porno ever. You're lucky I didn't puke."

"What's all the commotion?" asked Marcus, who had come out of his room and was standing in the doorway. "They just watched *Two Girls One Cup*," said Zoe.

Marcus chuckled and clapped his hands. "Oh, that's so old now. But I guess it's the kind of thing everyone needs to see once."

"No, no one needs to see it." Jessica glared at him. "Do people actually get turned on by watching people shit and piss and vomit in each other's mouths?"

"Maybe Anne knows." Linda waggled her eyebrows. My eyes widened. Zoe threw her arm over my shoulder. "Oh, leave Anne alone! Ignore Linda. She's an idiot."

I peered at Emily, who was smiling at Marcus. "Hey." She tucked her hair behind her ear. He nodded at her. "All right?" Then he looked at Zoe and I. "Enjoy the rest of the night."

He went out of the room. Emily burst into a peel of giggles. Jessica's hands were shaking, and Meg was lying on Zoe's bed with a pillow over her head. I felt horribly sick. Zoe frowned at Emily. "I told you to get over this stupid crush you have on my brother. He thinks all my friends are dumb."

"I can dream, can't I? He's much hotter than Chris Abeley! Does he have a girlfriend?"

Zoe snorted. "No, the only girl in his life is his PlayStation."

"True, though, Marcus is gonna be gorgeous when he's older," said Linda. Emily squealed. "He's gorgeous now! Oooh." She lay back on her pillows. Zoe picked her pillow up and whacked it at her.

"Hey!" Emily picked up another pillow off the floor, tossing it at Zoe. Meg lifted her head up. "We having a pillow fight now?"

"Apparently." Zoe jumped as I tossed one of her teddies at her head. "Hey, Anne's using stuffed animals now! This is war."

"You're on." Linda leaped up, and pillows, blankets, and teddies began flying around the room, erasing the memory of that awful video.

Chapter Seven: Girls Will Be Girls

I began to hang out with Zoe's friends regularly, and gradually became less self-conscious around them. I hoped my feelings involving Meg would go away, refusing to admit to them and not daring to let myself think about her. Most days, Zoe's friends came around after school, or we went to one of theirs. We all did things together, like going to the cinema or shopping or ice-skating. It was great, and for the first time in my life, I felt like a normal girl, out doing things with my friends.

Aunt Colette and Uncle Brian were not Christians. Neither seemed religious or God-believing at all. I still prayed, but I stopped going to church. It made me think of Mum, and the less I thought of her, the better. It made things less painful. But sometimes, flashbacks came to me, in my dreams or when I was studying or reading or hanging with Zoe and her friends.

"John, love, maybe you should take it easy? Three Desperados in ten minutes is a little excessive, don't you think?"

He let out a stream of false laughter. I froze mid-swallow.

"Is there a problem, my dear?" he said. "Do you have a problem with me drinking, is that it? Can't I enjoy a drink in my own home?"

She peered at me and put a piece of chicken on her fork into her mouth. "I'm just a little worried about it, that's all."

He slammed his fist on the table. "This is my house, and I will drink as much as I want to when I want to. You're not so pure, are you, Martinique?" he sneered. "Why don't we talk about you and your little affiliations?"

She looked anxious again. Crossed her eyes over to me. "I don't know what you're talking about—"

"Oh, you know exactly what I'm talking about," he said, coughing loudly.

"John, please, not in front of Anne—"

"You're my WIFE!" he bellowed, taking no notice of me. "I am your HUSBAND, not one of your pathetic boyfriends. Maybe I need to remind you of that." Belt unfastened. Her screams set in motion his night of terror. I ran to my room, cowering under the duvet.

I tried to forget about my dad, but still, I prayed for him. He was a monster, but if there was a God, he would want me to be loving and forgiving. I had to forgive my father for his sins, no matter how awful they were. *Didn't I?*

Thoughts of God and my Christian upbringing tore my heart as well as my head. I couldn't stop fantasizing about Meg. Were my feelings natural? Was it wrong for two girls to be together? Was it wrong for me to like a girl? The Bible said only men and women should be together, but I didn't think that was very fair. What about people who weren't Christian? What did they think? What did my aunt and uncle think?

Sometimes I let the thoughts just be thoughts and I would smile, imagining her and I holding hands together and walking along a sandy beach, drinking in the sun. She would whisper things in my ear and tell me I was the nicest girl in the world. And her breasts. I daren't think about them during the day, but at night, I held them in my dreams. At Zoe's bowling birthday party in March, Meg wore a revealing top, and I had to spend most of the time avoiding her. Lots of other girls from Zoe's class came to that. And a few boys.

"Have you ever had a boyfriend?" Zoe asked me once. I shook my head. "I g-guess I haven't really been around them much."

"But you've seen guys you think are cute, right?"

I shrugged. She glanced intently at me, then sighed. "There's this boy I *really* like in my class. William."

"Why do you like him?"

"He's great at football, and he's really funny, and once, he smiled at me and offered me his pen in Maths cos I'd dropped mine in the girls' toilets."

"Do you t-talk to him much?"

She scrunched up her face. "I'm too scared to talk to him. And he likes this girl in our year called Betsey Taylor." She flopped back on her bed, throwing her arms up. "Not that I'm surprised. Boys don't even know I exist."

"Maybe they're just nervous? Because you're really pretty."

"No, I'm not." Zoe was always criticising her appearance. Everybody loved her hair, including me, but she moaned about the spots on her nose or her lips being too small or her glasses, wishing she could just wear contact lenses instead, but she had been told her eyesight was too bad.

On occasion, Zoe would talk about Scotland and visiting her family there. I pointed out that most of her friends were white, just for the sake of curiosity, but also because there weren't many people of colour in Copperwood. "Yeah, cos it's a small town," she said. "It's way worse in Scotland, though, especially cos my dad's family lives far north in the middle of nowhere, not like Edinburgh."

"Have you ever…erm, experienced…anything b-bad?"

"Like racism?" She sighed. "I was ten, and I was with Marcus and two of our cousins, Ben and Jodie. We were all just walking to the shop, through some woods, and we passed this group of older kids. They all started staring at Marcus and me, and they said all these things — awful things. I'd rather not repeat them." She bit her lip. "Ben and Jodie got *really* cross and told them to go away and leave us alone. After they did, Marcus just laughed, calling them ignorant twats from the countryside. But I...well, it was weird. It's always a bit weird. Everyone stares at us. I hate how it gets made into such a big deal. Like...we're all human at the end of the day, ya know?"

I nodded. "I can imagine."

"It must be so different in London. I'd love to live there. I love cities, like London and Paris. I'd love to visit New York."

"Have you been to London?" I asked.

"Yeah, loads. And Paris. Mum never said anything about going to visit you, though, but then, I guess your dad wouldn't have liked it."

I didn't say anything. "Scotland's nice," she continued. "But there are just so few people who look like us. I swear, some of them have never seen brown people before."

"You're not even that brown." I put my dark arm next to her light one. "What on earth would they say about me?"

"Who knows." She told me all about the Highlands, and the cattle and sheep farm her uncle owned. She told me stories of family trips to the beach, visiting different countries, when Patrice introduced his first girlfriend to the family, and all the paintings her dad bought. She talked and talked and talked, and I listened. I loved listening to her tell me all about her life — about the kind of childhood I wished I'd had.

It was decided I would enrol in Copperwood Secondary School in September. Aunt Colette filled out all the paperwork. I would start year eight, attending school for the first time. I wasn't sure how I felt about it. Nervous and excited, but also calm. Like it was no big deal, almost anti-climactic.

Around July, things went wrong again. It was my fault. I'd spent months thinking and fantasizing about Meg. She drove me crazy, and I couldn't help it. I had moments where my face flushed and I lost my breath, almost like I was about to keel over. I knew I couldn't ignore it, and I hated myself for it. I daren't say anything to Zoe. I discovered what she and her friends thought about lesbians:

"Can you imagine if a girl just hit on you? That would be nasty."

"I know, right? Just no. So awkward. I don't know what I'd do."

"Yeah, it's not the same if it's a guy. At least we like guys as well."

"I'd rather have some idiot boy flirt with me than a girl. Any day."

We were all sleeping round Meg's house. Zoe's friends all had big houses, and Meg had a trampoline in her garden. It was great fun, though I tried not to stare as Meg bounced up and down. Instead, I focused on springing into the air. I stared at the summer sky as the breeze cooled my face. When I poked my head up, the others had gone inside, and Meg and I were the last girls jumping. She was smiling at me.

"Guess we have this all to ourselves." She hopped up and down like a rabbit, doing splits and spinning around. I laughed, even though my heart was hammering.

"Weee! I love this. It's so much fun! Come, let's hold hands."

I shook my head. "N-no, i-it's okay."

"Come on, Anne. Don't be boring. Take my hands." She held them out. I reached out, swallowing. She didn't notice the clamminess of my palms. We bounced up and down. I watched the birds flying over our heads as my black skirt swished below me.

"Do you always wear only black?" she asked. I nodded. "How come?" she asked. "Like, don't you get tired of it?"

I shook my head. "I l-like b-black."

"So, you're a goth then."

"N-no, I-I'm n-not."

"Y-yeah y-you ar-are," she said, mimicking my stutter. She pulled a funny face. "Look at me, I'm Anne, the *goth girl! Totally goth, yeah, you get me!*" I burst out laughing as she let go of my hands, jumping around. She stopped, both of us giggling like mad. She stepped towards me again, brushing her hair out of her face with her hand. She took my hands again. We regarded each other. I stepped closer to her. She tilted her head to the side, curiosity strewn on her face. I blinked, the smile leaving my face. Next thing I knew, my lips were on hers

my lips were on hers
and she was pushing me away
pushing me so hard, I stumbled
yelling, shouting, asking what I was doing
why did you do that? What's wrong with you?
calling me a disgusting lesbian
you bloody les, how dare you touch me
and she ran off the trampoline, screaming, running to Zoe, telling them all what had happened, and they all came out into

the garden, staring at me, shocked, and I didn't know what to do, I was stuck on the trampoline, barely able to stand up, my heart palpitating, and I had nowhere to run because they were all ogling me, but I managed to bounce off and run past them, back inside Meg's house, and Zoe called for me, but I just needed to get away, hide myself because I was an embarrassment and knew I couldn't hang out with them anymore.

My secret was out in the open.

I was supposed to go to the same school, but now I couldn't, and I didn't know what to do.

I went to Meg's room to fetch my bag. Aunt Colette had bought me an iPhone, and I was all set to call her to tell her I felt sick and ask her to pick me up. Zoe came up, but I couldn't face her. She closed Meg's bedroom door.

"Are you okay?"

"Of course not," I said, wiping my eyes.

"Do you want to talk about it?" She stepped closer, but I backed away, and the tears began to pour down my cheeks.

"Oh, Anne, please talk to me. I want to help you!"

"No." I wiped my face again. My phone buzzed. "Your mum's here. I have to go downstairs." I picked up my bag. Zoe stood in the doorway.

"Wait, please, you don't have to go. I know this was a bit shocking, but—"

"*Leave* me, Zoe, please." I stepped past her, racing down the stairs and leaping into my aunt's silver car as fast as I could. When I got home, I went straight to bed, even though I didn't fall asleep for hours.

The next morning, I went downstairs to get myself some breakfast. I wondered if Zoe had said anything to her parents.

Uncle Brian had left for work, and Aunt Colette was in the living room, reading a magazine. She smiled at me and asked if I was okay, showing no trace of surprise or shock. I went back upstairs, not sure what to do with myself. The obvious thing was to lose myself in the pages of a book, but my heart was still hammering.

I was sprawled on top of my bed when there was a faint knock at the door. Zoe crept into my room, carefully closing the door behind her. I put my eyes back on the page, even though the words fell over my head. Zoe sat down on the floor next to my bed. My room was spotless compared to hers.

"How are you?"

I shrugged and grunted. She twiddled with a bit of the rug. "You know, about what happened yesterday—"

"I don't want to talk about it."

"I *know,* obvi, it's awkward and all that. But I just want to let you know I'm not judging you. Honestly, I think it's better if we talk about it—"

"What about the others?" I put my book down. "I'm sure they're not exactly on your wavelength."

"Well..." she looked uncomfortable, "they're all a bit shocked obviously, cos none of us knew. Emily doesn't think it's, like, bad or anything. Same with Linda, though they kind of hadn't expected it. Jessica says it's weird and she's a bit so-so about it." We regarded each other. I didn't need to ask the obvious.

"Meg comes from a really conservative family. She didn't go to Copperwood Primary. She went to the Catholic school on the other side of town. Her parents are proper, like, traditional about things like marriage and that. They don't get that people can be gay and bi. And cos my parents are more accepting and tolerant and stuff, they don't mind as much. *I* don't mind." She sat up on my bed next to me. I sat up too. She held out her arms, and I gave her a hug. I closed my eyes.

"I'm not g-going to b-be able to h-hang out with you g-guys now," I mumbled while my body quivered. I wondered what was going to happen to me when I started her school. "This is all such a m-m-*mess*."

"It's not your fault," she said. "I'll talk to Meg. I'm sure the others will calm down." She leaned forward and put her slender arms around me. "How long have you known?"

I pulled back from her embrace. "I-I've always known," I said. "I j-just always saw g-girls that way, n-never boys. I t-thought there was something w-wrong with me. I mean — t-there is. I know it's n-n-not right."

"Don't be silly. It doesn't matter, you know."

I stared away from her, studying the topless poster of Taylor Lautner. "But it d-does matter. I used to think it was un-n-natural because that's what it said in the B-Bible and what they used to say in church. I was also b-brought up pretty religious."

"Do you still feel like that now?"

"I don't know. I don't know what to believe any more. S-Since...my mum l-left." I stared into space. "Sorry, I n-never u-used to stutter before I c-came here. My dad also said it was unnatural, that only m-men and women should b-be allowed to be t-together."

"But he's only going by what *he* was raised to believe," said Zoe kindly. "He's from an older generation. My mum used to think that too, when she was younger, that being gay was wrong and all that, but as she got older, she started accepting it. You can't choose or decide it. Like you can't choose if you're a boy, or black, or what colour eyes you have. We're just born with these things."

"But maybe if..." my voice trailed off. I wasn't sure what to say. "I'm not u-used to boys. Mum and I were so c-close. I never talked to my dad much. S-Surely if—"

"It wouldn't make a difference. It's not about that. I mean, you don't fancy your mum, do you?" She burst out laughing at my horrified expression. "Like, it's literally just who you're naturally born to like. Like, I *know* Taylor Lautner and I are meant to be." She waved a hand dreamily at him. I smiled, and the heavy feeling in my stomach lifted.

"It all just depends on how you feel. You can't make yourself like boys, even if you're not used to them. *I* barely talked to boys in primary school. Except for my brothers."

"I know this sounds bad, but I feel kind of weary around your brother. I mean, I know he's my cousin, but...yeah, I dunno."

"It's fine." She patted my arm. "The main thing is it's good you can talk about it. You shouldn't feel weird or afraid. If you'd have told me sooner, it would have helped. I mean, there's only so long you can hold things in for. You can't just let them build up and build up and build up until they get to a point where something awful and random happens and you don't know what to do."

I gave her a weak smile. "I guess you're right. You're so lovely, Zoe."

"Aw, thank you! We're family. If you ever need anyone to talk to, I'm here for you." She reached over and gave me a warm hug. "You have to take care of the people you love, otherwise why bother sticking around?"

Chapter Eight: School Daze

September came, and I was to start Copperwood Secondary School — my first time at a real school, with real boys and girls. In the nights leading up to it, I cradled my pillow, thinking of my mum and longing for her to hold and comfort me. I wished she could see me, age thirteen, on my first day at school.

I had to do this long test beforehand to find out my "capability," and whether I had studied the right things during home-schooling. I trembled as I walked into the hall. I had said bye to my aunt, who had gone with me into the office, and waved to Zoe and Marcus. Zoe had said I was welcome to hang out with her and her friends at break and lunchtime, and that she would watch out for me. Meg was still distant, but the others had calmed down. Linda asked me all sorts of questions about my sexuality, most of which I answered monosyllabically...or avoided.

I walked into this room, with children of different ages sitting at individual desks. I sat down at one of the desks and saw this booklet with a bunch of questions and sections to write down answers. Teachers stood around the classroom, walking past us. My imagination ran away with me and I pictured them as Nazi soldiers assessing us at a concentration camp, ready to toss those of us who did badly into the gas chambers and bring those of us who did well in "for effective use." My hands were sweaty and shaking as I unfolded the sheet of paper.

I peered at the questions. Thumbed through the sheets, blinking. Startled and slightly baffled, I began to answer them, writing out in full. They were so...simple? Basic? Obvious? I glanced at some of the others, mostly terrified and uncertain and scratching their heads and flicking their pens. Puzzled, I continued answering. They seemed like the sort of things I would have expected someone starting year six to answer, not year eight. I wrote in detail about Lady Macbeth's "unsex me here" scene from Macbeth, putting in quotes I'd remembered from the film, and a play and opera version I saw with my mum. I answered all the maths questions, checking them carefully. I stifled giggles at the simplicity of the science questions involving electricity and condensation and the carbon cycle. It was an absolute breeze.

"Are you okay?" one of the teachers asked as she came over, seeing my raised hand — something Zoe had told me to do if I had a question.

"Oh, yes, I'm f-fine. It's j-just…I've finished."

The teacher inspected the clock above her head. The test was supposed to last an hour and a half; I had finished within fifty minutes. She peered at me, then smiled. "Excellent. I'll collect your paper for you."

"B-But where do I go now?"

"You can wait in the canteen until everyone else has finished. Another teacher will mark your paper and decide which sets you'll be in for your subjects."

"Okay." I had no idea where the canteen was. I considered calling Zoe, but she would be having lessons. I asked her where the canteen was, and she told me it was straight down at the end of the corridor on my right. I got up, feeling the other kids staring at me as I walked out of the room. Gulping, I pushed open the double doors.

Relief hit me. The fact that I was starting school hadn't, but after the test, I thought if the work was that easy, it was going to be okay.

But…perhaps it had been deliberately easy. Real lessons could be awful. It wouldn't be like at home where I was free to read and research whatever I liked. Zoe had told me stories about teachers not letting you use the toilet or telling you off for eating even if you were starving or sending you out for laughing in class. I wouldn't be free like I had been at home. There were all kinds of rules.

I couldn't wear my usual black clothes. I had to wear Zoe's scarlet uniform: red blazer, red skirt, white shirt, and tights. Luckily, my black shoes were smart enough. You weren't supposed to wear dangly earrings, but Zoe said loads of girls still did and wore makeup, and no one really cared. That confused me even more. There were rules, but they weren't enforced?

"Well, it's like they *try* to enforce them," said Zoe airily, "but at the end of the day, they don't care that much. I mean, they're not going to exclude you for turning up wearing hoop earrings. They might confiscate them, but you'll get them back at the end of the day."

Still, to be on the safe side, I wore studs. I certainly didn't want my earrings confiscated. Zoe also told me you weren't allowed to use your mobile phones in class. I had spent the summer trying to work out how to use mine, fascinated by it and taking lots of pictures of Zoe and her friends. I didn't like taking pictures of myself because I always looked dull or stupid. Mum would have loved to mess around taking pictures of the two of us, posing and dressing up in random clothes. Sometimes, Zoe would thrust her arm over me and pull the camera to our faces, saying, "Let's take a selfie!" She and her friends all had Instagram accounts and they would pose and upload pictures of themselves.

I was too ashamed to tell Zoe I'd made an Instagram account of my own — an anonymous one — to gape at pictures of Meg. I couldn't help it. As much as she ignored me now, I still thought her incredibly beautiful. She never took a bad picture, always posing with her mouth pouted and chest stuck out, her hair long and sometimes clipped up on top with the rest hanging loose. I knew nothing would ever happen, but I couldn't stop thinking about her. I had never felt this way about a real girl before, a girl who wasn't a Disney cartoon.

I told myself even if Meg liked girls, she would never go for me. I was boring and quiet and nothing special to check out. I wasn't beautiful like my mum. But in my head, Meg kissed me and told me I was the most amazing girl in the world. I longed deeply for someone to feel that way about me, but I doubted it would happen, at least not soon.

There were girls all over the place at Copperwood, and boys too. They pushed and shoved each other in the corridors and sniggered when a teacher told them off. At first, it felt like being at a zoo, surrounded by wild animals. I walked with a hunch, feeling self-conscious and anxious. There were so many people of different shapes and sizes — tall, short, fat, thin, and some seemed far too old to still be in school. Some girls meekly wore their skirts hitched up their hips, then smirked after a teacher told them off.

I had passed my test well. I was put in all the top classes for every subject. Zoe marvelled at me when I told her this, as did Emily and Jessica. Linda nodded, and Meg rolled her eyes. I swallowed. I would have thought she'd be impressed or something...but why would she be? She'd made it clear she wanted nothing to do with me. I had tried to act normal around her, smiling, even making small talk, but most of the time, she acted as if I wasn't there. At least she wasn't in any of my lessons.

Lessons were a major problem. I'd thought being in the top set would make everything fine. I would be surrounded by clever people, and the teachers would hopefully like me.

My English teacher, Mr. Miles, told me off around twenty minutes into my first lesson. I had been explaining the plot of *Of Mice and Men* to Daria, the girl sitting next to me. Mr. Miles had walked up to me and stood in front of my desk.

"I-Is everything alright, s-sir?"

He wasn't pleased. "It's Anne, isn't it? Tell me, Anne, do you think it's polite to talk in my classroom?"

"B-But, sir, I was t-telling her about St-teinbeck's c-classic." My legs began to shake, but my brain thought fast. "You s-see, i-it's all about the Am-m-merican Dream, and Lenny and G-George's pursuit of it, and—"

He let out a hefty sigh. "It's very impressive you know the storyline, but I have been trying to explain the syllabus for this year and seem to be having great difficulties considering I can't actually hear anything over what you're saying."

"B-But...but I was talking quietly." I was so confused. "And i-isn't it a *good* thing to p-possess knowledge of a n-n-novel we are going to be s-studying t-two years from now?"

Out the corner of my eye, two boys and a girl were sniggering at me and mocking my voice. I sunk into my chair, mortified. Mr. Miles shook his head and told me to stand up and leave the classroom.

He came outside after a while and explained to me knowing the plot of *Of Mice and Men* was very good for someone of my age, but it didn't belong in a year eight classroom. It wasn't part of the syllabus and talking over the teacher was impolite. I nodded meekly, went back inside, and said barely a word for the rest of the lesson.

Syllabus. Curriculum. Timetable. I heard those words a lot. In geography, we were learning about the mountains of Mongolia and the different terrains within them. Eager, I raised my hand and began talking to Miss Parker about Mount Everest, Mount Kilimanjaro, and K2. She was impressed, but also said it was not relevant to the task at hand. I scrutinized the room and saw more people laughing at me. I felt foolish. I was just being *enthusiastic.* Was there such a thing as a tad too much?

I got more chuckles when I offered to read aloud in science, following the cheery tone of the text and trying to bring enough energy into my voice, like in a David Attenborough documentary. I lifted my head and saw even Ms. Charles was smirking at me, saying that was lovely, but somebody else could read now.

I didn't get it. I didn't get it for a while, not when Mr. Trane looked surprised and didn't know what to do with me after I finished the set maths equations within twenty minutes. I didn't get it in music when I sight-read the sheet music for *Gone in Seventy Minutes* within a tenth of the time and started showing everyone else how to do it. I certainly didn't get it in French when I tried my best to speak in a proper French accent like in *Amelie* or *Chocolat* while everyone else mumbled along incorrectly.

"How are you finding it all?" Zoe asked me a month in. I still mostly hung out with her and her friends, feeling too shy to join any other groups. I was friendly with some people in my classes, but they already knew each other, and I didn't want to intrude.

"It's weird. I don't think people here l-like me very much."

"That can't be right! I bet you're top of all your classes. Everyone's talking about 'that smart, home-schooled girl.'"

They weren't just saying that. I'd heard whispers behind my back, felt glances in the canteen. After maths, a boy in the corridor yelled, "Hey, you autistic or something?" at me. I gulped, running past him and stumbling. Some girl had stuck her foot out and her friends burst out laughing as I nearly collided with the floor. Standing up, I sniffed and rushed into the toilets, locking myself in a cubicle. I was in there for about fifteen minutes, rubbing my eyes with tissue. The mirror showed me my eyes were red. I walked out of the toilet, feeling more alone and miserable than ever. I let my shoes shuffle across the floor, barely glancing up until my body collided with another.

"Whoa, you okay?" A boy gazed at me with concern. He had floppy, dark blond hair and a blue jacket over his white shirt and tie, which hung long and loosely knotted on top. My pace quickened, and I tried to edge past him.

"Hey, hey, come on." He stopped in front of my path, putting his hands on my shoulders. "What's the matter?"

I shook my head. I didn't want to talk to anyone, let alone this strange boy. I still wasn't completely comfortable talking to boys. But he sounded gentle and harmless.

"You're Anne, the new girl, aren't you? The home-schooled one?"

"T-That's me." I coughed, then sniffed again. "Word t-travels fast. But t-then…it is a s-small school."

"Do you want a drink of water?" He unhooked his bag off his shoulders and took out a bottle. Nodding gratefully, I took a sip, making sure not to put my lips on the bottle top.

"You can drink straight from it, I don't mind."

I shook my head, swallowing the water. "I'd rather not c-catch germs. Bacteria travels at a rapid rate."

He smiled. "Yes, but you won't pick up much bacteria from sharing drinks. You can get more from touching door handles."

"I-If you s-say so." I handed it back to him. "Th-Thank you." I shrugged my shoulders. "I sh-should...my c-cousin...I s-said I'd m-meet her."

"Who's your cousin?" he asked gently. I surveyed my eyes from the floor to his face.

"Zoe P-Peterson."

"Oh, I know her. She's in my science and English classes. She's nice. I didn't know you were her cousin, I thought you were just friends. Like, I saw you hanging out with her."

"Yeah, she's t-tried to h-help me g-get through regular school. So far, i-it's not—oh, sorry." My eyes fell to the floor again. I felt like a babbling fool, but he just patted my arm. We began to walk out of the building.

"You need a step-by-step account of how to survive this place, especially if you're different in any way. I mean, it depends. Some people are nice, and some are twats. There are twats everywhere, you've just got to weed them out and ignore them."

"E-Easier said than done." I grimaced. "S-Someone called me autistic. I'm not. I kn-know what autism is; it's a condition where people h-have diff-fficulty with s-social interaction. I d-don't...I mean, n-not intentionally. I j-just had a very sh-sheltered upbr-bringing." I wondered if I should swallow my

69

tongue so I didn't have to speak. Luke simply nodded and patiently listened.

"It's such a stupidly rude thing to try to use as an insult," he said. "My dad has Asperger's and found it really tough to cope when he was in school because there was less awareness around it. You'd think people would be less ignorant. Why would they say that? Are you a maths genius?"

I laughed at his jokey demeanour. "No, but...I g-guess...well, when you're home-schooled th-th-there aren't any b-boundaries. S-See..." I waved my hands in the air, inspecting the floor as I spoke, "y-you're constantly learning new things, there aren't any l-limitations. N-No one's telling you to w...wait a few more years before reading up on something."

"Yeah, I get you. Sometimes, it's like school can hold certain people back on the things they could know. You're probably just ahead of everyone and they haven't realised it yet, and the teachers aren't quite sure how to handle it."

I shrugged. I didn't like putting it like that.

"So, it's your first time at a real school? You're like Cady Heron in *Mean Girls*."

I laughed. "I love that movie."

He held out his hand. "I'm Luke." I peered down at it, then shook it, hoping I seemed amicable. Zoe and her friends were hanging outside the canteen, waiting for me. Meg was laughing at something with Jessica.

"Are you going to be eating lunch with them?"

I flicked my head from them to him. "I-I mean, I was, but i-if...maybe..."

"I totally get it if you already have plans, but if not, maybe we could, like, eat together?" He scratched his head, and I realised he was almost as nervous as me. I smiled and nodded, saying that would be lovely, then walked over to Zoe.

She was thrilled when she saw me. "Hey! Are you okay? I was looking for you!"

"Yeah, I was just over there with L-Luke." I gestured my head in his direction. "He s-said he's in the same science and English class as you."

She frowned. "Oh, him? That really quiet weird guy?"

I raised an eyebrow. "W-Why weird?"

"Oh, he just...well, he just is. You know how it is."

"N-No, I don't." I glared at her. I didn't like the expression on her face. "W-What do you mean weird?"

"No, nothing. Just forget about it. Are you going to go hang out with him then?"

"He s-seems lovely." My eyes flickered over my cousin and her friends.

"He's just a strange guy, that's all," said Emily. "Like, he's always humming or mumbling to himself, and he stares into space a lot. And he hardly talks to anyone."

"H-He spoke to m-me. A-After those other people w-were making f-fun of me."

"Oh, good, maybe he fancies you." Meg's voice was catty. "I remember he went to my primary school and he was always standing around by himself. Shame you'll have to let him down gently and tell him he's not your type."

"Shut *up*, Meg!" said Zoe fiercely. She turned back to me. "If you want to go hang out with him, that's cool. Just, like, be careful."

I didn't say anything. I felt both infuriated and upset. It wasn't fair to make judgements about someone you never bothered to talk to. What gave them the right to ostracise others like that?

I went back to him, and we went to the canteen, chatting and ordering helpings of pizza and apple juice. I told him all about what being home-schooled was like. He told me after a while you got used to the crazy whirlwind of school.

"It's a lot better when you have good company," he said, nodding at me. I smiled back, though I was concentrating on cutting neat little triangles off my pizza with my knife and fork.

"I got bullied in primary school," he said to me. "It was shit. But you suck it up. I guess what doesn't kill you makes you stronger and all that."

I shook my head. "W-Why did they p-pick on you?"

He put his fork down. "Because I'm gay."

That was a shock. "What? Oh my God, s-so am I." It just slipped out. We stared at each other, then burst out laughing.

"Wow, that's funny. Yeah, I went to Saint Aquinas. It's right on the other side of Copperwood. I had a crush on this boy and told him I liked him like an idiot, and…well, yeah that didn't go down well. My parents are cool with it, though, thank God. When I started secondary school last year, I decided it would be better not to tell anyone."

"I c-can't believe people would do that."

He shrugged. "It's just ignorance. People don't understand. But yeah, it's been difficult here. I mean, I find it hard to relate to most people, and I feel like I can't be friends with any of the boys without doing something stupid. I was pretty close with this girl called Susie, but then she moved back to Poland in the summer."

"So, h-how long have you known?" I asked him.

"Oh, I've known all my life," he said. "Yeah, it's just one of those things you realise. I mean, I found keeping to myself helps. But I don't like being alone all the time, you know."

I nodded. That, I could relate to.

Chapter Nine: Spinning

I began to spend most of my time with Luke. People said things, making snide comments about the two of us, but we just laughed it off and ignored them. I liked him a lot. He was easy to be around, and I could tell him anything.

Almost anything.

I told him things had been tough between my parents while skipping over the details. I said my mum had left and I had no idea where she was. He was very sympathetic and said it sounded like I'd been through a lot.

"But what about your Grandma, or any of your mum's old friends?" he asked me. "Won't they wonder where your mum is?"

"W-Well, my mum and g-grandma didn't really get on much. They sort of lost contact after she married my dad. M-My dad didn't like Mum ha-having friends or going out much." I paused. Luke stood, not rushing me.

"He was very controlling," I said slowly. "Anything he told her to do, anything he made her do, she d-did it. The only freedom she had was when she snuck out..." I blinked hard. "I know it was wrong, but when she'd g-go out to meet guys, it was the only thing...th-the only thing she could do to get some k-kind of...c-comfort." My brain started to fizzle like warm ginger beer was rushing through it. The playground began to resemble a distorted fairground mirror, and suddenly, my breath quickened.

"Anne, are you all right?" Luke's voice echoed above me, but I barely heard it. The ground was floating from side to side, and then the world faded from blue to grey to white. I fell to the ground, carried by angels, drifting towards the sound of my mother's voice.

When I opened my eyes, I was in the medical room. Luke, Zoe, Emily, and Jessica were standing there, as well as an elderly woman with a white dress and cap. I assumed she was the school nurse. I was lying down on a sofa, and there was a towel and cup of water next to me. A voice said, "She's okay."

I began to sit up. "No, you stay down, love. There now," said the nurse. "Your temperature's up a bit. Must have been this heat. Unusual for this time of year, but who's surprised these days in this country? Cold and raining in June, hot and sunny in October." She patted my arm. "I'm not surprised you fainted, love. I've had all these kids coming to me complaining about being ill, and I'm telling you, it's all these weather changes."

"Mmm." I closely observed my friends and cousin. "H-how l-l-long...?"

"I didn't know what to do." Luke swallowed. "Like, you were talking, and then your eyes were all glazed over and you passed out. A teacher had to carry you here."

"Which teacher?"

"It was Mr. Trane," said Emily.

"Oh, m-m-my maths t-teacher." I shuddered at the thought of him picking me up and carrying me. I hoped the entire playground hadn't seen or noticed. Zoe handed me a cup of water. "You should drink something. To get your temperature back to normal."

I sipped the water, lying there while they all crowded around me. Thankfully, they had to slip off to lessons, and I stayed curled up. I think I fell asleep at one point. Then the nurse said my aunt had come to pick me up.

I was taken home and allowed to have the rest of the day off. Zoe and Luke both texted, asking if I was all right. I didn't know what to do with myself for the rest of the day. I lay around in my room, picking up the sheets for my geography homework, then tossing them aside. I wasn't in the mood to do schoolwork. My eyes swivelled to my desk. I got up, pulling open the drawer where I had stored photographs of my mother and me. I opened them, my hands trembling as if I was clutching forbidden treasure. Tears dripped onto the photos as I took in each one, turning over one after the other. The questions lingered in my throat. *Where are you? What did he do to you?*

One day, in December, shortly before the Christmas holidays, I mentioned my mum to Luke. I hadn't mentioned her since I had fainted.

"I think about her every day," I said. "Sometimes, I talk to her at night. I ask her for help with things, to guide me and say what to do. She always gave such good advice." She would know what to do about Meg, or the fact that all the other students thought I was strange and most of the teachers didn't really know what to make of me.

In one R.E lesson, I ended up in detention. We were assigned a task that involved us having to get up and walk around the classroom.

"B-But, sir, we're not supposed to leave our seats. What about that time when I'd wanted to go to the toilet?"

"Excuse me, Anne?" He folded his arms and tapped his foot. The whole classroom was quiet.

I cleared my throat. "I don't mean to be rude, it's just that we're told we're not allowed to leave our seats, so why can't I just do the work in my seat? I mean, what's the use of having these rules if we can just break them whenever? It's all very confusing."

I was sent straight to the headteacher's office. Luke laughed his head off when he heard. Fortunately, I'd been staying out of trouble thanks to him. Mostly, I kept my head down and completed the work as quickly and quietly as possible. I tried to push myself far into the background so nobody would notice me.

Christmas was much more fun with Zoe and the family than it had been with my parents. Our Christmases had always been forced, as if we were all characters in a play where we hadn't quite memorized our lines. We usually went to church in the mornings, Mum would cook, my dad would tell her how great the food was, then we would watch a film, and my dad would drink and slump on the sofa. At least the morning sermon mellowed him.

My aunt and uncle had a huge tree, played loads of music, and Agatha cooked and cooked and cooked. We had roasted meat and potatoes and vegetables and delicious cakes for dessert. Zoe patted her flat stomach. "Every Christmas, I gain, like, a stone. Maybe some of it will go here this time," she said, patting her chest. That made me laugh. Her birthday was on December 24th, and she always celebrated at home with the family as a joint birthday and Christmas celebration. "My friends are usually busy or away this time of year anyway," she said.

I met Patrice, who was down for the holidays. A tall, gangly boy with messy curly hair and pimples on his forehead. He was a lot quieter than Marcus and Zoe, spending most of his time texting his girlfriend or in his room fussing over homework.

After we all exchanged presents, Zoe and I went up to my room. I wanted to give my gift to her in private.

"Those earrings really suit you," she said, gently playing with the blue crystals dangling from my earlobes. "You like the books too? I went with Mum to the LGBT teen section and thought they could, you know, help."

"Zoe, it's all wonderful. I love my new coat as well. You're honestly the best cousin ever."

Smiling, we sat down on my bed. I handed her a small wrapped parcel, which she tore open. It was a framed photograph of her and me, taken when we went bowling with her friends. The frame was studded with red and blue gemstones. "I hope you like it. I just wanted to give you something you could remember."

"Anne, I love it." She beamed, stroking it with her fingers. "It's great. I'll put it on my bedside table. Aw, now I have a piece of you in my room!" She gave me a hug. "I'm so happy you came here."

"So am I."

On New Year's Eve, my aunt and uncle had a massive party. I was planning to make myself scarce in my room. Zoe and Marcus snuck secret glasses of wine, giggling like mad. Patrice shook his head at them.

"Up to no good, you two?"

"Oh, don't tell on us." Zoe burped, then burst out laughing. "Want some?"

"I'm good." Patrice gestured to the can of Guinness in his hand. "You're not joining in?" he asked me.

I shook my head.

"That's sensible. You guys should be more like your cousin — especially this one." He ruffled Zoe's hair. She squealed and leaned against her big brother, telling him how much she loved him. He caught my eye and laughed. I tried to laugh too, but then thought of my mum and the last time we'd cuddled up together on the sofa at Christmas and played some silly word association game. Dad had been passed out in his study, full of food and gin.

I ran upstairs and leaned against my bedroom door, crying. I picked up one of my new books, needing a distraction until Zoe knocked on my door. "Anne, is everything okay?"

Sighing, I crawled away from the door and sat in front of my bed. She peered her head around, then walked inside...or swayed. "Hey, how's it going?" She plonked herself onto the floor. I frowned at her. "Are you d-drunk?"

"No. Not really." She shook her head too vigorously, burped, then laughed. "Anne, don't you want to come downstairs? You're missing the party."

I shook my head. "Not really a p-party person."

"Well you *should*. It's *fun*." She clambered up onto my bed. "Whatcha reading? Oooh, that book I picked out for you. Is it good?"

"Yeah. Really good." I placed it facedown. She put her arm around me. "What's wrong? You look sad."

"I'm fine."

"Is it the book?"

"No, it's n-not the book."

"Please don't be *sad*." She rubbed my back. "Because you're my cousin, and I love you, my lovely, lovely cousin. And I *love* having you to stay and my friends love you—"

"Your f-friends d-don't l-love me."

"Yeah they doooo! How could they not love my Anna? My Annie?" She rested her head on my shoulder. "Annie, Annie, Annie, get your gun. Have you seen that movie?"

"No." Suddenly, my own breath was stuck in my throat. I could feel tears bubbling up in me. I tried to push them down.

"Annie, I can see you're sad. Please tell me what's wrong. I promise I am here for you. I love you so much. You're the best cousin ever."

I became Niagara Falls. She was being so sweet to me, but I couldn't pretend. "I m-m-miss my mum s-s-so m-m-much," I stuttered between sobs.

"Awww, Annie." She pulled me close to her, and I leaned on her shoulder and cried and cried and cried.

Chapter Ten: Change of Plans

I was dreading the second term of school. I tried to kid myself that it was a new year — 2014, a clean slate — but the only thing that made me excited was seeing Luke, who had spent the holidays with his relatives in the countryside. My main thought was to keep my head down and stay out of trouble.

Within a week, I was sent to the headteacher's office. I wondered why. He shook his head at me, telling me I couldn't wear those earrings to school. They were my new sapphire-crystal ones. I hadn't even realised I'd been wearing them. I took them off, but he asked to confiscate them. I blinked, nervous, wondering if he was being serious.

"But, s-sir, these were a C-C-Christmas present."

"You can have them back at the end of the day. I need to take them now. Come on." He must have been in his fifties and wore a sharp pressed suit and had tired blue eyes. He held out his hand. I stared down at it in horror. "W-What if you l-lose them?"

He opened a drawer in front of his desk. "These are other students' pieces of jewellery and various items. Your earrings will be safe. Hand them over please."

I didn't think it was fair. They were my earrings, nice expensive ones. Why couldn't I just leave them in my pocket? I didn't think he had any right to take them from me. "I p-p-promise I won't w-w-wear them again. But th-they're *m-mine* a-and—"

"Anne, please," he said, sighing. "You can come here at the end of the day and collect them from me. If you don't hand them over now, you will be in detention after school and I will be calling your aunt and uncle."

"For w-wearing e-earrings?" This was getting more ludicrous. "T-They're just earrings. I d-d-don't see what all the f-fuss is about."

"They're not part of our school uniform!" He didn't sound angry, more exasperated. "Listen, you're a highly intelligent young girl, excelling well in all your subjects, so I hear, which is fantastic. But I know you have been home-schooled your entire life, and you're not familiar with the way things work in an institution. There are rules, and those rules must be followed. It's not about what you think, or what I think, it's about the rules set in place. If those rules are not followed, we would have anarchy. And that's no good, is it?"

I cleared my throat, speaking as slowly as I could manage. "Actually, sir, anarchy or anarchism is a system in which there is no g-government, but it's not intending to be chaotic. So, if the rules aren't f-followed, but there's no one in charge and students governed them-themselves, that would be a form of anarchy, but if students are di-disciplined enough to follow their own rules, according to their own needs, that would not b-be chaotic. It would be anarchy, but anarchy d-doesn't mean the same as d-disruptive and chaotic. So, you've actually used that word in the wrong...erm, c-c-context."

He blinked hard, gobsmacked, unsure whether to laugh or send me home. I had no idea where it had come from, or why I had even said that. "Are you trying to get smart with me?"

"I'm c-certainly not try-trying to get s-stupid with you, s-sir."

"Just please get out of my office. You can come back at the end of the day to collect your earrings." He waved me away. I stood up to go off to my next lesson.

Later at lunchtime, I told Luke what had happened. He couldn't stop laughing. I slapped his arm.

"D-Don't laugh at me. Those were an expensive Christmas present. W-What if he accidentally loses them or b-breaks them or something?" I glared into space. "It's not f-fair. They are *my* earrings. He shouldn't be allowed to t-take them."

"He's gonna give them back to you," said Luke, taking a swig of water. He offered me the bottle, and I shook my head. We were leaning on the bars in the playground, near the science block. "I just can't believe what you said. Is that true, about anarchy or whatever?"

"Of c-course it's true. Why would I make it up? I read it in this book about p-p-political systems. It explains them all in simple terms — capitalism, socialism, anarchism, theocracy, democracy..."

"Mmm." He sounded uninterested. "One time, I got my earphones confiscated. It happens to everyone."

"Well...I d-don't like it. I don't like all these r-r-*rules*!" I spat the words out, frustrated at my unclear diction. I breathed in deeply, slowing my speech. "They're unfair and rigid. I mean, I understand you have to have s-some rules, like respecting others and not yelling in the c-corridors, but surely we should be allowed to w-wear what w-we want?" I bent my head, scanning over my uniform. "I don't agree with uniform. How am I supposed to express my indi-di-di..."

"Individuality?" he said helpfully. I smiled weakly at him. "Without my earrings, I'm just another drone."

Luke shrugged. "I dunno, I'd say you're pretty individual to me." Luke never wore the blazer. He always tied it around his waist, or had it slung over his arm. He said it made him feel too hot, even in winter. "You just need to get used to it, that's all."

"I c-can't. I don't l-like it here." I was in a slump. "And it's not just the uniform. It's everything. I don't *belong* here."

"Story of my life," said Luke cheerfully. "Oh, don't beat yourself up about it. Just give it a bit more of a chance."

I paced up and down, tapping my chin. "My cousin Patrice goes to L-Lakeland. You know, it's a b-boarding school, across in the Lake District."

"Cumbria?"

"No, it's a t-town sort of near Highwood and Milton K-Keynes. And it's tiny. Bas-sicaly encompass-sses the school and the c-c-city c-c-centre, which has Lakelandssss Sh-Sh-Shopping M-Mall — oh, for G-God's sake!" I balled my hands into fists and put my head in my hands. Luke put his arm around my shoulder.

"Hey, cheer up, mate. So, you want to go there?"

I nodded. "Patrice likes it a lot. He st-started going when he was tw-twelve. He was here for a year, but he was having problems at home, like arguing with his p-parents a lot and staying out late. I had no idea. He was so m-mellow and relaxed when he was at ours over Christmas. Anyway, they decided to send him to the boarding school to s-s-straighten — help him out, and he's been there ever since. He's doing his A levels there now."

Luke nodded, then frowned. "But you don't know anything about this place."

"You can wear whatever you like."

"Anne! That's not a good reason for starting a new school."

"I know, I know. It's just an i-i-idea — a thought I was having."

He hopped down from the bar. "I know you don't like it here, but *I* don't want you to move away. You're the first good friend I've had since Susie moved away. You've only been here a term and a bit. Can't you just give it a chance? It's not so bad."

I gave him a hug, but deep down, we both knew I wasn't happy there. It wasn't just the uniform. The school wasn't right for me. Maybe *school* wasn't right for me. Boarding school would be more like being home-schooled. You'd still have to go to lessons, but you got to live there. And Patrice had said there was much more freedom, and teachers were less restrictive and more relaxed. He said he'd messed around a lot at first, but after a couple years, really got down to it and learned way more than he had at day school. To me, it sounded perfect. Away in a nice, small town, like something out of Beatrix Potter. And I'd be far away from Meg.

I barely hung out with Zoe and her friends at school anymore. They were all friendly when they saw me, apart from Meg, who remained icy. Zoe could be as nice about it as she wanted, but Meg didn't seem like the type of person to pass up a grudge.

Later at home, I found myself on Zoe's laptop searching Lakeland online. For a staunch city girl, the charm of this town seemed strange, yet plausible. The website showed a sunny blue background with a bunch of happy, smiling students standing outside a grey brick building. I clicked on a slideshow of pictures of the school. It spread across acres. I imagined me and my future girlfriend lying by the river, eating ice-cream; talking about life and our dreams. Maybe we could buy a house in Copperwood; so much cheaper than London.

There was a knock at my door. Zoe bounded inside. "Helloooo! Just saying dinner is nearly ready. You still on my laptop?"

"Oh, yeah. Is th-that okay?"

"Sure. No probs! What you looking at?" She crouched on the floor next to me in front of her desk. "Oh, Lakeland. Yeah, I heard you asking Patrice about it. It's nice, isn't it? Mum actually took me there, like on the open day when I was in year six, but I didn't really want to go to boarding school even though it's not that far."

I drummed my fingers on her desk. "Erm, Zoe, I'm s-sort of...well, I've been thinking...I think I'd like to visit it myself."

She cocked her head to one side. "How come? You thinking of applying there?"

"Well...I mean, you know I'm not really ha-happy at Copperwood, and I know you're there and I have Luke, but I don't really...well, I haven't really settled in, and...yeah."

She had a big smile on her face. "I think you'd really like it. It sounds like a great idea, and the deadline for applications isn't 'til March, I think. We could all go visit if you'd like, you, me, and Mum."

I was glad she was being so supportive. "It seems like it would be more your thing —less restrictive, more independence, you know? Plus, you get to live there, so it would be like being home-schooled again."

"That's exactly what I was thinking." I peered at the site again, sighing. It had to be wonderful. "I'd love to go there. But I'd be st-starting year nine — or upper fourth, as they call it."

"You can start at any year. They *do* usually get over-subscribed quickly, though. It's such a good school, and it's one of the most popular boarding schools because it has a mix of state school and private school students. I think the ratio is like sixty-forty or something. But yeah, you should go for it. And you can say your cousin goes there. If you've got family there already, it gives you priority. And you're black. Not trying to sound rude or anything, but that gives you a big advantage for, like, diversity. And you're gay! Hey, you can use that in your favour!" She started jumping up and down.

I shuffled my feet uncomfortably. "Well, whatever gets me in, I g-guess."

"Oooh, this is so exciting! I'm so happy for you! I can't wait to tell Mum! We can book an open day right away!" She danced out of my room. I had to admire Zoe's enthusiasm and optimistic attitude when it came to…well, everything.

Chapter Eleven: Lakeland

A week later, Zoe, Aunt Colette, and I went to visit Lakeland.
They wouldn't have any open days until late February, but
Aunt Colette had said we could use going to visit Patrice as an
excuse for exploring the grounds. We got the train as it was
much quicker than driving. Zoe chattered about how much I
would love it and what a lovely place it was. It was an
especially chilly day. I felt very snug inside my Jane Norman
coat and silver pashmina scarf.

Through the window, I observed the passing hills and
cows grazing in the farms. Maybe living in the countryside
one day would be nice. Peaceful. In a quiet area somewhere in
England with my girlfriend...or wife. We could adopt children
or have our own via sperm donation. Funny, I had never
thought of the appeal of living in the countryside, but then,
Richmond wasn't as harum-scarum compared to the rest of
London. Certainly not in comparison to Clapton or the West
End.

When we reached Lake District Station, we got out. The
air smelled freshly of green and blue. Zoe was clamouring for
something to eat, so Aunt Colette bought her and me
chocolate croissants. They were soft and firm, without pieces
of the bread crumbling all over the place.

We walked out of the station and into town. It looked like
it had been carved by the hands of a carpenter on opium. The
footpaths were clean and freshly swept, paved with silver
concrete, and the buildings were modern with cars hauled in
front of them. The school was right at the end of the town, so
my aunt said we could hire a cab to take us up there, and then,
on the way back, have a walk and explore around. There
weren't many people queuing up, so we were able to get a cab

quickly. We got inside, and I peered out the window, marvelling at the view. It really resembled a fairy-tale town; all cobbled streets, narrow roads, and little independent vintage shops and cafés. Zoe nudged me and pointed to some geese walking by the river. The river really was beautiful and ran through the whole town along the side of it. There were willow trees framing the edges of the river on the riverbank. A couple people were sitting there, chatting, but few were around, probably due to the cold weather.

The cab drove to the school. It was an enormous building. In fact, there were several buildings — a main one at the front, then some more I could see around the back and sides. I guessed those were the dormitories. Zoe said it was even bigger around the back. There was more grass around the sides, and more geese and mallards trotting around. Zoe said there were even rabbits.

The cab driver drove into the car park and dropped us off there. My aunt paid him, thanked him, and then we got out. We walked out of the car park and into the main building, all new and modern on the outside. Inside was nice and warm, and there were three receptionists standing behind a long desk. One of them was on the phone, and another was typing something on the computer. The one who was free smiled at us.

"Hello there, can I help you?" she asked. "Hello," said my aunt. "We're here to visit my son, Patrice Peterson."

"That's fine. Can I see your ID please?"

My aunt handed the receptionist her driving licence, then checked something on her computer. "That's all good, thank you. Please sign the visiting book."

"My niece here is also thinking of starting Lakeland in September," said my aunt. The receptionist's smile broadened. "Oh, how lovely!"

"Yes, so we were wondering if we could have a wonder around whilst we're here?"

"Of course, so long as you don't disturb students whilst in their lessons."

"May we also speak with the head teacher?"

"Mrs. Saydes is usually busy, but you can find the application information on our website. If you want, I can have a guide give you a tour of Lakeland, or would you prefer your son show you around?"

"I think my son will probably give us a tour," said Aunt Colette. She and the receptionist laughed.

"No problem. Please wear these visitor badges all day. Visiting hours close at six p.m. — eight p.m. for sixth formers. Have a wonderful day!" She waved at me. "Maybe see you in September!"

I smiled at her, then the three of us walked through to the main building.

"Patrice said he was going to meet us at the canteen," said my aunt, peering at her phone. Zoe jumped up and down.

"I remember the way! It's this way." We walked through a corridor with lots of classrooms and notice boards. There were students sitting inside, listening attentively to the teachers speak. I saw artwork pinned up, and poems and pictures of smiley students, and quotes like, *"You can succeed at anything you put your mind to."* Zoe said we were in the arts and humanities section, and there was another section for maths and science, and one for technology and home economics. And then the sports block. P.E was compulsory once a week for everyone apart from sixth formers, who could choose to do it as a subject.

We walked through the corridors and pushed open the doors into the massive canteen. I got a shock when we walked in. It was brighter and even noisier than Copperwood, and these students looked much older. I couldn't even tell who was in my year. Everyone was wearing their own clothes and standing around, laughing, watching stuff on their phones, and playing music. Some were sitting at huge tables, texting. A girl threw something at a boy, who dodged out of the way. Three boys screamed, "Lad, selfie!"

It was more ethnically diverse than Copperwood, but the majority were still white. A simple observation. Zoe waved when she saw Patrice, who was coming over to us accompanied by a thin, freckled girl wearing glasses. He hugged all of us.

"Oh, this is Helen, my girlfriend," he said to me. "Hi," she said. She kissed Patrice on the lips, then walked away to her friends. I peered at my aunt, who didn't seem bothered by seeing her son kiss a girl in front of her. I wondered why that thought even occurred to me. I really didn't know how people were supposed to act in front of one another. Was this a terrible idea? I'd be stuck here in a place filled with teenagers and wouldn't have the comfort of my aunt's house to run to. I might not even have a Luke to complain to or laugh with.

"Should I show you around then?" Patrice said to me. "Give you the grand tour?"

"Mmm." They were all watching me. I'd gone off into space again. We left the canteen and walked down another corridor, past more classrooms.

"So, we have lessons every day like normal — well third, fourth and fifth formers do, but sixth formers don't," said Patrice.

"W-Why do they call it third and fourth form r-rather than year eight, year nine, and that?" I asked. Patrice shrugged. "No idea. I guess because it's always been called that. Something to do with early British schools. I think it was only when secondary moderns and comprehensives were built they started year seven, year eight, etcetera. But I dunno. You'd have to check that."

We walked up some stairs. I was marvelling at how big it all was. Much bigger than Copperwood, and more spacious. "Arts and Humanities are across here and upstairs. On the top floor there's Philosophy and Psychology but that's only for sixth formers."

"So, there are th-three floors?" I asked.

"Yep," said Patrice. "But massive corridors with like fifty classrooms on each floor. Everything is huge here, but you get used to it. It also gets pretty crowded what with students rushing forwards and backwards from lessons."

We walked past some music classes. Violins squeaked in one class; guitars strummed and drums clashed in another.

"Do sixth formers ha-have all their l-lessons here too?" I asked.

"Yeah, we all have our lessons in the same buildings, but at different times," said Patrice. "In sixth form, you do less subjects and you have less hours."

Zoe squealed, tugging my coat. "Hey, look at this!" She stood outside a door, peering in. The rest of us followed. A drummer, guitarist, keyboardist, and singer were playing "Diamonds" by Rihanna. It sounded amazing. The singer had a great voice, and the keyboards and guitar went well together.

It sounded different. The drummer had "funked it up," as my dad would say. It was just the four of them in the room, practicing together.

"Whoa, cool!" said Zoe. "I'd love to be in a band, but I'm not talented. I can't sing or play anything."

"You could always learn," said Aunt Colette, ruffling Zoe's hair. We moved along.

"Yeah, music is really good here," said Patrice. "Everything is, really. Every penny that comes in goes into the school, and there are seriously well-off kids with well-off parents here. The ones from poorer backgrounds can get scholarships, but they have to be seriously smart. It's a good school, and fair in who it admits."

"You have to p-pay fees to come here?" I asked my aunt.

"It's state funded education, but you have to pay for boarding," she said.

"H-how m-much is that?"

"About two thousand pounds per term."

Wow. That seemed like so much money to me, but then, I guessed Patrice's parents could afford it. If my going here had been a problem financially, they would have said something.

An uncomfortable thought occurred to me. "Erm, i-i-is my d-d-dad sending you any m-m-money?" I took a deep breath. "F-For me. Does he know I'm going to b-boarding school?"

Patrice and Zoe went quiet and waited for their mother. "I haven't spoken to him much, but he's been sending money since you arrived." My aunt paused. "He actually helped with Patrice's fees for years."

"Really!" Patrice said, shocked. "You never told me that! I've never even properly met Uncle John."

"He's a difficult man." Now my aunt appeared uncomfortable. "Maybe it's best not to talk about it. Let's try to enjoy the rest of the day — the grand tour, as Patrice is so wonderfully giving us." She forced a laugh.

He showed us the rest of the arts and humanities department, then we walked back downstairs through the main building to the other block, which had all the maths and science classes, then the back block, which had graphics, design and technology, food technology, media, film studies, and ICT. A girl and two boys came laughing outside one classroom. They were around my and Zoe's age. The girl had black choppy-layered hair, and was wearing a white top, short black skirt, and black fishnet tights. I was surprised those kinds of clothes were allowed. She also had a tattoo on one arm, though it must have been fake. One of the boys was short and dark-skinned like me, and the other had neat blond hair and wore glasses. He was saying something to the girl.

"No way. Like, no way, Simone. I'm *telling* you, you totally got called out for not doing the homework."

"But I *tried!*" She had a louder, more hysterical laugh than Zoe. "What's Mr. Clarkson gonna do anyway? Dumb-arse. He makes such empty threats with that 'list' of his. 'Stop messing about or your name's going on the list'! Oh, please."

"Haha, him and that list," said the black boy. "He never does anything with it anyway."

"*No one* ever does anything," said Simone. "What's he gonna do, call my parents? Yeah, like they'll give a shit." She stopped when she saw us. "Hi! You all right? Are you visiting?"

"Yeah, we're visiting," said Zoe. "My brother's in the lower sixth."

"Oh, cool!" said Simone. The boys spluttered with laughter. "Do you *have* to say hi to every person you see?" said the blond boy. "Sorry about her. She's weird as hell."

"Oh, we're all weird," giggled Simone. "Life would suck if we were all normal!"

"Couldn't agree more," said Zoe cheerfully.

"See, she knows!" said Simone. "Anyway, we gotta get to our next lesson. See ya! Enjoy your visit!" She trotted off with her friends.

Aunt Colette laughed. "What a funny girl. But what on earth was she wearing — especially in this weather? Mind you, I've seen students wearing all kinds of things here."

"Yeah, I mean they try to emphasise 'appropriate' clothing, but then because you live here and go here at the same time, people just end up wearing what they like," said Patrice. It reminded me of Copperwood; people just aimlessly breaking rules. At least no one would confiscate my earrings.

"That's most of the building," said Patrice. "Shall we go grab some food? I'm hungry."

"Sounds good. Anything else you'd like to see?" Aunt Colette asked me. I shook my head. I had been overwhelmed enough for one afternoon.

We went and had some lunch in a nice little café in Lake District Town. We had a pleasant view of the river. I was a bit disappointed we hadn't seen any rabbits. I liked rabbits. They were little and cute and fluffy.

"Are you allowed to keep p-pets at the school?" I asked Patrice.

"No," he said through a mouthful of his sandwich. "Sometimes people try to bring their pets in, or keep animals, but it's not allowed. A girl I know had a pet gerbil. It got confiscated. Someone even had a tarantula once."

"Oh *no!*" gasped Zoe. "That's horrible! I hate spiders! Why on earth would anyone want to keep one as a pet? Oooh." She shivered, scratching her arm. My aunt laughed. "Oh, dear. Yeah, I'm not one much for spiders either. They can be creepy."

"I don't mind them," said Patrice, shrugging. "I feel like it's sort of a stereotype, like we teach people to be afraid of them from a young age because most people are scared of them, so we start associating them with fear. There's nothing actually wrong with spiders. Most of them are harmless in this country."

"Yeah, they don't b-bother me so much," I said. "They used to t-terrify my m-mum though." A memory came to mind of one of the rare times I saw my dad laugh. There was a big spider scuttling along the kitchen floor, and Mum shrieked with terror while Dad was doubled over in laughter. I remember getting rid of the spider by chucking it out the window. Afterwards, my dad put his arm around my mum, twirled her around, patted my head, and called me a hero. I can't remember if he'd been drinking. He'd been in a good mood, so it was unlikely.

Thinking of my mum made my mouth go numb. I felt the world slow around me and couldn't finish my sandwich. I started blinking rapidly, then felt my body collapse.

I blinked, turning my face up. Zoe had a shocked expression on her face, and Aunt Colette also appeared worried. Patrice helped haul me up back onto my chair.

"Are you all right?" asked Aunt Colette. Zoe held my hand and rubbed my shoulders. I felt a grey cloud run through my soul, like the world has lost all its light.

"I think you had a panic attack," said Aunt Colette. She seemed concerned. "And they said you fainted at school that time. Do you think it's because you mentioned your mother?"

I nodded. I wanted to cry, but the tears couldn't come, and I couldn't cry in front of them even though they were all gazing at me with kindness and concern.

"Anne, you know you can talk to us about her any time," said my aunt. "It's better to let stuff out, remember?"

"You must be missing her. It's only natural. Don't you have a number for her or anything? I mean...she just left?" Zoe sounded forlorn.

I sniffed. "I th-think my d-dad...d-drove her away. Mum and I were very c-close. She loved me. And he t-*took* her from me." I burst into tears. Zoe pulled me towards her, letting me cry all over her jumper. "I'll never s-see her again." I sobbed and sobbed. Zoe soothed me. "I'm sure you will."

I wished I believed her.

Chapter Twelve: Boarders

Over the next several months, I filled out my application to Lakeland, along with a letter of recommendation my aunt had persuaded my English teacher to write. I spent as much time as possible with Luke. My uncle had bought me a laptop as a late birthday/Christmas present. Usually on my birthdays my dad would buy me some expensive jewellery or give me a hundred quid to spend as I liked. Mum and I would always do something together. One year, we got on lots of trains and busses and went all around London, pretending to be tourists and observing people and making up stories about their lives.

"So, that man is a robber, and the woman is his sidekick." *She pointed to a couple on the train. "They're off to conduct the Great London Robbery."*

"And they're going to be very slick about it, right?" I *said. "You see how neutral and non-suspicious they seem? But they've actually got walkie-talkies in their bags and sacks to stuff all the money into."*

Mum laughed. "And they're ready to call their back-up anytime — so they can make a quick getaway."

"Of course."

That summer, we all went on holiday to Cornwall for two weeks, instead of Scotland like normal. I breathed in the sand and the sea and the fresh country air and decided it didn't matter if God had created the world's beauty, or if it came as the earth evolved.

I was accepted into Lakeland. I was to start in September, a few days after turning fourteen. I began having nightmares again, of my dad battering my mum with a hammer or stabbing her. The walls were thick, and Zoe was a heavy sleeper. Marcus heard me a few times, glancing my way at the breakfast table. I wondered what I would do at boarding school. You had to share a room with someone else — only sixth formers were allowed their own rooms. What if I screamed in the night and woke them? At least girls and boys had separate dorms. The girls were in one block and the boys were in the other.

Patrice had shown us his dorm and said there was a bathroom with shower cubicles on each corridor. There were some rooms with their own shower, but you had to pay extra for those, and they were only available for sixth formers. I tried to imagine standing in a cubicle with strange girls next to me, naked, water raining down their lathered skin.

My aunt drove me up there, along with Zoe, who went back to school the day after I started. All my stuff was in the car. Moving on again. The first day was just people either returning to board and starting afresh, and there was to be an assembly for newcomers. We'd also get given our timetables and assigned classes.

I had said bye to Luke before going. We promised to stay in touch.

"Will you wr-write to me as well?" I said. Luke laughed. "What, like letters?"

"Yes. We can be p-pen p-pals." We both giggled at my stutter. I smacked his arm. "But what if I have nothing to write about?" he asked.

"Then y-you can write 'dear Anne, life's cool, not m-much is happening, I'm just letting you know I'm alive.'"

He laughed again. "If you say so." We gave each other a hug. "I'll miss you," he said. I would miss him too. I hoped he would write.

I said bye to all my family too. I was overcome with tears again and had to run upstairs to my room. Marcus gave me a giant hug and lifted me up, saying it had been great to have me around and that I'd mellowed his sister out. Uncle Brian also said it had been lovely having me. I couldn't believe they had let me stay with them and given me a life. If only I had known them before. If only Mum had known...perhaps she would still be around. But there's never any use wondering what might have been.

Uncle Brian and Patrice helped move all my stuff into Aunt Colette's car. Patrice wasn't due to start for another few days. He said he would watch out for me when I was there; the same thing Zoe had said when I started Copperwood. I was grateful, although I presumed it would be difficult if he was studying a lot.

Zoe was babbling in the car journey about how excited she was for me to be starting this whole new chapter in my life.

"I bet you'll love it there," she said. "Does this feel weird? All these changes?"

"Yes," I said.

Aunt Colette chortled. "Of course it will. You've been through a lot, dear, but you've dealt with it all incredibly. We're all so proud of you, you know."

"Like, *so* proud of you," said Zoe.

Her friends had all wished me well. They had been surprisingly kind to me, even Meg. Or maybe they were just happy I was going. Zoe said her friends had really liked hanging out with me, but maybe she was just saying that to be nice. I couldn't really think of a good reason as to why anyone would want to be in my company. But then...Luke had. He liked me. And Zoe liked me…but we were family; she was supposed to.

"Gosh, this traffic," said my aunt, blaring her horn. "Bloody hell, it's everywhere."

"Guess everyone has the same idea," said Zoe. "Oooh, there could be people in other cars starting Lakeland too! Who knows, you could end up best friends with some of them! Isn't that weird?"

"I suppose." I hadn't really thought about it. I had thought more about meeting a girl. It plagued my thoughts. Would I meet a girl here? Would I meet a girl anywhere? But what girl would want me? Why would anyone want someone as dark and dull as me?

"Oh, good, we're picking up speed," said my aunt. Zoe was sitting in the back with me, and my bags and suitcase were all in the boot. My aunt's massive handbag sat on the seat next to her. She put on the radio, whistling along.

"I *hate* this song. Nicki Minaj is so shit," moaned Zoe, as her latest single, "Anaconda", came on. "And it's so catchy too! Now it's going to be stuck in my head!"

"All the music you guys listen to today is bad," said Aunt Colette. "When I was young, we had *real* music. People used to go discos and dance. Those were good times."

"I do listen to real music!" protested Zoe. "I listen to One Direction! They're awesome!"

My aunt burst out laughing. "One Direction is not real musicians, Zoe. They're a manufactured boy band."

"They're the best."

"You only like them because you f-find them attractive," I pointed out. "If they were ugly, you wouldn't think twice."

"I like them cos they're hot *and* have good songs," said Zoe, jumping up as a One Direction song came on the radio.

"Oooh! I love this! Wow, this song is so old now! I wish *I* lit up somebody's world like nobody else!"

"That bass line is the same as that song from *Grease*," said my aunt. She began to sing "Summer Nights." Zoe sang too. They both sounded off key and out of time with the One Direction song playing in the background. It was funny, though. I slid down in my seat, staring outside the window at the other passing cars. I thought about what Zoe had said. Suppose there were students out there on their way to Lakeland like me? Boys I would potentially meet, and girls...

"Hey, Anne, let's play 'I Spy,'" said Zoe. "I spy, with my little eye, something beginning with...C!"

"Cars," I said. She gasped. "How did you know?"

"Because you always pick the most obvious suggestions."

As we drove off the motorway and pulled into Lake District Town, I felt my tummy gnaw away at itself and my knees began to quiver. We drove towards the gaping school gates; thrown wide open like they were welcoming the world and his wife inside. Upper third to fifth formers started today. Sixth formers started in a few days. The first assembly was for Key Stage 3 — upper third and fourth formers — and then fifth formers had their assembly later. It was confusing trying to remember to say third and fourth rather than year seven, year eight, and the like.

A bunch of smiling students were on hand, ready to help escort newcomers to their dorms and carry luggage up. Patrice said these were prefects, and they had them in every year. They ran the student body and had to help all the new students, make sure people weren't going outside after dark, that sort of thing.

I inspected all the other students, the new and returning. I gulped. Zoe was jumping up and down. "Isn't it exciting, knowing you'll be meeting all these people in a homier environment?"

I nodded, trying to ignore the fear flooding through my tummy.

"Hello there!" said two smiling girls. "I'm Heather, and this is Lisa. Do you guys need any help with anything?"

"Oh, yes, thank you," said my aunt. "Where do you find out where your room is?"

"I'll check now." Lisa scanned over the clipboard in her hand. "What year are you in?" she asked Zoe and I, peering between us. Zoe pointed to me. "She's the one starting."

"I'm st-starting y-year nine — I mean, up-upper f-fourth," I stammered. Lisa laughed, but not unkindly. "It's confusing, isn't it? Don't worry, you'll get used to it. Upper fourth girls. Quite a few new ones this term."

"What year are you girls in?" asked my aunt.

"We're upper fifth," said Heather. "GCSEs, eek! Not fun. I miss Key Stage 3. What's your name?" She peered at me.

"A-Anne Mason."

Lisa scanned down the sheet, then smiled. "Great! You're in room 104, and you're Upper Fourth Form 2."

"W-Who's my roommate?" I asked uncertainly as the girls helped haul our baggage towards the boarding house. "Oh, don't worry, she'll be another newbie like you," said Lisa. "They put all the new students in the same rooms first term, so you'll be fine. You're sharing with a girl named Sarah."

"Okay," I said. Zoe skipped around. You'd have thought she was starting, not me. I kept glancing around at everyone. They were all getting out of their cars or talking to prefects.

Some were scared, some upset, some happy, and some indifferent.

Heather and Lisa escorted us to the girls' boarding house. Both boarding houses were behind the main building. Only sixth formers could go into the opposite sex's boarding house after lights were out, but Patrice said people still snuck out and some of the prefects let you off.

Lisa pressed the button to call the lift. She waved to some other girls behind us, also escorting people inside. A bunch of us stepped into the lift — parents, new students, and prefects crammed in, all of us strangers. We stepped out into the corridor.

"Room 102, Room 103 — ah, here you go!" said Heather. She pushed open the door to 104. The first thing I saw was a girl sitting on a bed with her mum, dad, and two anxiously hovering prefects. The girl was howling.

"I DON'T WANT TO LIVE HERE! I WANT TO GO BACK HOME!" she screamed. "Now, Sarah, we've talked about this," said her mum. "We said unless you got your grades up, you'd be sent to boarding school."

"But I tried, I really did. I promise if you let me come back home, I'll be good!"

She sniffed and noticed the five of us who had just walked into the room. I spread my fingers at her in an awkward wave.

"This is Anne, your new roommate," said Heather brightly. Sarah's parents clapped their hands in enthusiasm. "See, this is the girl you'll be sharing your room with! Isn't that exciting?"

Sarah shook her head and pushed past us, running out of the room. Her parents ran after her. The two prefects shrugged and followed.

"Every year it happens," said Heather. "There's always that one kid, that one crying kid who insists they don't want to be here." She and Lisa placed my things down. "She may end up having to go back home, but it depends on the situation."

"Oh dear," said my aunt. "If that were to happen, who would take the room?"

"Another student could move in here if they're unhappy with their current roommate. It's happened before."

Zoe sat down on the free bed. I took in the room properly. It wasn't huge, but big enough for two people, with two beds, two bedside tables, two chests of drawers, a large wardrobe, two desks with chairs, and a sink. Zoe opened the wardrobe. "Cool, there's a mirror on the inside door!" She started striking poses at herself while I bit the skin of my thumb, wondering what I was doing in this strange place. There was also a cupboard with plenty of storage space. I noticed a little white card on each of the bedside tables.

"These are your room keys," said Lisa, handing me my card. "You simply tap it on the door handle to lock it and tap it twice to unlock. Simple."

"W-What's going to ha-happen to Sarah?" I asked nervously.

"Don't worry about her," said Heather. "She'll be fine. We'll give you some space to unpack now and settle. When you're ready, you can come down to the assembly hall for the welcome talk. Hope you enjoy the rest of your day!"

They both left as cheerily as they had entered.

Chapter Thirteen: Roomies

I inspected the room, sitting on the bed. Another new home. Zoe was jumping around, opening the cupboard and sitting on the swivelling desk chairs and peering out the window.

"Oooh, you can see the garden from here! Cool! Come see Mum!"

Aunt Colette smiled. "Oooh, nice. There's a garden and vegetables growing and a fence — over in the distance, there's a football pitch. How lovely."

"I d-don't really l-like football," I said. I hugged my knees to my chest. Zoe laughed. "I'm sure you don't have to play football! You get to pick what extra-curricular stuff you want to do. Gosh, you're so lucky! I almost wish I was coming here."

Aunt Colette glanced at her watch. "We should probably go downstairs to the assembly hall," she said. I stood up, shivering inside my coat.

"You okay, Anne?" Zoe linked her arm through mine before we walked out the door. I remembered to lock it with my room key card. We saw other students and parents making their way downstairs to the assembly hall. They were talking amongst themselves loudly, but I barely heard anything. If it hadn't been for Zoe's arm curled around mine, I would've sworn I was floating across the ground like a ghost.

We had to go into the assembly hall for this welcome talk, and then collected our timetables. It all skimmed past my head like a blur and by the end of it I was yawning, wanting to just go to my room and lie down and be away from all these people. My Aunt and Zoe walked along with me across the corridor and outside the main building. Both were talking to me, but I barely heard them. My body had gone heavy, and the world was full of background noise.

We stood outside the building. Most of the other parents were leaving. I saw them, but didn't notice them. They were nothing but an amalgamation of shapes and faded colours. Zoe squeezed her arms around me. "Remember you can call and message me whenever!"

I nodded. "Of c-course."

"Aw!" Her body snuggled warmly against mine and I suddenly wanted to cry, not wanting my cousin to leave me all alone in this unfamiliar place. She felt safe and full of love. "Let me know how your first day of lessons go tomorrow!" She stepped back from me, holding my hands in hers. "You'll be fine, I know it. You're super smart."

"Take care, darling." Aunt Colette hugged me, and then I blinked rapidly and swallowed. She smiled, and then her face fell and flicked to Zoe's. "Is everything alright?"

"Yeah, I j-just need some r-rest. Been a long d-day."

"Mm. Well, we'll come visit loads of course, and we'll see you in the half term and at Christmas anyway." Zoe hugged me again and blew me a kiss, and they went back to their car, leaving me alone.

I stepped into the lift, up to room 104. The door was already unlocked, so I guessed Sarah had decided to stay after all. I pushed open the door and jumped.

"...because this girl decided she doesn't want to be here, blah, blah, blah, I'm bunking with this new girl...yeah, you *know* I hated sharing with Katie last year. She was such a bitch. Gosh, tell me about it! But whatever. New year, and all that. Fucking GCSE options and all that crap. Everyone knows upper fourth is a blast. It doesn't really get serious 'til *next* year..."

A girl was sitting on the bed meant to be Sarah's, talking loudly on the phone. Her suitcase was wide open on the floor, along with a bunch of bags and a black shape that resembled an unopened guitar case. Hair products, bath products, and makeup spilled onto the floor and along the top of the chest of drawers. She smiled at me. I recognised her. Black, choppy-layered hair. Green eyes. Red lipstick. A white cut-off top, a tiny black skirt, tights, black shoes. There was a tattoo of roses on one arm. I saw her when we came to visit.

"Hey!" she said to me. I was still standing by the door. "*Basically,* the girl who was supposed to be here decided she doesn't want to be here anymore, because she was so upset about leaving home. She's gone back with her parents and they're gonna decide what to do, blah blah blah, but this room was free and I absolutely *hated* the girl I was going to be sharing with this year, so I literally begged to be put in a different room. They normally let you share with your friends, but I applied late because I'm so frickin' unorganised, and they put me with this annoying bitch who isn't even in our year, she's in the year above, and I was just telling my friend about it and yeah." She flicked her hair out of her face while I grunted and sat down on my bed.

"So, you're Anne, right? Anne Mason, new girl?"

I nodded.

"That's cool. I'm Simone. Simone Van Pyre."

For the first time that day, I found myself laughing. Maybe it was her full-on personality or her surname or a release of tension from the entire day — I didn't know. She laughed too.

"Yeah, I know, it sounds like *vampire*. I tell people I'm Mona the Vampire. *Watch out!*" She curled her fingers like she was making a claw. "My dad is from Holland, hence the 'Van.' We go there like every year to see his family. But yeah, we're gonna be roomies! You get to put up with me all year."

"Mmm." I took off my shoes and lay down on my bed, facing upwards.

"Sorry about the mess," she said. "I can be really messy. It's something I'm gonna try to work on this year, don't you worry." She started whistling. "So, whereabouts are you from? Like, which city?"

"Erm...L-London," I said. "B-But I've—"

"Oooh, I'm from London as well!" she squealed, clapping her hands. "Which part? I'm from Kensington. Proper posh. You should see my parents. They sent me here because they hoped it would straighten me out." She rolled her eyes. "They don't 'approve of my lifestyle.'" She had her fingers raised in air quotes.

"Mmm." I closed my eyes, wondering if it were possible to drown her out. "I'm f-from Richmond."

"Oh, I *love* Richmond! It's beautiful! Old Deer Park is so pretty! And the houses! You go there, and it's like a little village, like it isn't even part of the city. How lucky for you to grow up there! Mind you, this school's weird. Like, half the kids here come from well-off places like us, then half are from shit-holes. Most people come from London, cos it's near, and then a few are from Surrey or Brighton or other small random towns nearby. Guess it makes sense. Why would you come all the way from somewhere like Liverpool to a boarding school at the bottom of the country? Still, Lakeland has a great reputation. It's really—"

I lay down on my bed, taking off my shoes while she prattled on. She was worse than Zoe.

"I might go see some of my mates in a bit. Do you want to come?"

I peered at her and shook my head. My eyes were closing. I heard her shoes clacking around the room. She was muttering to herself and whistling. I groaned inwardly, turning over. This was going to be a long year.

Chapter Fourteen: New Friends

I woke up the next morning to the sound of Simone snoring. She still had some bags strewn around the floor, but the room was overall tidier. I checked my phone on my bedside table. 6:30 a.m. There was still two hours until registration. Simone was in the same form as me, hence why she had gotten the room so quickly. I rolled onto my back, staring up at the ceiling. Today was my first day at school. Again. Only, this time, I was living here. Aunt Colette and Uncle Brian and Zoe weren't here to take care of me. I was on my own.

Zoe and Aunt Colette had texted me several times, asking if I was all right and getting settled in. I sent them standardized responses; that everything was fine, and I was adjusting to my new surroundings. I listened to Zoe's voice note, laughing at her complaints and then wistful at the sound of her voice. I suddenly longed for Zoe to be in the room with me, accompanying me to my lessons. What if people laughed at me again? What if nobody liked me or I couldn't make any friends?

I needed something to give me courage. I pulled open the top drawer of my little bedside table and took out the photos, flicking through the glossy images. "I wish you were here, Mum," I whispered. "I miss you every day."

I wondered how my dad was doing. My hand tightened around my phone. I still had his number. I opened my contacts to where he was listed, feeling my chest tighten at the thought of sending him a message. Instead, I selected the options from the drop-down menu and blocked and deleted his number. There was no point. What could I possibly say to a drunken middle-aged man who was supposed to be my male role-model? I pictured him slumped over his desk, two empty bottles of whiskey next to him. I pictured his bloodshot eyes and drool all over his shirt, my mum no longer there to iron his clothes.

An hour or so later, Simone's alarm went off. I had just returned from the shower. A few girls had been in there with their towels wrapped around them. I had ducked my head and gone into a cubicle with my shower gel and scurried out again as fast as I could, trying not to make eye contact.

Simone stirred as I was pulling on my clothes. She yawned, switched off her alarm, then pulled her duvet cover back over her head, groaning. I shook my head. I went to the wardrobe. Simone had taken up most of the space with her clothes, mine all pressed against the side. My end resembled a bat cave. I picked out a black, long-sleeved dress, tights, and underwear from the chest of drawers. As I got dressed, I glanced at Simone, who was still lying in bed. It was 7:46. If she didn't get up soon, she'd miss breakfast and be late for registration. I walked over to her bed, tapping her.

"H-Hey," I said. "You'd better get up, or you'll m-miss br-breakfast."

She mumbled something inaudible. "C-Come on," I said, tapping again. "It's qu-quarter to eight."

She ignored me again. At least I tried. Sighing, I went over to where my earrings were on top of the drawers. I picked out some dangly silver ones, then opened the wardrobe. I put on a silver necklace Uncle Brian had bought me. I smoothed my hair, still tied up in its usual bun and cane-rolls. It was a nightmare when I had to comb it once a week. I peered again at Simone's bed. It was almost eight. I walked over to her.

"C-Come on!" Just my luck to have such an exasperating roommate. "Simone, come on, g-get out of b-bed or you won't be able to eat anything until br-break time."

"I can't be bothered," she mumbled. "Just go without me."

"B-But you were s-supposed to sh-show me…" My voice trailed off. I squeezed my eyes shut, then opened them again. "Our f-form room? U4 2? I don't know w-where it is."

"Ms. Handells is our tutor," she mumbled. "She teaches art."

"Come on," I pleaded, tugging at her sheets. "Come, let's g-get something to eat. I don't want to g-go down by myself." I was starving. She didn't move again. I rolled my eyes at the ceiling.

"Fine, I'll m-meet you downstairs." I put on my black shoes, grabbed my bag, and went downstairs to the canteen.

I was mad at Simone for leaving me all by myself. I decided she was a real pain. I would try to find some friends who were less irritating. I gulped when I walked into the canteen. There were students everywhere, of every year. They chatted loudly, all confident, except the smaller upper third students who seemed as scared as I felt.

I collected a tray, joining the line to get breakfast. The dinner ladies were much friendlier than the ones at Copperwood. I selected scrambled eggs on toast and hash browns with tea. I didn't know where to sit. Because of the lack of uniform, it was so hard to tell how old everyone was. Some of the bigger students could have been in my year or they could have been fifth formers. Everyone roughly my age was sitting with groups of friends.

I felt stupid, just standing there holding a tray. I walked around a little, trying to find a free spot where I could sit by myself. I felt angrier at Simone for leaving me all alone. Why did she have to be so lazy?

I noticed a group at a table in the centre of the room. They were all laughing loudly, waving their phones around. Some of them were yawning and complaining about how they couldn't be fucked to be back this year.

Then I saw her. A girl at their table. She was talking to one of the other girls. Calmly, not loudly. She had a white, heart-shaped face, and a pink tank top on. And her hair…long, soft, bright natural red, as if she'd been kissed by flames. There was something comforting about her face — something gentle. She tucked shiny ginger tendrils behind her ear, then smiled at the girl she was talking to. Her friends struck me as brash or lazy, but she blended in. Like she had nothing to prove. She turned her face, and for a moment, noticed me. I turned away quickly, feeling like an idiot.

"Anne!" somebody yelled at me from behind, making me jump. It was Simone. I glared at her. "You f-finally made it out of b-bed."

"Yup," she said, yawning, clearly oblivious to my hostility. She was still in her pyjamas and carrying a tray with only a bit of fruit and yoghurt and a cup of coffee.

"Come on. I'll introduce you to my friends." We walked past the table with the girl to a different group of girls and boys. I recognised two of them.

"Ey, look who just rolled out of bed!" a boy with messy brown hair and equally messy clothes called out. Simone stuck her tongue out at him as we sat down. "Quiet, Steve."

The blond boy wearing glasses sniggered at her. "Why the hell didn't you get dressed?"

"She overslept again. Lazy bitch," said a pretty girl with a strong cockney accent. Simone groaned. "Can you guys please leave it? Maybe I like wearing my pyjamas to registration."

"Yeah, that's what you had to do last year cos Ms. Handells kept giving you detention for turning up late," said the blond boy, making everyone else laugh. Simone cleared her throat.

"Guys, I would like to introduce you all to my new friend and roommate. This is Anne Mason." She smiled, pointing to me. They all cheered, "Welcome, Anne!" I felt extremely bashful.

"Sorry about this lot, they're a bunch of weirdos," Simone said to me.

"Yeah, we're the weird kids," said the black boy sitting next to her. Simone slapped his arm. "Right, I want you to all go around the table and introduce your names. Let's start with Melvin."

"But you just said my name. Does that mean I need to say it again?" said the black boy. Simone slapped him again whilst he burst out laughing. "And say your surnames too please. Let's bring in some formalities."

"Oh, you want us to bring in formalities?" said Steve. "What's this all about?"

"Can you idiots *please* shut up for five fucking minutes and be civilised?" snapped Simone. "My friend here is a very civilised young lady from Richmond."

"Oooh, you're from Richmond? So, you're all posh like this one then?" said the blond boy. Simone glared at him and turned to Melvin.

"Okay, hi, I'm Melvin Marshall," he said, waving at me. He was nice-looking and had an easy-going demeanour. "His dad's Richard Marshall, the radio presenter on BBC1," said Steve. Melvin shook his head at him. "Why'd you have to say that?"

"Hey, you should be proud of it, man!"

The blond boy was next, sitting opposite Melvin. "Hi, I'm Roger Puffin, and I'm the coolest person at this table—"

"Don't listen to anything he says," said Simone. I laughed nervously. Roger stuck his tongue out at her. He wore thick-framed glasses and his blue polo T-shirt was tucked into his trousers, which I imagined were as stiff as cardboard. I imagined his mother had pressed every single item of clothing he had before he came to school.

"I'm Steve Smith," said the boy next to him, the opposite of Roger with his greasy brown hair and rumpled clothing. "I'm way cooler than Roger, as you see."

"Except she *won't* see, cos no one's cooler than me."

"I'm way cooler than you both," said the cockney girl, rolling her eyes. She was next to Steve. "Hi, darling, I'm Canel Batuk."

"If you want to piss her off, call her Kanel or Canal," said Roger, shrieking with laugher. He and Steve high-fived each other whilst Canel yelled at them. "It's pronounced *Janel,* teachers can't tell cos of the spelling innit, so they pronounce it like 'Kanel.' It's a Turkish name." I nodded. She was gorgeous. She had big brown eyes, olive skin, and thick, curly brown hair with blonde bits at the end. Simone clapped her hands and reckoned me. "You've met my crew now. Welcome, my darling."

"Hey, guys, we'd better get going. It's nearly time for registration," said Roger. I stood. "D-Do we l-leave our trays here or t-take them?" I asked.

"Leave them. The dinner ladies will take them," said Simone. Canel rolled her big eyes. "We're *supposed* to take them. It's kinda rude to just leave 'em like that."

"You're lucky, you have a laid-back form tutor," said Simone. "She's got Mr. Oseni, the English teacher. He's lovely. I had him last year for English. Hopefully we'll have him this year too." She gasped when she saw it was just gone half eight on the huge clock on the wall. "Crap, Ms. Handells is gonna kill us. Come on, let's go."

Chapter Fifteen: Lord of the Flies

Ms. Handells did not "kill" us since it was only our first day, though she rolled her eyes at Simone for turning up in her pyjamas. Simone only smiled sweetly. She, Melvin, and I were all in the same form. We sat together while Ms. Handells let us talk amongst ourselves. She asked us what GCSE options we were thinking of choosing for fifth form.

"English, maths, and double science are compulsory," said Simone. "You can do triple science if you want — that's optional."

"Canel's picking that cos she wants to go into medicine later," said Melvin. He shuddered. "I hate science. It's so boring and confusing."

"I'll say," agreed Simone. "I'm deffo picking music and drama. And maybe geography. You know we can do GCSE psychology now? That would be so cool!"

"Y-You p-play the guitar, r-right?" I asked, remembering the case in our room. She nodded. Melvin nudged her. "Yeah, she's awesome. She plays guitar and sings. She's in a band."

My eyes widened. Simone giggled. "Well, *sort* of. We spent last term trying to sort ourselves out. We haven't actually performed in school or played any gigs yet."

"W-what k-kind of mu-music?" I persisted. "Sorry, I ha-have a slight st-stutter." I wiped my hands on my dress. Simone and Melvin regarded me patiently, like Luke had.

"We're called Radio Silence," she said. That made me laugh. "I just thought it sounded like a cool band name," she said. "We're kind of emo-punk. Think My Chemical Romance, Paramore, All Time Low, Bring Me the Horizon..."

"I d-don't know any of th-them," I said. Melvin laughed again at my confused expression. "Yeah, this one's a proper emo," he said. "Have you seen her tattoos?" He lifted her pyjama sleeve. Simone flexed her arms.

"Hey, it's fake, duh. My parents went mental when they saw it." I examined the rose with the thorns. It was pretty in an alternative sort of way. I noticed something else on her arm: thin, horizontal scars travelling upwards. I blinked at them. She didn't appear to notice. "I've got a tramp stamp too," she said.

Melvin burst out laughing. "No way."

"Got it over the summer. My parents don't know."

"W-what's a tramp st-stamp?" I asked. Smiling, Simone turned around and lifted the bottom of her pyjama top. On her lower back was this cool flowery design with a picture of a butterfly intertwined with hearts. My eyes widened. She turned back around, pulling her top down.

"W-why's it called a tr-tramp stamp?" I asked.

"Cos she's a hooker," said Melvin. Simone smacked his arm. "It's just some stupid stereotype that if you have a lower-back tattoo, you're easy or slutty or whatever. Obviously, mine aren't real cos you can't get real ones until you're eighteen." She rolled her eyes. "It's just nonsense said by people who get pissed off by anyone who tries to be different."

"Oh, okay." I thought her tattoos pretty, and wished I had the confidence to do something like that. My parents once said something about tattoos not being classy and deeming them common. I'd never seen the fuss about it all; they were simply works of body art.

"So, what kinds of music do you like, Anne?" Melvin asked me.

"Erm…soul, jazz, the st-stuff I grew up with, I guess. You?"

"Oh, I like pretty much anything," said Melvin. "As long as it sounds good or has a good beat."

The buzzer went off then. Time for us to head to our lessons. We collected our things. I had maths first period. I didn't mind any of my subjects. I'd been decent at all of it back in Copperwood. Simone and Melvin also had maths and moaned about it. They were in different classes. Ms. Handells gave Simone another telling off for not wearing proper clothes and said she needed to get changed at break time. She didn't sound too annoyed with her, though.

I got through my first day okay. It wasn't that different from Copperwood, except teachers seemed more laid back and classes were smaller. The work seemed more challenging, which was good. I liked the fact that we were going to be doing the Cold War in history. Teachers were all talking about GCSE options and what subjects we had to pick. I wasn't sure yet; there wasn't anything I particularly loved or despised.

I saw the red-haired girl at lunchtime again. She was going to fetch her tray. I jumped when I saw her. She gave me a little smile, then walked back to her table. I tried to stop staring at her. I wondered if Simone knew her or had ever spoken to her. I couldn't bring myself to ask.

My last lesson was English. Simone and I were in the same class. She did a thrilled jump. "We have Mr. Oseni! You'll love him. He's one of my favourite teachers." We were standing outside the class. Simone had changed into tight blue jeans and a black crop top showing off her "tramp stamp." I heard a few girls snigger behind us.

"Hey, Simone, you sucked off any guys lately?" said one of them. I turned around. I recognised them; they had been sitting at the same table as the red-haired girl. Simone glared at them, then went pink as other people laughed. "Yeah, nice tramp stamp," said a boy.

"I heard prostitutes mainly get those. All she needs now is a tongue piercing and she'll be ready to hand out BJs for money." A tall girl with braids, dark skin, and a nose stud nudged her mates as they all sniggered. I don't know what came over me, but I walked up to her. "I think it's nice." I spoke very slowly and clearly, careful not to trip on my words.

The girl stopped laughing. She raised her eyebrows at me. "Huh?"

"My friend's tattoo. I think it looks nice on her," I said. "A-And you should stop making fun of her."

The tall girl flicked her braids out of her face. "Or what?"

I racked my brain, then ogled her piercing. "I heard g-getting your nose pierced on the right side makes you a prostitute in s-some countries, so maybe you need to re-think yourself."

The girl gasped. A bunch of kids laughed. "Aww, she got you, man!" they called out. She put her hand to her nose, then glared at me. "And who the fuck do you think you are?"

"My n-name is Anne. A-Anne Mason."

She kissed her teeth and stood closer to me. My heart beat increased, but I remained cool, ignoring the sweat on my palms. She scanned me up and down.

"You new here, A-A-Anne Ma-Ma-Mason?" she mocked. I nodded.

"I'll be watching you, stuttering know-it-all. Don't go disrespecting me like that again. You don't fucking know who you're talking to."

"I'll b-bare that in mind." I stepped back. Her friends regarded me like I was dirt. I swallowed. Simone turned to me. "Thanks for that," she said, "but it wasn't the best idea."

I shrugged. I'd seen worse. Simone opened her mouth, but Mr. Oseni arrived. He unlocked the door, and we stepped inside. Some teachers assigned a seating plan in alphabetical order, but he said we could sit where we liked. Simone and I sat at the front next to each other. At Copperwood, everyone had tables, but here, we all had our own desks, which I liked. Mr. Oseni welcomed us to upper fourth top set English and told us we were going to be studying *Lord of the Flies.* Excitement zipped through me. I loved that book. We were going to be reading it in class, watching the movie, then analysing its cultural and historical significance. Somebody behind Simone and I raised their hand.

"Sir, why are we studying a book about flies? Or is like *Lord of the Rings* but with flies?"

I burst out laughing. "L-Lord of the Flies isn't about flies," I said. "It's a metaphor for these boys who get stranded on a d-desert island after their plane crashes and slowly become crazy and think a beast is c-coming to get them. This non-existent 'beast' is the lord of the flies, the flies being all of the n-nasty insects and bugs that surround the island as well as the boys' terrified imaginations. There's one p-particular scene where one of the boys sees a pig's head on a stick and thinks of it as the 'lord of the f-flies.'"

I coughed after blurting all of this out. Simone smiled at me, miming an air high-five. I heard some of the mean girls from earlier mutter some comments. Mr. Oseni nodded, impressed. "That's a very good summary of the story, in a nutshell," he said. "And what's your name?"

"A-Anne. Anne Mason. I-I'm n-new."

"Hello, Anne," he said kindly. "Welcome to our class. It's good to have you here. To all the newcomers, welcome, and I hope we have a really good year and enjoy ourselves."

Something hit the back of my head. I turned around and picked it up. It was a rumpled piece of paper. I opened it.

KISS-ARSE.

How charming, I thought. I turned around, scrutinized the girls, then scrunched it up and put it in my bag.

Chapter Sixteen: School Social Hierarchy

"I was going to tell you earlier," said Simone when we were back in our dorm room at the end of the school day. "Those girls you were talking to…they're horrible. It's better to just avoid them or avoid talking to them."

"Don't worry. I'm no st-stranger to bitchy or horrible girls," I mumbled. I was sitting back on my bed. Simone was sitting on hers, stretching her legs out. "They're, like, the populars. They all sit at this massive table at lunch, you might've seen them."

"Ma-Massive table?" I thought of the red-haired girl. "What are their names?"

"The one you were talking to, with the nose piercing, that's Olivia. She's, like, the leader. Last year, she and Emma, this other girl in their group, kept yelling at me in P.E and calling me 'flat chest' and other stupid stuff. By the end, I just bunked P.E."

"Didn't you t-tell your parents? Or th-the teachers?"

She shrugged. "What were they gonna do? Everyone loves the populars. They hardly ever get into trouble. The boys do, but not so much the girls. Anyway, the other two in our class were Tasha and Kim. Kim's proper spoilt. Her dad practically funds a third of this school. I used to know her before I went here, cos she's from Kensington as well. She used to be a right snob, and now she tries to act all down-to-earth." Simone kicked off her shoes, clearly annoyed. She certainly wasn't a "right snob." I'd have hardly guessed she was from Kensington if it weren't for the mildly plumy accent.

"W-What about the others?" I asked. "I-In that…erm, group."

"There's Amelia. She's pretty annoying and really dumb, like *really* fucking dumb. Melvin had to sit next to her last year in history and he said she thought World War II happened five hundred years ago when there were dinosaurs."

I stared at her blankly. "B-But there weren't d-dinosaurs f-five hundred years—"

"Exactly."

"Oh." I laughed. "Who else?"

"Jacinta…she's all right. Emma's awful. Then there's Karen, she's kinda quiet. I don't really know her."

"Okay." I wanted to ask which one was which.

"Don't worry, I'll point them all out to you at lunch some time," she said. "So you know to stay away from them. And the wannabes, and the roadmen…"

"Sorry?" I wasn't following. Simone shook her head. "I'll show you tomorrow at lunch. Do you want to come to Canel's room to watch a couple movies? The others are all there."

"Th-That sounds nice."

"We're thinking of just staying in today, especially since it's raining. We'll chill there for the rest of the afternoon and evening."

"W-What about prep?" I asked.

She laughed. "Anne, no one goes to prep. Only fifth formers and sixth formers cos they have actual exams. A few of the nerdy kids go, but that's it. There's no point going now. It's the start of the year and we don't have any work. Best to go later when we actually have tests and all that."

"B-But…w-won't the teachers check?"

She shrugged. "Nah, not really. They're not that bothered. I mean, they say they are, for, like, standards and all that, but honestly, they're pretty chill. Don't worry about it."

I *was* worried, especially since I wanted to make a start on the reading for *Lord of the Flies*. I wanted to re-read the book myself, even though we were going to be reading it in class. I thought I could start on some of the analysis and character themes. I really wanted to impress Mr. Oseni. I liked Ms. Handells, and most of my other teachers seemed fine, but Mr. Oseni was my favourite so far. He seemed very gentle and enthusiastic, and even though we'd only had one lesson, I hadn't heard him raise his voice at all.

"See, I *told* you he's great," Simone had said to me after. It had been a good lesson — minus the note. I'd ripped that up and thrown it in the bin.

Canel's room was across the corridor from ours. Her roommate was a girl named Fatima, who was always out. Canel reckoned we'd have the room to ourselves for the rest of the evening.

"Do you know where she goes?" asked Melvin as we all made ourselves comfortable.

"Kind of. I think she just goes into town a lot to the shopping centre and meets friends," said Canel. "Plus, she writes for the Lakeland paper and travels up to Highwood to go Mosque, and she goes to the library a lot. She's just proper busy. Like, she's nice, but she's in and out constantly."

"Means we can just chill in here then," said Roger. Simone, Melvin, and I were sitting on Canel's bed, while Canel, Roger, and Steve were on cushions on the floor. Canel was opening Netflix on her laptop. They'd brought a ton of snacks. I got déjà vu of being with Zoe's friends.

"Ha-Have you g-guys ever seen *Two Girls One C-Cup?*" I blurted out. They all gaped at me. Simone burst out laughing, Melvin groaned, Roger and Steve began making stupid noises and miming things, and Canel pointed her finger at me. "You know what, my older brothers made me watch that, and I am *not* fucking going through that shit again. No frickin' way."

"Oh, go on, let's all watch it now for a laugh," said Steve.

"Are you *mad?* Fuck that shit, that's nasty," said Melvin. "Some fucking weird fetish, man. People are fucked up."

I gasped. "I w-wasn't sug-suggesting…just w-wanted to kn-know if any-anyone else ha-had s-seen…"

"I think everyone's seen that," said Simone. "I met the director once. He actually asked if I wanted to be in a porno."

"Rubbish," said Roger. "You never met the director."

"Yes, I did!" she yelled. "I did, honest. But I turned it down because I didn't want people seeing me in it. He actually thought I was eighteen."

"She wouldn't even have needed to audition. She could just go as she is," said Steve, nudging Roger.

"All right, guys, what are we watching?" said Canel. "And no fucking pornos."

"Let's watch *Divergent*," suggested Melvin. "That's supposed to be really good."

"Isn't that just like the new *Hunger Games*?" asked Steve.

Simone squealed. "Oh, I love *Hunger Games*. *Mockingjay* is out soon! Yes, guys, we are so watching that."

"We'll watch *Divergent* then," said Canel. "Everyone cool with that?"

We were cool with it, and it was a fun movie — another teen dystopia where America had been blown up. I liked the main character, Triss, better than Katniss from *The Hunger Games*. Steve and Roger kept taking the piss and making random jokes. Simone had to kick their backs to tell them to shut up.

"God, Four is so sexy," said Canel, referring to Triss's love interest.

"Yeah he is," said Simone, "but what kind of fucking name is *Four?*"

"His real name's Tobias," said Melvin.

"Yeah, but still, of all nicknames, give me a number!" said Simone. "What's his sister called, Five? Is he gonna name his son Seven?"

"He doesn't have a sister, you idiot," said Roger.

"I shagged a guy who looked like him once," said Simone. "His name was Mark. He rode a motorbike. God, he was so fit."

"You *never* shagged a guy who rode a motorbike," said Steve. "That's such bullshit."

"Erm…yeah, I did. It was back home. He was nineteen."

"How old we were you when you allegedly fucked him, twelve?" asked Roger.

"Thirteen, actually. It was in the summer," said Simone, sticking her tongue out at him.

"Don't listen to her, Anne. She's chatting shit," said Canel. "When she first got her tattoos, she tried to convince us they were real."

"You idiots believed me," said Simone.

"No we didn't," said Melvin.

After the movie, we played a game of Monopoly. Canel seemed to take it much more seriously than the rest of us and moaned every time she lost money from a property. Melvin had to tell her to calm down several times while Roger, Steve, and Simone just found it funny. I was a bit alarmed, watching her get all worked up like that over a game.

We played for about an hour, then went downstairs to get dinner. I was still worried about missing prep.

"A-Are you s-sure we won't get in tr-trouble?" I asked Simone as we stood in line to collect our food. She rolled her eyes at me. "Yes, Miss Paranoid. No one gives a fuck."

"B-But won't that ef-f-fect our grades?"

Simone scoffed. "Anne, we've had one day of lessons. Even the sixth formers don't shit their pants about missing the first day of prep. What are you going to do anyway, colour code your timetable?"

"I j-just wanted to catch up on some reading for English."

She smiled. "Ah, I see. Trying to get into Mr. Oseni's good books already. By the way, what was on that note that bitch Olivia gave you?"

"N-Nothing. I tore it up. She j-just called me a know-it-all — n-nothing too surprising." I guess I took it as a given. I was far more anxious to find out who the red-haired girl was. I was hoping she wasn't one of the nasty or stupid ones. No, surely she was peaceful and content. Or maybe I was imagining things.

The next day at breakfast — Simone was fully dressed this time — I got a grand tour of the various cliques of Lakeland. We had spent the previous evening after dinner watching *This is the End* and discussing how best to survive an apocalypse. Simone and I were standing at the side of the canteen, where we had an unobstructed view of all the tables. Students seemed to sit according to year group, so the lower third students clumped around the front whilst fifth formers were more spread out at the back. There seemed to be less students as the year groups progressed. Sixth formers ate in the sixth form block.

She pointed to the largest table. "That lot is the populars — Olivia, Tasha, Kim, Amelia, Karen..." Karen. That was her name. The red-haired girl. I studied her, gazing at her gentle blue eyes and smile. She was laughing. Her hair was tied back today, and she had on a red jumper and green earrings, which brought out the orange flames cascading down her back. She resembled a cute Christmas decoration lit up by a candle.

"Yeah, so you want to avoid them. Don't piss any of them off, and whatever you do, *don't get with any of the guys.* Seriously, this one time I snogged him — you see, Michael — and Tasha tried to come after me. She was just angry because he'd fingered her behind the boys' boarding house for a bet, only she didn't know it was a bet, and anyway, she heard about my nineteen-year-old boyfriend with the motorbike — Anne? Hello?"

"Yes, s-sorry? I was listening."

"You do that a lot, you know."

"Do what?"

"That. Zone out. Disappear. Stare into space? It's like you're permanently high or something. *Do* you smoke weed?"

I frowned. "Erm…n-no, I don't."

"Oh, fair enough. Then again, you're not the type. You're too straight edge."

I wasn't sure what to say to that.

"I tried it once with some older mates of mine," she said. "It was great. We just lay back and listened to Bob Marley." She laughed. I raised my eyebrows. Like the others, I was beginning to question the validity of anything Simone said.

"Anyway, let's move along here. *That* lot is what you'd call 'wannabes.'"

I laughed. "D-did you give them that nickname?"

"Yep," she said. "So, the populars and the wannabes basically hate each other. The populars are the ones who are the loudest, most boisterous, don't study too hard, and take the piss out of everyone else. They're not all stupid — a few of them are smart enough to be in our English class, they just act like they don't care. Half of them have parents so rich, they fund half the school, while the other half came from 'impoverished backgrounds' or whatever and just make the rich ones feel cool and 'street.'

"The wannabes wish they were the populars. They have their own drink ups and parties. They try to cheek the teachers, but they never get away with it, and they just try to act like the populars, but fail miserably. Take Natalie for example." Simone pointed to a pretty girl with light brown skin and long braids who was staring at herself in her phone mirror.

"Her Instagram page has over nine hundred followers and half of her pictures are of her eyebrows. She's so shallow her reflection is practically see-through. And check out Chloe, her best friend. She acts like Natalie's pet, always kissing her arse and all that, but she's secretly jealous of her and insecure because Natalie's prettier and going out with a guy who was in my music class last year. He raps and makes beats." Simone pointed to someone else.

"And that guy, Roy — *everyone* thinks he's gay because he only ever chills with the girls. I hardly ever see him talk to any guys. He's on Instagram as much as Natalie. He's in like half her pictures and they have sleepovers together, but in a friendship sense. I've never seen him with a girlfriend."

"That doesn't automatically m-make him gay." I frowned.

"Oh, no, but you know how people talk," she said.

That annoyed me. "There's nothing wrong with being

gay."

"I know there isn't. I'm bi."

"Sorry?"

"I'm bi. I like girls and guys. Most people are, apparently. They say all girls are a bit bi."

I wasn't sure. Being with a boy seemed alien to me.

"W-Who's next?" I asked her. This was strangely intriguing.

"Around the corner, there's that group of guys." We moved around some other tables, hanging back so no one could see we were talking about them. They were all so engrossed in conversation — and food — they wouldn't have been able to tell; plus, we weren't the only ones standing around.

"Those are basically the nerdy guys. You know, sit around all day on their iPads and play their consoles, get really awkward around girls, probably won't have sex 'til they're in their twenties..."

"Simone!" I laughed and shook my head. "Don't be so mean. You c-can't make those kinds of assumptions about people."

"People make assumptions about me all the time. That's what you *do* at our age. See, Roger, Steve, and Melvin are all twats, but they're funny and laid back. They're not awkward. They won't freeze up if they so much as breathe near a girl or see a can of beer. This lot is boring as fuck."

"Have you even ever sp-spoken to any of them?" I thought she was being a bit prejudiced. It reminded me of when Zoe had called Luke "weird" without ever having interacted with him.

Simone shook her head. "It's not really about that. I mean, yeah, obviously I'm sure they're decent people. But this is just how we all see each other. You were home-schooled, right?"

"Yeah, then I w-was at my cousin's school f-for a bit."

"So, you should have seen it then. It's shit, and I am taking the piss a bit, but this is how it is. Everyone knows their place in the school social hierarchy — know it, but don't show it. We can try to say, deep down, each one of us is a model, or a nice guy, or schizophrenic, or a smart girl, or…I dunno, a druggie, but truth is, that's all bullshit. It's like in *High School Musical* when they all sing 'stick with the status quo.' Or in *Grease* with the T-Birds and the Pink Ladies."

"Those are American m-movies," I said. "They exa-exaggerate."

Simone put her arm around my shoulder and patted me on the back. "Ah, but sadly, my gal, there's truth inside the lie. Teenagers are fake superficial pricks. We're all thinking the same things about each other."

I peered around the room at all the boys and girls sitting at their socially assigned tables, eating their meals and laughing, and wondered what went through their minds when they looked at one another — or when they looked at me.

"Just move along." I checked the clock. "We've got t-ten minutes 'til registration."

"All right, all right. Oh, shit, you better beware of that lot. The roadmen — also known as wastemen, or plain dickheads. If any of those prats ever come up to you and try to chat you up, come to me and I'll tell them to fuck off." She pulled a disgusted face at the group of burly boys wearing big jackets and trainers and chains around their necks, checking out the girls around the canteen and laughing about stuff on their phones.

"Yeah, half of them will end up in prison. All the insecure girls fall at their feet and get called slags for sucking them off. Most of them hang about in detention, so if you're lucky, you'll never have to speak to them.

Now, over there, are some of my people — goths and emos. Those two are in my band. Most of them piss me off with their Tumblr and Instagram accounts talking about how depressed and misunderstood they are. I mean, sure, all teenagers are depressed and misunderstood, but they sort of go overboard with it." She lowered her voice. "Caitlin over there actually campaigned to have about fifty genders added to the school registration list."

I knotted my brows and cocked my head to one side. "Okay, *now* I know you c-can't be serious."

"I swear to you, I'm not even joking. She told me!" Simone put her hand to her mouth. "She even asked me to sign her petition."

"Yeah right."

Simone flicked her hair. "Fine if you don't believe me." She nodded towards a corner. "That lot is considered plain losers."

"By w-who exactly?"

"Erm, the rest of the school? They're the most unpopular people. You don't even want to go near any of them. Disabled people, slow people, *boring* kids who no one likes or talks to or invites anywhere. They don't exist to the rest of us. It's fucked up, but like I said, that's how it is."

We moved away from their table. I felt sorry for them and wished things weren't like this. Did everyone buy into this absurd social segregation?

"And lastly, you have us. The irrelevant, the misfits…whatever. We're not popular or unpopular, we stay out of everyone's way, don't get involved, and keep to ourselves. Again, if we disappeared, the populars and wannabes wouldn't give a fuck."

"W-Why should we c-care what they think?"

"They make up half our year group," she said sadly. "And they're the ones who run everything and decide how everyone else is going to see you. We're a mish-mash of smart kids, artsy kids, and weird kids who don't belong to any group. We're the *others*."

I scanned the room, observing Karen, and the populars, and all the other various groups and sub-types. I took in the other kids who sat around us, also "irrelevants," just a different group.

"So, do you get it now? Roughly? You see how screwed up it all is?"

I regarded Simone. "Yeah, I get it."

Chapter Seventeen: Watch Your Back

Just because Simone had pointed out — without meaning to — that Karen was way out of my social league, didn't mean I couldn't still think about her. It wasn't like I hadn't fancied a girl totally out of my league already. Karen wasn't as striking as Meg, but she hung around with girls who would make mincemeat of me. Still, I didn't have to tell anyone. I certainly wasn't going to tell Simone, who might blab to our friends — my newfound circle of friends. They didn't seem like the kind of friends who would judge me for being a lesbian; they didn't seem like the kind of friends who would judge me at all. I was relieved. I felt less on edge around them then I had around Zoe's friends.

She sent me frequent messages asking how I was doing and if I was settling in and if it was all going well. She kept pestering me to get Facebook, but I didn't want to be found on the internet. I certainly didn't want my dad contacting me.

I also messaged Luke as often as I could. He'd started hanging out with another group of girls in our year who he said were all right, but different from me. I missed him. I said I would meet up with him for sure at half term when I went back to my aunt's.

Lakeland was more laid back than Copperwood and felt homier. But it was strange, moving around so much from one place to the other. I started to feel as if I really were on some sort of drugs.

I tried to stay out of the way of the so-called "populars," but they seemed weirdly interested in me. I would pass them in the corridors, and they would stop, stare at me, and then burst out laughing. In English, they'd pull faces at each other whenever I spoke, mimicking my stutter. I tried to ignore them. Karen didn't join in. She hung back, trying not to get involved. One time, she threw me an apologetic expression and walked past with her friends. I knew I had no chance with her, but I couldn't stop thinking and dreaming about her. I so longed for the romantic company of someone. Just thinking about her made me smile. I knew I had to find a way to get to know her better.

In the meantime, I was doing well in all my subjects. My teachers were all nice, but I especially liked Mr. Oseni. He was so kind and never got angry with anyone. He really liked my work too. I tried so hard on my analyses of the cultural themes within *Lord of the Flies*. We watched the movie in class. I loved Piggy, the smart boy who tried to hold everyone together, but ended up getting ridiculed by everyone else. We were given a table to complete on the different themes in the film and asked to come up with our own. We also had to read the book aloud in class — something I wasn't fond off after being ridiculed at Copperwood. Most people mumbled along the lines.

I grew fond of Simone. She was still full-on, but the kind of person you got used to after a while. I still had to practically drag her out of bed to come down to breakfast, though.

"Simone, come on," I said one day. I wanted to hurry down so I could try to get to the canteen and stare at Karen. So far, my interactions with her consisted of staring and turning away if she caught me ogling her so I didn't seem like a creepy person who stared at people. I doubted she'd think much of it. Half the time she'd be chatting to her friends. I needed to get a good seat where I could have a pleasant view of her without turning around.

Simone was lying under the covers. I lifted her duvet off her face. She had a purple eye mask covering her eyes.

"Mmhurph," she said, pulling the duvet back. "Come on, darling," I said, playing mother. "You need to be fresh for today. You've g-got band practice later."

"All the more reason to skip registration."

"You can't skip br-breakfast, though." I pulled her covers up again. "The m-most important meal of the day."

She lifted her eye mask, glaring at me. "You're such a kill-joy."

I shrugged. "I try my best."

She got up, giving me a little shove. I laughed. She made me laugh a lot.

We managed to get to the canteen in time, joining the rest of the group. Thankfully, there was a seat next to Canel where I could gaze at Karen. She was lovely in a pink jumper with a silver necklace, silver matching earrings, her gorgeous hair fanning fire when it caught the light.

Canel waved her hand in front of my face. "You all right there?" I jumped, realising I had my fork just below my mouth, with a piece of uneaten french toast sitting on the edge of it. I gulped it quickly.

"S-sorry, j-just—"

"Zoned out. She does that a lot," said Simone, knocking back an espresso. "I'm telling you, Anne's secretly a stoner. She has spliffs hidden away in her drawers. I can smell it at night."

"I think she's more of a goth," said Roger, nodding at me. "You always wear black, hardly speak, and look permanently depressed."

"Hey! That's mean! Anne doesn't look permanently depressed! Oh, ignore him," said Canel. I felt baffled. Roger shook his head.

"I didn't mean it in a bad way. Like, you know that lot?" He pointed across the room to the "emo kids," as Simone often referred to them. "Maybe you should start hanging out with them."

"Oh, leave her alone. Anne isn't a goth, she's just quiet," said Simone.

"Yeah, and you never shut your mouth," said Roger.

Simone shrugged. "Takes one to know one."

"We're all a bit weird anyway, that's why we sit at this table," said Melvin. "Apart from me, of course. You guys are nuts. I'm the only sane one here."

"Your dad's a minor celebrity. That automatically makes you a problematic child," said Steve.

Canel burst out laughing. "Yeah, maybe you'll end up like Jaden Smith!" They all roared with laughter. I whipped my head around the table, attention from Karen diverted.

"W-what's the j-joke?"

Simone whipped out her phone, typing in "ten of the craziest Jaden Smith tweets." "You know Will Smith, right? And his son, Jaden?"

"Well…yeah, of course."

"Check the shit he posts on Twitter." Simone cleared her throat. *"How can mirrors be real if our eyes aren't real?"*

"I bet he was fucking great at physics," said Canel as we all roared with laughter. Simone continued. *"You can discover everything you need to know about everything by looking at your hands."*

"Does that mean if I stare at my hands all day, I'll become a genius?" said Steve. He nudged Roger. "Maybe you should take that one into consideration."

"Oh, I love this one," said Simone. *"Most trees are blue."*

"I think he might be colour blind," said Melvin.

"Or maybe he's just blind, considering he doesn't have eyes," said Canel, wiping the tears from her eyes.

Even I found the tweets funny. "W-What is wr-wrong with him?" I asked.

"He thinks he's some kind of modern-day philosopher," said Simone. "He even said if he was white and not Will Smith's son, he'd be the greatest philosopher of all time."

"Nah, mate, he'd still be an idiot," said Roger. Canel was still laughing. I thumped her on the back. "Quick, everyone! Canel's dying! Someone call A&E!" said Steve.

"What's so funny over here?" We shot our heads up. The voice wasn't coming from our table. Olivia, Tasha, and Kim were standing above us. Canel's laughing changed to coughing, then died. Everyone turned away, suddenly silent.

"W-We were just talking about J-Jaden Smith," I piped up. Olivia nodded, pouting. "That sounds interesting."

"Anne, can we talk to you for a sec?" asked Kim. She was wearing bright red lipstick which clashed with her bleach-blonde hair. It was cut into a bob, framing her ivory face. I peered between the three of them. Tasha was the prettiest, with light brown skin and curly hair and her eyes outlined with black eyeliner. Olivia had taken her nose ring out. Pity. It had suited her. She had on tight skinny jeans and a black crop top, showing off her athletic figure.

"O-o-kay." I swallowed, deciding I wasn't going to be intimidated by them. They were like an evil girl band. Olivia gave a chirp of false laughter. "A-Are you g-g-gonna st-stand up th-then, A-Anne?"

"Hmmm?" I blinked at them, ignoring their sniggers.

"Well, we're obviously going to talk to you in *private*," said Tasha, rolling her eyes. "You're smart, you should understand that." They were all baring their teeth at me in what was supposed to be friendly smiles. The hairs on the back of my neck stood on edge. I shook my head.

"But we need to talk to you *in private*," said Olivia, playing with the end of her braided extensions. She smiled sweetly. "Come on, don't be difficult. Be a good girl and come talk to us."

I shifted focus between the three of them, then back to my friends, who all faced away. Simone regarded me empathetically. Feeling rightly apprehensive, I stood up and swallowed.

"Great!" said Kim. "Come on then."

I started walking with them when a small girl wearing a flowery Ed Hardy jacket pushed into me, knocking her tray of food all over the front of my clothes. The girl gasped, covering her mouth. Kim, Tasha, and Olivia were sniggering.

"Oh my gosh, I'm so sorry!" the small girl said to me. "Are you okay? God, I'm such an idiot. So bloody clumsy! I'm such a midget, I can never see where I'm going."

"Emma, you fucking *dumbarse*," said Tasha. "Look what you did! You knocked your food all over the poor girl's dress! That'll take ages to wash out!"

"Lucky you're wearing black. At least black doesn't stain so much," said Kim. They were all talking. I glanced between the four of them. I recognised the name Emma, and her face. Of course, it had been a set up. I peered at my black dress. There was cereal splattered on it, as well as tea and smudges

141

of chopped banana and apple. I got a tissue, trying to wipe it off. Everyone was staring and pointing and laughing. I noticed Karen, gasping in shock. I wondered what she was thinking. I had managed to seem a total idiot in front of her. The loser girl. One of the "others." Of course, I would never have a shot with her. I would never have a shot with any girl.

I ran past everyone out of the canteen and main building. I wanted to be alone. I wanted to bury myself under my bed covers for eternity. I would disappear forever into my mattress and blend into the cotton, ceasing to return.

I was running so fast, I barely heard my name being called behind me. I ran into the girls' boarding house, stepping into the lift. I walked through the corridor to my bedroom. I pushed open the door. The door was locked. I'd left my key card in my coat pocket. As if things couldn't get any worse. I sat on the floor, hugging my knees to my chest.

"Anne?"

Simone was standing above me, holding my coat and bag. She looked as if she wanted to cry for me.

"You always put your key in your coat pocket. I reckoned you wouldn't be able to get back in."

I stood up. She handed me my possessions. I mumbled a thank you, then started to sort through my coat pocket, but Simone had her card ready and tapped the lock. She let me go in first and followed.

"Are you all right?" she asked.

I threw my coat and bag on the floor and sank onto my bed. "Yes, b-b-besides the fact that I'm c-covered in br-breakfast cereal and b-bits of f-fruit and tea."

"It'll wash out," she said. I pulled off my dress and pulled on my black nightie. "I'm just g-going to s-sleep all day."

"You don't need to do that." She came and sat next to me. "That was horrible what those bitches did. I *told* you they were vile."

"Mmm."

Simone wrapped her arms around my neck and leaned her head on my shoulder. "It'll be okay. Everyone will have forgotten about it by, like, tomorrow. Accidents happen. It did seem like an accident."

"W-Well, it w-wasn't."

"Yeah, we know that." She sighed. "Emma's a dwarf cunt. I hate her. She and Olivia are the worst. I'm so glad I'm not in their P.E class this year. Emma's captain of the girl's football team and made sure I was always picked last."

I grimaced. Thankfully, I was useless at sports.

"S-S-Simone, I n-need to t-t-tell y-you s…" I groaned and squeezed my eyes shut. She pulled her head off my shoulder, letting me whack my fists against my duvet.

"It's okay. Take your time," she said gently.

"W-Well…I'm not r-really sure h-how to p-put it." I sighed and chose my words carefully. "There's this p-person I l-like."

"As in, have a crush on?"

"Y-Yeah."

She raised her eyebrows at me and smiled. "Oooh, who is he?"

"W-Well…it's a g-girl."

She shrugged. "Okay. I'm bi; I don't really give a fuck if you're straight, gay, or what not. So, who is *she*?"

"Th-That's…th-the problem. Sh-She's one of…the — the p-popular girls."

Her eyes widened. "Oh God, don't tell me it's Tasha. She is hot, but she's nasty, and I'm not even gonna lie, she's a frickin' slag."

I shook my head. "No! No, it's K-Karen."

She blinked, trying to remember who Karen was. "Oh, her. The quiet girl. Yeah, she seems all right. I don't really know her, but then I guess that's cos she's never pissed me off. She doesn't seem like a bitch. But she does hang out with a bunch of girls who just knocked cereal all over your clothes."

"I d-don't know what t-to do." I slumped forward. Simone moved her arm off my shoulder, concerned. "I mean, it's cute you like her and all, it's just..."

"She'd never like me. I'm a st-stuttering idiot."

"Don't be silly."

"I just made a f-fool of myself in f-front of everyone."

"It wasn't your fault!"

"Still."

"Hmm." Simone patted my bed sheets. They were plain; the only white piece of cotton I owned. Simone's were covered in cool black and blue and red patterns with swirls and stripes all over them. She sat back on my bed, leaning against the wall. I shifted slightly to face her.

"I don't know what to say, Anne. If you like her, you like her. But getting involved with any of the people in that lot is a bad idea. Best thing is to stay out of their way and eventually they'll get tired and move onto someone else. They're only picking on you because you're new. But if you start hooking up with a mate of theirs, it could really mess things up."

Chapter Eighteen: Karen

There was one room with washing machines and dryers in each of the boarding houses. The room was massive, with about a hundred machines and dryers, but this was to be split between five to six hundred girls. I tried to wash my clothes once a week, but there were some girls who did washes daily and ended up getting told off by Matron. Matron was the school nurse, who also took care of the students in each year. There was Matron and Assistant Matron, and both had their own offices in the girl's boarding house. They were smiley, plump, jolly women who had loud voices and could get seriously cross if you got on their wrong sides.

I shoved my cereal-covered dress into the machine, poured in the powder, and turned it on. I sighed, leaning against it as it whirled. The room wasn't that full, considering most girls were in lessons. People typically did their washing on the weekend, so I tried to avoid the rush by washing mine during the week.

"Hi."

I opened my eyes. Someone was talking to me. A soft girl's voice. She was standing next to me, several inches taller, and very thin like Simone.

She played with the silver necklace around her neck, matching her starry earrings. She was smiling anxiously at me. "Are you okay? I saw what happened earlier in the canteen."

I swallowed, nodding.

"I'm sorry that happened to you. I thought that was awful. My friends can be a bit…mean sometimes." She scratched her head. Her hair was like orange silk, framing her heart-shaped face. She had some spots of acne on her cheeks, but they oddly suited her, making her more real rather than flawless.

"Anyway, are you all right?" She peered at the machine. "Washing your clothes up?"

"Y-Y-Yes," I managed. "A-And, th-thank you. I'm…erm, f-fine."

"That's good."

There was a pause. We regarded each other, then turned away, not knowing what to say. "D-Don't you ha-have a l-lesson n-now?" I asked her.

"Yeah, but I needed to do some washing," she said. "Plus, it's English, and I'm shit at English."

"Oh." I wasn't sure what to say to that. "Th-That's a shame. English is my b-b-best subject."

"Lucky! My favourite is drama. I'm good with art and graphic design, but not stuff to do with writing. I'm dyslexic."

"Oh, okay." I nodded. That made sense. "L-Lots of p-people are. D-Dyslexic, I mean." I peered at the floor, hating myself for being so awkward. But she gazed warmly at me, without judgement.

"Yeah, it's annoying. Stupid word too. I can't even spell it."

"It is an odd word — f-for someone who st-struggles to read and write." I laughed. She laughed too. "I didn't m-mean that…erm, b-badly," I said.

"No, it's okay, I know what you meant. It's fine. I get extra exam time and help because of it."

Blue eyes. Like tranquil pools of water. "Why aren't you in your lesson?" she asked.

"I d-didn't feel up to it. After wh-what happened earlier."

"You shouldn't let them get to you. It'll settle down."

Why do you hang out with them? I wanted to ask. How could someone so kind and gentle befriend such awful people?

"By the way, my name's Karen," she said, but I already knew that. "And you are?"

"Anne."

"Well, it's been lovely talking to you, Anne. I should head back. I need to make my next lesson. It's maths and I've already missed it twice in a row. Not that they care much here. It's not like day school, but I need to keep my grades up or my parents will be on my case." She gave me a little wave. "I'll see you later!"

I leaned against the washing machine, barely able to catch my breath. I realised I was smiling, and not because I felt I had to. It had been a long time since I had last smiled for real. We had had an entire conversation, and she didn't think I was weird or sad. She had spoken to me like I was a normal person.

I spent the next forty minutes sitting on the floor staring into space and day-dreaming scenarios involving Karen and I while my dress washed. I pictured her taking my hands and bending down to kiss me. I imagined the feel of her lips on mine. I imagined touching her body and putting my hands under her clothes. It made my skin flush.

I shook my dress and took it back to Room 104 to hang up. I could have put it in the dryer, but I didn't want to stand around waiting for it, and I didn't want to run the risk of seeing someone I didn't like in the laundry room. I started to feel hungry; it would be lunchtime in about an hour. I wondered if I could grab something and eat in my room to avoid being in the canteen. Perhaps if I bought a sandwich and crisps instead of a hot meal, I would be okay. That seemed safer.

For the rest of the day, I lay around my room, staring at the wall and trying to flick through *Lord of the Flies.* Around half three, Simone came into the room. She flung the door hard and threw her bag onto the ground.

"God, Anne, I've been so worried about you! Have you missed *all* your lessons today? Mr. Oseni was wondering where you were."

"Oh." I was sitting on the chair by the window, gazing into space. "I-I've been fine."

"I should hope so! Anyway, you'll never guess what. I'm so stressed out about my band. Cerys, our drummer, quit because she said her parents were pressuring her to focus more on work this year and she was failing half her modules last year. And one of my guitar strings broke, so I have to go get that fixed because I'm stupid and can't do it myself." She let out a huge groan. "I swear, I need a new guitar. I asked my parents to get me a new one for Christmas, but they said it's 'impractical.' What do they want to get me instead, a frickin' typewriter!"

"Why a typewriter?" I said, momentarily confused. "They went out of date d-decades ago."

"I dunno, it was the first thing that popped into my head." She sat on her bed and rubbed her eyes. "Anyway, have you been all right today? What you been doing all day?"

I shrugged. "Washed my dress. Lazed around. Tr-Tried to do some homework." I swallowed. "I sp-spoke to K-Karen."

She perked up. "Karen, as in the girl you like? Oooh, where?"

"I-In the lau-laundry room."

"When you were washing your dress?" She looked excited. "How'd it go?"

I smiled. "We just...t-talked. Sh-She was saying some-something about bunking English because she's d-dyslexic."

"Oh, Melvin's dyslexic. Loads of people are. It's really common. I have a cousin who's dyspraxic. He gets a lot of help at school. He's like ten."

"Mmm." I realised I was still smiling. Simone squealed. "Aw, man, you really like her! This is so cute!" She was so bouncy, her black hair shook everywhere. "But remember what I said, be careful. Her friends are all bitches."

"Yeah. I wonder why she hangs around with them?"

"Popularity. That's literally probably the only reason." She lay back on her bed and sighed. "God, this fucking guitar, man. Don't be a musician, it's so stressful."

I pulled my chair closer to her bed. "Is th-that what you want to do long-term?"

"Hopefully. If I get good enough."

"I'd l-love to hear you play s-sometime."

"I would play for you now if my guitar string wasn't broken. I don't know how to fix it. Mr. Smithers handles problems with instruments." She sat up. "Do you want to go for a walk? Around the school grounds? Have you seen them properly yet?"

I shook my head. "Th-That would be nice." I hadn't been out all day, and I was starting to feel a bit isolated. I got my coat whilst Simone took something out of her drawer and put it in her bag. She picked up her coat too, then we went outside.

The Lakeland grounds were beautiful. The grass was clipped to perfection and there were hedges cut in shapes surrounding the school's domain. We walked by some pretty mermaid shaped fountains spouting water from their mouths. There were other people from school sitting on the benches and walking around the gardens. I shivered in my Jane Norman duffel coat as I took it all in.

Simone opened her bag and took out a small box. I gaped at her and realised what it was. She took out a cigarette from the pack and put it between her lips. My eyes widened as we stopped walking. "W-W-What are you doing?"

"Just having a smoke." She took a lighter from her pocket, lit it, and inhaled. She breathed out white smoke.

"W-Why are you s-smoking?" I asked. "That's r-really b-bad for you."

She inhaled again and breathed out. "I don't do it that often, just occasionally. It helps with anxiety."

"W-What are you a-anxious about?" I asked.

She shrugged. "I dunno. Life. My music. People."

I stiffened as I watched her exhale. "Do your p-parents know? D-does anyone else?"

"'Course my parents don't know. They don't know anything. Roger smokes now and again, and most of my older mates do back at home. It's no big deal."

I had seen my mum smoke occasionally. She'd sneak one of dad's cigars or his Marlboro Lights and go out in the garden. She had drummed into me that smoking and drinking were terrible habits and I should never do it. Hearing my dad's awful chesty cough was enough to put me off.

Simone continued smoking, shrugging it off and not seeming to care. She threw it on the ground when she finished and stamped on it. She saw me staring at her and let out an exasperated sigh. "What do you want me to say, Anne? We all have our vices."

"Are you okay?"

"What do you mean?"

"I mean in general." We resumed walking. "Like, w-with your arms." I made a gesture towards my own arms. "I s-saw the scars."

"Loads of people cut. It's no big deal."

I scoffed. "Yeah, like smoking. S-Self-mutilating is t-totally c-cool."

She glared at me. "Why do you care?"

"Because we're friends. H-How long has that been g-going on?" I mimed cutting my arms.

"About a year, I think."

"Are you, like, unhappy?"

Her voice was piercing. "Are you?"

"What d-do you mean?"

She stopped walking and surveyed me. "We've all got problems. We just cope with them differently, that's all."

That annoyed me. "What are you t-talking about? You h-hardly even know me."

"I know more than you think. For God's sake, we sleep together." She stood still. I raised my eyebrows at her, and she gave me an embarrassed glance. We burst out laughing.

"Sorry, that came out wrong," she said. "I didn't mean..."

"It's fine, I know w-what you meant." I rubbed my tummy. It felt good to laugh. She put her arm around me. "You know, if there's anything you ever want to talk about, you can."

"S-Same with you."

She smiled at me, but she didn't meet my eye. I looked away from her too.

Chapter Nineteen: Secrets

Mr. Oseni handed me back my work with lots of ticks and a comment saying, "Well done, keep up the excellent work." A warm thrill swam over me. Simone nudged me. "Get you, teacher's pet."

"Sh-Shut up. How did you do?"

"Good, but I couldn't seem to nail the question about Biblical Allegories. I didn't really get the whole 'Bible' theme in *Lord of the Flies.*"

"I think it's more c-conceptual, like the beast is meant to be symbolic of the devil. But yeah, it is tricky to tell. You know *Narnia*? That's b-based on Christian Mythology."

"Oh yeah, like Aslan is supposed to be Jesus!" said Simone. "I love *Narnia.*"

"Me too."

The girls behind us were bickering in protestation. "Sir, what is wrong with this? I explained the whole difference between civilisation and savagery. Piggy and Ralph represent civilisation. Jack and Roger represent savagery!" It sounded like Tasha. Simone sniggered.

"I think you just needed to explain it a bit more," said Mr. Oseni calmly. "You all generally did well, but there are few things that need to be touched on. That's why we're going to go through each of the questions now."

After the lesson, I hung back, deciding to take a long time to put away all my things. I didn't want another run-in with Karen's awful friends. They gave Simone and I a few scalding glares as they left but didn't say anything.

Simone and I were among the last to leave. As we were walking out, Mr. Oseni called my name. "Anne, if it's okay, I'd like to have a quick word with you."

Simone grinned at me. "I'll see you in the canteen, genius."

"Yep." She walked out whilst I stood in front of my English teacher's desk. He was smiling at me. "You've been doing very well, Anne. You've got a real gift for writing and interpreting literature."

"Th-Thanks, sir."

He opened his drawer. "Are you involved in any societies or extra-curricular activities?"

I shook my head. I had thought about taking piano lessons again or doing a drawing class, but I was overwhelmed enough with all the changes and getting used to being at Lakeland.

"This will be perfect then. I was thinking about assigning you a little task — think of it as a potential extra-curricular activity. It's not compulsory, and only if you agree with it. I trust you're a very avid reader?"

I nodded.

"Well, I was thinking about assigning you a book, shall we say per term, to read and review? This is only for literary purposes and because your reading is clearly advanced for your age." He took out a fat book with a man's face on the cover. "This is *Native Son* by Richard Wright. I read it when I was seventeen. It may be a little advanced for you, but I feel you'd be able to handle it."

I glimpsed at it. "W-What is it about?"

"A poor young African-American man named Bigger living in urban Chicago during the 1930s. He gets wrapped up in a tricky situation, and that's all I'm going to tell you."

"I-Is it a bit like *To Kill a Mockingbird,* only f-from the perspective of the black person rather than the w-white person?"

He smiled. "You could put it like that. *To Kill a Mockingbird* is one of my favourite books. *Native Son* is told in third person, but yes, it is all from the perspective of Bigger rather than from the perspective of a child."

I held the dense book in my hands. "Th-Thank you. I'll t-tell you what I think as soon as I f-finish."

He smiled again. "I know you will."

I left his classroom, feeling flushed with pride. I couldn't wait to start reading. I bounded along the corridor, sensing a spring in my step. It was a feeling I hadn't felt in a long time. To make matters better, Karen was approaching my direction. She gave me a little wave.

"Hey! You're looking happy," she said. I beamed at her. "Y-You know what, I am!"

"What are you happy about?"

I held up the book in front of her. "M-Mr. Oseni g-gave me this to read as extra homework."

Karen's eyes widened. "That sounds awful!" She peered at the front. "*Na-tive Son*. What is it about?"

"This poor black man who g-gets into trouble in the 1930s." My eyes were shining. Karen was talking to me, I had a huge new book to read, and Mr. Oseni adored me. Karen laughed. "It's about racial tension? Well, it's huge, but you're smart, I guess you'll like it. Rather you than me!"

I felt a surge of confidence. "Y-You know, if you ever w-wanted, I c-could help you out with reading. C-Considering you're dyslexic. We c-could m-meet in the library after l-lessons sometime."

A rush of joy spread across her face. "That would be great! I'll think about when would be good and get back to you. Gosh, I'd need it. If I fail English this year, I'll have to re-take it before I do the GCSEs next year. They won't let you take the GCSEs unless you pass the upper fourth exams. I have to get a C or I'm screwed."

I was nodding as she said this, barely listening. "G-Get back to me when you can then." My stomach rumbled. I needed to meet Simone and the others in the canteen. My feet practically glided across the ground. I barely registered the world as I walked into the canteen and picked up a tray heaping with macaroni cheese, juice, and apple pie. I sat down with my friends at their table.

"Someone's in a good mood," said Simone as I sat next to her. Canel grinned at me. "What you so gassed about?"

They were all gaping at me. "I-Is it really that big of a deal for me to be happy?"

"You aren't usually that smiley," said Melvin.

Simone nudged me. "Any particular reason?"

"Yes!" I picked up my book and put it on the table. "Mr. Oseni assigned this book for me t-t-to read as extra homework!"

Simone peered at it while the others chortled in mock-horror. "Wow, Anne, you really are a nerd," said Roger. "No one else would get that happy over a book."

Simone was studying the inside cover. "Interesting. It'll take you a while to churn through that. I wouldn't mind having a skim through after you."

"You're as nerdy as her!" said Steve.

Simone rolled her eyes. "Shut up, Steven. I think the word you're looking for is smart."

"Oh, all right, we'll let the smart people go sit at their own table!" said Roger.

Canel shrieked with laughter. "Should we all just get up now and leave Simone and Anne by themselves?"

"Guys, come on, don't take the piss," said Simone. "There's nothing wrong with being intelligent."

"We're just teasing. We can't all get the best grades in everything," said Melvin.

I released an embarrassed cough. "Oh, I w-w-wouldn't say I get the best g-gr-grades in *everything*. I'm n-not that good at d-drama or design and t-technology."

"Yeah, but you do well in everything else," said Simone. "Maths, science, geography, history, French, English, music..."

"When you were home-schooled, how did it work?" asked Canel. "Did your parents teach you everything or give you books or what?"

"I ha-had some private tuition for maths, English, and French," I said. "My m-mum took me out a lot to m-museums and art g-galleries and the zoo and would identify d-different things with me. And we had a piano at home. My dad sh-showed me how to p-play some things."

I had forgotten that. It *was* my dad who taught me the piano initially. After that, I picked it up myself and had some private tutors. He really was great at it. It was a shame he didn't use it more as an emotional outlet. Maybe then things would have been different.

I got started on *Native Son* as soon as I got back to my room. Simone was fiddling around on her guitar. It was a long black and white electric guitar almost as big as her. A sharp twangy noise sounded. She groaned.

"Eurgh, I've broken the string again!" she said. She leaned back against the wall by her bed. "I'm such an idiot."

"C-Can't you take it to the music technician to fix it?" I asked.

"Yeah, but I'm always going. These strings are shit. They're always breaking. My uncle got me this one three years ago. He plays bass in a band. My parents were so annoyed because it was an electric and they said it was 'impractical' and I was being 'wrongly encouraged,' blah, blah." She reached over to the drawer by her table and took out a clear bottle. I glanced up from my book, then did a double take. It was a glass bottle.

"What's that?"

"What?"

"W-What's that you're drinking?" I put my book on my lap. "W-Why do you have a g-glass bottle for water?"

She shrugged as she put it to her lips. "Plastic is bad for the environment."

"Yeah, b-but why do you leave it in your drawer?" I sat up straight on my bed. "W-With your cigarettes."

She swallowed. "I don't *know*, Anne. Why do you care where I leave things?"

"Can I have some? I'm a b-bit thirsty."

"Don't you have your own water?"

"Bottle's empty."

"Fill it up. We have a sink. Or go to the water fountain." Her skin was flushed.

I got off my bed and went and sat on hers. She was watching me, half nervous, half irritated. "I-Is that r-really water?"

She rolled her eyes. "Jesus, why are you always interrogating me? That's sure what it feels like. Or are you some sort of undercover investigative journalist?"

"Funny. W-What's the matter with you, Simone?"

"What's the matter with *you*?" She banged her bottle on the top of her bedside table. Some of the liquid fell out. The bottle had traces of sticky white paper on it, indicating the label had been peeled off.

I stood up. "I don't know what's going on with you, but I know there's s-something. You oversleep, you smoke, you always act f-funny or j-jumpy like you're off somewhere else—"

"At least I don't look permanently stoned!" She jumped off her bed. "You're such a hypocrite. It's something to do with your dad, isn't it? Why would someone go live with their aunt and uncle when they've got a rich father who can take care of them and more?"

"My life is none of your business."

"I hear you yelling about your mum in the night, you know. Calling for her."

I froze. "A-A-And?"

"What *happened* between your parents? If it's really bad, you can tell me."

"No."

"No?" We stared at each other. *What is the matter? What are you hiding?*

"My d-d-dad's an alcoholic," I said. "It's n-not a g-good road to g-go down."

"I'm not a fucking alkie," she said.

"I never said you were," I replied, speaking slowly. "Just that it's not a good road to go down. D-Drinking, that is. Social dr-drinking's okay, but not when you're...alone."

She shrugged. "Whatever. I don't do it that often." She slumped her shoulders and sat back down on her bed, next to her broken-stringed guitar. I sat down on the stool in our room.

"He'd g-get v-violent when he drank. And aggressive."

"Did he hit her?"

I nodded. She nodded too. "I'm sorry."

"It's okay," I said, even though it never would be. "She l-left after that. Ha-haven't seen her since."

"After what?" said Simone.

"She left after...after he h-hit her one too many times." I started shaking. Simone looked concerned.

"Anne, are you all right? We can stop talking about this if you want."

I could barely hear her. My eyes started twitching and blinking. My breath began to shorten, and I clutched my chest, struggling to breathe. Simone stood up, scared, saying something to me. The room slowed and my head went sluggish. I blinked rapidly, then my body went heavy. I tumbled off the stool. Simone yelped. She ran out the door and across the corridor whilst I lay on the floor. I was gasping, terrified I would choke to death. I couldn't move. Was it possible to forget how to breathe?

Moments later, someone came running into the room. It was Matron. Simone was behind her. Matron held a brown paper bag. She put it in my hands. "Take slow, deep breaths." Her voice was soothing. "In for five, out for five."

I blinked at her, trying to keep my breath steady. Simone watched as my breath hastened up and down. "It just happened...we were just talking...she fell off the chair..." Her words echoed in the background.

"Don't worry, lots of people get panic attacks." Matron had her hand on my shoulder. "Everything is going to be okay, you can do this."

Gradually, my breathing calmed. Matron helped me to sit up. Simone also rushed to my aid. They helped lean me against Simone's bed, and Simone put her pillow behind me.

"Do you have any water?" asked Matron. Simone nodded at the sink. "I'll fill up Anne's water bottle."

I held the bottle between my lips, drinking leisurely as the room returned to focus.

Chapter Twenty: Face Off

Simone was peering at me nervously after Matron left. I sat up on the chair.

"Do you feel all right now?" she asked. I nodded, then rubbed my head. My mouth was numb and heavy, like a magnet was pulling it down. I rubbed the sides of my cheeks with my fingers.

"My mum used to get panic attacks, really badly, for like two years," said Simone. "None of us really knew what brought them on. Sometimes they could be really scary. She'd be all fine one minute, then the next, she'd be screaming or gasping or shaking and unable to move or talk properly. We got used to them after a while."

"You d-didn't know what c-caused them?"

She shook her head. "My parents don't really talk. Not to me, or even much to each other. We all sort of shut our feelings in and deal with our problems ourselves." She gave a fake, strained smile. "That's the best way to be, apparently."

I frowned. "That s-sounds r-really unhealthy."

"It's just life, I suppose. Nice suburban upper-middle class families are supposed to behave like that. I'm sure you can relate."

I thought of my dad and how everyone used to coo over him in church and marvel at how we were the perfect model family — as if they didn't see the bruises on Mum's face and arms, or the quiet, guarded way I seemed to shy away from people.

"Yeah, I kn-know what you mean." I took another sip of water. "I don't know w-where my mum is. I don't know if my dad…" I couldn't elaborate further. Simone watched me, patient and attentive. "She just vanished. I n-never understood w-why she stayed with him."

"Sometimes, when people are in abusive relationships, it's hard to let go," said Simone. "You become dependent on the person. It's a bit like a drug." She peered down at her arms. "Or other things. It has a hold on you, and even though you know it's bad for you, being without it somehow feels worse."

We blinked at each other. She bit her lip. "I know it's bad, like self-harming and smoking and all that. I'm not an idiot. I mean, I told you a while ago when we were talking about the cliques about all my emo mates who do that kind of stuff. Thing is, it's stupid. It doesn't help or solve anything."

"So, w-why do you do it?"

She scratched the back of her neck. "It makes me feel better. It's soothing. Like, I get these feelings — like I'm drowning and can't claw my way out, like I'm being sucked into this black hole. And no one understands. People just say stuff like 'oh, you're too young to feel stuff like that, life hasn't really begun to fuck you over yet.' So, I don't bother saying shit, or I try to make jokes or make things up because people find you more entertaining if you're telling stories, even if they aren't true."

"The age thing is s-silly. I d-don't believe you c-can't feel things at a certain age. No one knows w-what you've been through or what you've seen. We're all different people. Experience ha-has no age." I peered down at the ladder forming in my tights and stroked it with my fingers.

"You don't have to lie, you know," I said. "You don't ha-have to exaggerate. I mean, you're interesting enough w-without needing to make things up. You're certainly w-way more interesting than me."

"Am I?" she mumbled. "I don't think I am. I think people see me as some stupid girl who doesn't shut the hell up. I mean, I get all emotional and dramatic about things without meaning to, it's just the way I am, and I think most people just think I'm weird or annoying. Even my friends. You know how we all take the piss out of each other and it's fun and that, but sometimes, it does kind of get to me. I think to myself, do these people even like me or do they just hang out with me because they find me entertaining and are secretly having some private joke about what a loud-mouthed crazy girl I am?"

"You are a little crazy." I smiled. "But that's okay. It's c-cool to be a bit crazy. You're fun. I'm boring."

"You're not *boring*, Anne. You know so much about everything. You're definitely one of the smartest people I know. You're probably going to become the next mayor of London or some all-knowing professor — or an investigative journalist." She giggled. "Journalism would suit you. You're good at English. I'll just be singing on the streets for coins."

"I r-really w-want to hear you play."

She stood up. "Come, let's go to one of the music rooms. I'll play you a song there with a guitar that isn't retarded."

We left our dorm and started towards the main building where the music rooms all were. Simone linked her arm through mine, and I felt warmth flood through me. Not like what I felt when I saw Karen, it was more comforting and loving, like coming home.

As we entered the arts block, sounds of laughter came from girls at the other end of a corridor. Simone froze, and her arm stiffened. Emma, Tasha, and Karen were coming our way, the three of them lost in loud chatter. Goosebumps rippled over my body at the sound of Karen's gentle, carefree voice mixed with the hard cackles of her friends.

"Quick, up the stairs," said Simone. We hurried up to the second floor where the music rooms were. Unfortunately, Olivia and Kim were standing right outside one of the rooms, chatting to some boys in the upper fifth.

"Oh, *hey*," said Kim, waving at Simone and me. She wiped her sweeping blonde fringe out of her face, revealing makeup so thick, you could peel a layer off her skin. Olivia was quiet, watching us with a small smile on her face.

"Well done for today, A-A-Anne," she said. "Mr. Oseni really likes you. You're getting to be really in with the teachers. Maybe I should get you to do my English homework for me"

"Yeah, cos you're so shit at doing it yourself," said Kim. Olivia laughed and gave her a shove. "Eh, fuck off!"

The boys turned and nodded at us. "You all right?" said the more handsome of the two. I examined the floor, but Simone smiled at him. "Yeah, we're fine."

"Gonna play some tunes, yeah?" he asked. Simone giggled.

"Oh, yeah, you play guitar innit?" said Olivia, putting her hand to her mouth. "Gonna provide us with some entertainment?"

"Oi, Liv, you're here already, but I thought the two of yous were jammin' out by the canteen?" called Tasha from behind us, making us jump. I turned and Karen's gaze met mine, but she quickly looked away.

"We're just chilling with our two favourite girls," said Olivia, her arm wrapping over my shoulder like a cold snake. "You two are pretty close, always laughing and chatting together, linking arms — are you going out?"

"Oh my God, you would make *such* a cute couple!" Emma burst out laughing. "Simone and Anne, power lesbian couple!"

They all hooted with laughter, even Karen, though her eyes flashed empathic anguish.

"I'm not a lesbian," said Simone.

Olivia ruffled my head. "Is Anne then? Are you gay?"

I didn't have time to say anything before Tasha clapped her hands at my expression. "Oh my God, she *is*! Anne, are you actually gay?"

"There's nothing wrong with it, you know," said Kim.

Tasha glared at her. "I never said there *was*. I just think it's cute for people to be themselves."

Heat seeped into my cheeks. I stared at the floor, avoiding Karen.

"Sometimes, I wish I was gay so I didn't have to deal with you fucking men," said Kim, tapping one of the boys on his forehead.

"I think lesbians are hot," he said. "Get a couple girls getting it on together, then have them finish me off."

"Mmm, you'd love that, wouldn't you?" said Emma.

Tasha kissed her teeth. "Boys are such perverts. You just want to see two girls together and then go wank off to it in your room."

"Well, if the girls like it, who am I to say anything, you know what I mean?" he shrugged, smiling. He had a stiff jawline and dark gelled hair and wore scruffier clothes than Steve.

He grinned at Simone, who smiled back. "I'm bisexual," she said.

"I think Jacinta's bisexual. Should have seen the way she was watching me the other day when we were getting changed to go to Amelia's party." Kim shuddered. "I swear, I was like girl can you stop checking out my arse."

"Well it *is* a great arse, for a white girl," said Olivia, moving her arm from my shoulder and giving her mate a tap on the bottom. Kim squealed, and the boys clapped and cheered.

"Fuck *off,* Liv!" snapped Kim while the others laughed. "Why do you do stuff like that?"

"Because you love me," she said. I started to try to walk away.

"So, Anne, what do you think of Lakeland?" asked Emma. I swallowed and turned to look at them all. "It's nice. Lessons are decent."

"All the fucking teachers love you. They're like 'oh, Anne, she's so smart, she's like the smartest girl ever, let's give her a medal.'"

"It's not my f-fault teachers would r-rather teach intelligent and attentive st-students," I said, clenching my fists.

Emma sniggered, and Tasha glared at me, her hands on her hips. "What you tr-tr-tryna say, that we're d-d-d-dumb?" Emma laughed at Tasha's mockery of my voice.

I shook my head. "Th-That's not what I m-meant."

"You need to watch yourself," said Olivia. "Sometimes, you get too rude, and we don't appreciate that."

"Well I d-don't appreciate you m-making my friends and I f-f-feel like sh-sh-shit..." my voice trailed off while the girls laughed.

Simone came up to me. "Come on, Anne, let's just go back to our room," she said, tugging at my dress sleeve.

I didn't move. I stared Olivia straight in the eye, clenching my fists. "You guys think you're it, but all you do is try to control what everyone else does so they think they have to f-fear you. Do you even care about each other, or are you just friends to p-p-present some sort of image?" I stood closer to Olivia, who glared at me like I was an insect she wanted to squash.

"You're really asking for a slap, smart-arse," she said. Her mates roared.

"Go on," I said, keeping my voice steady. "I dare you. H-Hit me. Right in the face."

"Eh, come on, girls, let's not fight in the hall," said the boys. A soft voice piped up.

"Liv, you've got volleyball practice later, remember?" said Karen. "Probably better to get an early dinner and not mess up your shot."

Olivia's eyes flickered over to Karen's, then back to me. Kim pulled her arm, and Olivia slapped it away. "All right, let's go." She began to walk away, still glaring at me. "I'm fucking watching you, you stuttering coconut. You hear me?"

I watched them watch me, their stares poisonous. All but Karen's, which was apologetic.

One of the boys shook his head. "You girls need to learn to chill, man. Always starting drama with each other."

"Yeah, guys don't have that as much. Still, I understand. She was way out of order." The ruggedly handsome one smiled at Simone, who smiled back. "Yeah, girls can be full of shit. That's why most of my friends are guys."

"Guys can be shit too," he said.

Simone chuckled. "People just suck in general."

"Yes, they fucking do, you're telling me. Especially when you get to our age. You realise all your friends are just fake as hell."

"Better to just have no friends." The boys both laughed, and Simone laughed with them. I didn't laugh. I stared back at where the girls had been — where Karen had been.

"Anyway, I was gonna play my friend a song. I'm in a band," said Simone.

They sounded interested. "Oh, really? What's it called?"

"Radio Silence."

"You'll have to play for us some time," they said. Simone grinned, and likely would have stayed talking to them if I hadn't coughed, evidently disgruntled. She waved bye to them and we went into a practice room.

"They were nice," she said as she picked up an electric guitar and plugged it in to one of the amplifiers. I shrugged.

"I dunno. W-Why were they talking to the others if they were so nice?"

"You need to be less suspicious of people, babes. Not everyone is an arsehole." She strummed the guitar. It suited her, her choppy-layered hair hanging down her shoulders; faux tattoos on display.

"Do you want a m-microphone as well?" I had a flashback of my mum singing around the house and suddenly felt a sharp ache in my chest. Simone looked worried. "You okay?"

I shook my head, sitting down. Simone set up one of the hanging microphones onto a mic stand and picked up a guitar tuner resting on the amplifier. She peered at me, but I shook my head again, wanting to leave the thoughts at the back of my brain. She strummed fully, then smiled at me.

"This is a song I wrote last year, about when Prince William and Kate had their son George and the tabloids were all over them. Pisses me off that the royal family always get

so much coverage, despite having more than millions will
ever have and barely paying tax." She grinned. "It's basically
a kind of anti-monarchy song — kind of sarcastic with a bit of
a Sex Pistols vibe."

"Got it," I said. She kicked her heel on the ground, then
began to play a heavy series of chords, which made me jump.
She threw her head back, shrieking into the microphone, then
set off into a highly charged number. I nodded along, wishing
I had some earplugs to muffle the sound. It wasn't my kind of
music, but she was full of energy, had a good, strong voice,
and played well. I couldn't help smiling as I watched her
passion pour into the music.

"There's your outlet, crazy-girl," I told her afterwards.
"Go forth and let the world eat your heart out."

Chapter Twenty-One: Winter Fire

A few days later, I was sitting in the school library, a third of the way through *Native Son*, making notes. I felt utterly immersed in the sad world of Bigger and the injustices African-Americans had to face. There was something darkly comical about what had happened to him as well, as if the author was laughing at how ridiculously cruel and unfortunate his situation was. Maybe behind every work of fiction that gazed upon the cruelty of humans was a writer laughing with bitter contempt.

I didn't notice her come in until she stood in front of me and cleared her throat. I jumped, deep in the world of the story. Lifted my head and there she was. She wore a green jumper, jeans, gold hoop earrings, and that beautiful hair lit her up from both sides like a phoenix.

"Hey, Anne."

I blinked and an electric current ran from my head to toes, pausing to sink my stomach. "H-Hey, Karen. D-Do you...erm, h-how are you?"

"Fine, thanks." She pulled up the chair and sat down in front of me. "Listen, about the other day—"

"Don't w-worry about it. I've already f-forgotten." That was a lie, and we both knew it. The expressions Olivia and her friends had been shooting at me surpassed gun wounds.

"I wish my friends didn't have to be like that," she said. "I don't know why they have to be so unnecessarily cruel to people. They just laugh about it. I hate having to just stand there and go along with it."

"Why do you? W-Why do you hang out with them?"

She peered at her bitten pink nails. "I mean, they're not all bad. They can be fun and kind of cool."

"Yeah, I'll believe that when I see it," I muttered, flicking my book page. Karen leaned forward and took my hand. The lightning current returned. She stroked my fingers, her skin cream against my liquorice.

"My parents aren't well off," she said. "We're working-class. I know there are a lot of lesser-off people who go here, but I had a lot of real trouble growing up. I'm from Lewisham, and there are all kinds of gangs and stuff around where I live. My older brother got involved with a bad crowd, and my parents didn't want me to go down that route, so they sent me here.

"Liv, Kim, and Emma…they all have money, and they used to buy me clothes and pay for me when we went out on weekends. I dunno, they took care of me. I mean, I was a bit awkward and shy, and they were there. Plus, back in primary school, people used to make fun of me because of my hair. They'd call me 'ginger minger' and say gingers have no souls. I used to sit by myself a lot and talk to the younger kids because I was too scared to mix with those my own age."

I leaned forward and stroked a thread of her hair out of her face. She didn't pull away. "Th-They were idiots. Your hair is beautiful," I said. "It's like w-winter fire."

She smiled, and spots of pink flushed upon her cheeks. We cast our eyes away.

"W-What happened to your b-brother?" I asked.

"He was in a gang that used to deal drugs to the younger kids round our estate. He got caught and ended up having to go to a detention centre. He's been there for the past nine months."

"Oh, gosh. H-How old is he?"

"Sixteen. Almost seventeen. And I'm worried. If he keeps it up, when he turns eighteen, he'll be eligible for adult prison." Her face fell. I took her other hand, stroking her delicate fingers. She smiled at me, and I smiled back.

"I'm s-sorry to hear all that," I said. She was gazing deeply at me, and I pretended to inspect my book. "It's really hard w-when things happen to your family. B-But how could you afford to come here? Did you g-get a scholarship?"

She laughed and shook her head. "I'm not smart enough. No, my mum has kidney failure, so she can't afford to work, and I'm dyslexic, so we applied via the disabled family's scheme. My dad works in waste management. It was better for me to go to boarding school and get out of that shit hole. My parents don't pay anything, and I get a special maintenance allowance from the government. Although, it's less than it would have been under labour." She scowled. "Those fucking Tories don't care about people like us."

My dad voted for the Conservative government. I didn't know much about politics or the party system — Mum never voted, claiming it didn't change a thing. I had assumed I would vote for the Conservatives as well since that was our main constituency in Richmond. I decided it would be wise not to mention this.

"But yeah, so I guess hanging around with people like them helps me a bit. I try to keep my head down and get on with stuff. I miss my dad a lot, though. I love my mum, but because of her illness, she never has much energy. My dad's amazing. We always do random stuff together, like go for walks or watch movies or just have long chats about politics and society and stuff. He's clever, reads a lot. That's what bugs me about struggling to read. He used to read to me a lot when I was younger."

"That s-sounds lovely."

"Yeah." She beamed, and I felt another pang in my stomach, but this time, it was envy. I wished I could talk that way about my father. I had money, but Karen had a dad who loved and cared for her and took care of her mother. I knew which I would rather have.

"What about your family?" she asked me. "What are your parents like?"

I cleared my throat and shuffled my chair forward, removing my hands from her gentle grasp into my lap. She patiently waited.

"My dad's..." What could I say? Horrible? Fucked-up? A monster? "Tr-Troubled... He dr-drinks a lot. And used to h-hit my mum when I was growing up."

"Shit." She put her hand to her mouth. "I'm so sorry."

"I g-grew up in Richmond. It was nice. I mean, our h-house was huge, and I was h-home-schooled. Mum and I were super close, I guess like you and your dad. I had this one good friend when I was little, Lucy, and she l-lived in the house next door. One day, I told her about the hitting, and I think her parents got freaked out about it. They moved away. Some older couple moved in afterwards."

"Oh, God," she said. "So, what happened? How come you came here?"

"W-Well, my dad..." I wondered how to squeeze the past four years into a few sentences. "He and my mum ha-had this fight, they went out, and she didn't come back. He said she was gone and I p-probably wouldn't see her again..." My hands were beginning to shake. The room swelled around me in a cloud of fog, and my chest had tightened. My eyes started the rapid blinking.

"Anne? Are you all right?"

"I th-think…I'm ha-having a p-panic attack. It happens, w-when I, like, m-mention, my m-m-mum…" Shaking, unable to speak. I was simply rocking back and forth, my hands clutching my thighs.

"Do you want me to get someone?" Karen whipped her head around, then stood up to fetch the librarian. Ms. Daniels was an old lady with short, white-blonde hair. Déjà vu struck of Simone getting Matron to help me and calm my breathing. Karen ran to fetch me some water.

Fifteen minutes later, I returned to normal. Karen was crouched on the floor, leaning against me and holding my hand. Ms. Daniels sounded concerned. "Have these happened before?"

I nodded. "L-Last time Matron came to my room, and she gave me this br-brown paper bag."

"The brown paper bag is always a good thing. Helps with the breathing. Do you know what brings these on? Have you gone to the doctor?"

"Erm, y-yes and no. But I don't r-really want to t-t-talk about it."

"Oh." She stroked her chin. "I mean, it would be better to, just to stop these from happening again. With things like this, they tend to recur until you properly sort them out."

I can't sort it out, I wanted to say. But I just nodded. She stood up, checked that I was all right, and went back to the desk.

Karen faced me. "Is there anything I can do?" Her face was close to mine, gazing worriedly into my eyes.

I shook my head. "M-Maybe we should g-go back to my dorm. I feel a bit w-woozy."

She nodded and helped me gather my things into my bag. A sudden thought dawned on me. "Will your f-friends s-see us?"

She shook her head. "Nah, they've all gone shopping. We usually go out to the mall on the weekend, or sometimes to Central London. I wanted to Skype my parents, so I didn't go. Plus, I hoped I might be able to see you."

My heart did a little dance in my chest. She held my arm as we walked out of the library. Simone usually rehearsed with her band on Saturdays, so I knew she wouldn't be in our room.

I took out my key card from my coat pocket when I got back in and opened the door. Karen's eyes widened as she observed the room.

"Yeah, my r-roommate is really m-messy," I said. She laughed. Simone's clothes and makeup and hair products were scattered all over her side of the room. By contrast, my side resembled a hotel suite.

"Is that...Simone?" she asked, squinting her eyes. "The short emo girl?"

I nodded. I sat down on my bed and exhaled deeply. I kicked off my shoes. Karen sat a few paces away from me, and I tried to ignore my racing heart.

"Your sheets are so soft." She stroked her fingers over them. Simone had posters of bands I didn't know next to her bed. I had nothing.

"Whoa, Dolce and Gabbana!" She leapt up and gazed at the table on my chest of drawers. "My mum would kill for this. She loves perfume."

"It was a p-present from my aunt. I moved in with m-my aunt and uncle after m-my m-m-mum...left." I inhaled deeply. "I haven't seen my dad since the beginning of last year."

She nodded, marvelling at the jewellery and perfume and books on my drawers and desk table. "You have such lovely things." She brushed her fingers along my necklaces hanging on my little Crinoline lady.

"I'm sure you d-do as well," I said.

She grinned. "Yeah, most of it is stuff my mates have bought me."

I hugged my knees to my chest. "It seems a bit…I dunno, al-almost manipulative, them buying you things and g-getting you in as their friend."

She sighed. "I try not to think about it. It is what it is, really. Anyway, let's not talk about them." She flung herself back onto my bed, then smiled at me. I smiled back. We both giggled. She leaned forward, taking my hand in hers again. Our palms rubbed against one another.

"Is this okay?" She bent her head forward, kissing my hand. I nodded. She moved closer. "What about this?" She moved her head to mine and kissed my cheek. I felt my insides turn from ice to mush, melting my soul.

I nodded again. She stared at me, her face still, her lips inches from mine. "How about this?" Then, we were kissing. Her lips felt as soft as her voice, and I could taste her minty lip-balm. She held my hand in hers and put her other on my back. Her tongue began to intertwine with mine, and I knew I wanted to hold onto this moment forever.

Chapter Twenty-Two: Piper and Alex

We must have dozed off on my bed, because the next thing I heard was an, "Oh," from Simone as the door opened. Karen and I blinked and sat up. We had been curled up on my bed, her arms wrapped around me like a protective cocoon. It was the happiest and most relaxed I'd felt in a long time.

Simone didn't make a big deal out of it, bless her. She just nodded at us, then put her guitar case back next to her bed and asked if I was going to come and have pizza and watch *Orange is the New Black* in Canel's room. Her eyes flicked to Karen.

"You can come too," she said. Karen glanced from Simone to me. "Would that be all right? I wouldn't be, like, intruding or anything?"

"N-Not at all!" I said.

"Our friends are cool, really accepting," said Simone. "We're a bit weird, but then isn't everyone?"

"Being weird is way better than being samey and boring," said Karen. "I like weird."

"I'm just going to take a shower and change," said Simone. "I always get really sweaty after rehearsals."

I looked at her, and she stared down at the floor and started rummaging through her drawers. It dawned on me that she sounded slightly off, and she was fidgeting with her hands.

"Are you all right? H-How was your rehearsal?" I asked.

"Good." She nodded. "You guys should head over. Canel and the others are all there already. Don't wait for me."

I wasn't sure, but Karen bounced up, linking her arm through mine. We walked out of my room. "I love *Orange is the New Black*. Alex Vause is my fantasy girlfriend. She and

Piper make such a cute couple, way better than Piper and stupid Larry. I can't wait for season three to come out next year."

"Yeah, we're ha-halfway through season two," I said.

Karen closely surveyed me. "Is everything all right?"

"Mmm?"

Karen stopped walking and turned to face me. She put her hand gently on my shoulder. "Are you feeling sad about your mum again?"

"Oh, no, no. It's not that. It's just…Simone."

"What about her?"

"I j-just…" I sighed. "I mean, she's a bit…unstable, I guess. U-Unpredictable. I just w-worry about her."

"I think we're all a bit unstable," she said gently. "Neither your life nor mine has been a stroll in the park."

"Yeah, but, like, she dr-drinks, for example. By herself. I saw vodka in her drawer. And she s-self-harms, and she smokes."

"It's probably just a phase," said Karen, though she sounded worried. "Is she getting any help?"

"Sh-She doesn't seem to have much support. I don't think she's c-close with her family. Her parents don't really talk, and she doesn't have any siblings. She has a bunch of older f-friends back in Kensington, and I think they all t-take drugs and go out to raves, and she tries to g-get in with them."

"So, she's just having fun. Me and my mates have gone to a few raves before," said Karen. "Though, to be honest, I don't drink much or take drugs, so I'd just be bored and awkward." She giggled.

"But it's not r-really about that," I said. "It's like she's tr-trying to fill some sort of empty void and be something she isn't, like she doesn't r-realise she's enough already."

Karen stroked my cheek, and my insides crumbled, as if the touch of her hands could wipe away my worries. "Don't worry about her. It's not your job to. You have enough of your own shit to deal with. I'm sure she'll be fine. I mean, my brother was all into that stuff as well, but what could I do about it? Worrying about people isn't going to solve anything."

"It's just r-rubbish, isn't it? People think being our age is all simple and we d-don't know anything about life. No one takes our problems s-seriously or realises how awful and hard things can be. We're just st-stupid kids who know nothing." I squatted down on the corridor, glaring into space. Karen crouched down beside me, stroking my hair.

"Your cane-rolls are so cool. Do you do them yourself?"

"Yeah. My mum used to do them for me, but then I l-learned myself." I lifted my fingers up to my head and began to undo my bun, letting it fluff out behind my head with my cane-rolls detailing on top.

"Like Alicia Keys," she said fondly. I laughed. "I look n-nothing like Alicia Keys. She's gorgeous, and I'm a d-dull nerd."

"Nerds are sexy," she said, kissing my forehead. I gazed into her eyes, then kissed her again, not caring if anyone saw.

Canel, Melvin, and Steve were on Canel's bed, locked in a heated debate about who was prettier, Piper or Alex. Roger was sitting on a cushion on the floor. They all said hello, then glanced at Karen. Melvin leapt up and shook her hand, introducing everyone. The two of us sat on the floor next to Steve.

"Here, have some pizza. There should be enough for everyone, even though Steve and Roger tried to eat all of it," said Canel.

"Fuck off. We never eat all the pizza," said Steve, slapping Canel on the arm. Melvin raised his arms up and put on a funny voice. "Steven, please be civil with ladies present."

"Where's Simone?" asked Roger, pushing his glasses up.

"She's coming. She just w-wanted to change after her rehearsal," I said.

"Is her band going to play at the Christmas show?" asked Melvin.

I shrugged. "I think that's the p-plan. She's just been having difficulties f-finding people to commit. I think they've got a full band now."

"Simone's sick at guitar," said Roger.

Steve leaned forward and flicked his shoulder. "Oi, oi, mate, you should be her groupie."

"Shut *up*," said Roger.

Melvin shook his head at Karen. "Sorry about this lot. They don't know how to behave in front of normal people."

"That's okay. I'm not normal either," said Karen, grinning. She put her arm around me. I noticed the others staring.

"Karen, who do you think is more attractive, Piper or Alex?" asked Melvin.

Karen smiled. "Yeah, getting a gay girl's opinion is a good idea."

"Oh, are you two together?" Canel voiced what everyone else was thinking. I nodded. She squealed. "Aw, that is so cute! Not gonna lie, I was kinda wondering."

"Can we not make a big d-deal out of it please?" I said. Karen kissed me on the cheek, and Steve and Roger cheered.

"No, we're not going to get it on in front of you," Karen said, laughing and flicking her hair. "Okay, I was telling Anne earlier Alex is my dream woman, so I would have to go with her because Piper annoys me."

Canel and Roger cheered, while Melvin and Steve shook their heads. "No way, man," said Steve. "Piper is hot. Alex looks like a man."

"You look like a troll," said Roger. "Nah, Alex is goals. Her tattoos are sexy."

Hm. A smile crept onto my face. A far-fetched thought, but it made sense; Alex wasn't the only dark-haired female with tattoos and a feisty attitude. Simone was sort of similar to Alex; blunt, smart, loyal...did Roger have a thing for Simone? The way he made fun of her, shot her glances at lunchtime, and they hung out together a lot. I couldn't have been the only one who had noticed. The thought deepened as he sat up in excitement when she walked into the room an hour later while we were eating ice-cream and had almost finished another episode.

"Eh, look what the cat dragged in!" he yelled. She rolled her eyes at him.

"We saved you a couple slices of pizza, but they're probably cold now," said Canel. Simone sat down on the floor next to Roger. "Don't worry about it. I'm not hungry."

"Where've you been? What took you so long?" asked Melvin.

Simone shrugged. "Just had shit to do."

"She was watching gay porn," said Steve. Melvin sighed and rolled his eyes at him. "Why do you always have to come out with such bullshit?"

"Are you all right anyway?" asked Roger. Simone nodded. She smiled at Karen and I, still curled up on the other side of the floor with Karen's arm around me. It was warm in Canel's room, but Simone was wearing a thick hoodie and leggings. She took out her phone and smiled at something on the screen. Roger leaned over, and she yanked the phone away.

"Who you texting?" he asked.

"I wasn't texting anyone. Mind your own business," she said.

He pretended to be offended. "Is it a guy?"

"Fuck off, Roger," she said. I watched the two of them. If Roger did fancy Simone, she clearly had no idea.

Simone slowly became more elusive, although I didn't really notice because most of my mind became occupied with Karen. I told Zoe all about her and took a picture of the two of us together to send to her. Zoe was delighted. We had a WhatsApp video chat and she said she couldn't wait for me to come back home for Christmas. She and my aunt visited me a couple of times during that first term and brought food and a few new books. Zoe was thrilled I was having a wonderful time. She wasn't having as much luck with boyfriends.

"I wish *I* was gay, then I wouldn't have to deal with stupid boys," she said to me as we walked around the Lakeland gardens one afternoon while my aunt sat and made some notes on a paper for her lecture.

"Boys aren't stupid, Zoe." All the straight or bisexual women I knew seemed to complain a lot about boys — Zoe, Simone, my mum. "And being g-gay isn't all sunshine and roses. Remember what ha-happened last year with Meg?"

"Meg's a bitch. She doesn't hang out with us anymore," said Zoe. That took me by surprise. "She hangs out with some other rude girls in our year now. They all take pictures of themselves and post them on Instagram and go out to house parties with people in year eleven. None of my friends talk to her."

"See, girls are just as bad as boys, in a d-different way."

Zoe giggled. "Maybe. But I dunno. Boys are so hard to figure out. They act like they like you, then they ignore you — or make fun of you."

"They probably find girls j-just as confusing. Anyway, I'm sure you'll meet a nice guy at some point."

"I've never even kissed a boy yet," she moaned. "I just get so awkward around them."

"I hadn't kissed a girl until I met Karen," I said. Karen had had one other girlfriend before me. She'd had boyfriends too, in primary school, which was when she'd realised she was gay.

"Just relax and let things be," I said. "Things ha-happen in their right time."

"Mum says I'm too young. She didn't have a boyfriend until she was seventeen. She says none of it means anything at our age."

Chapter Twenty-Three: Autonomy

There was one afternoon I won't forget. It was awful and incredible and comical all at once. Karen and I had been seeing each other for about a month, spending most of our time in my room or in the library or the Lakeland gardens. Anywhere her friends wouldn't find us.

But she was hanging with them less, and my friends and I more. They were bound to notice.

I hadn't given it much thought at first. She was like a delicious red velvet cake after an unappetizing meal. I felt like my heart was bouncing around the school walls, and everywhere the air was rosy pink. She made me feel like a little girl again, playing silly games with Lucy in our magical land of Pachidale. I knew I never wanted to lose the feelings I felt when she gazed into my eyes and held my hand in hers. I loved seeing our skin together — brown and white, dark chocolate and creamy milk.

She began sitting with us at mealtimes. First, it was just on weekends, but then it was during the week. Emma, Tasha, and Olivia stood up and walked over to our table. Tasha and Emma were smirking, but Olivia was furiously offended.

"Karen," she said, standing over us, her slender arms on her hips. "What the hell are you doing?"

Everyone stopped giggling at Steve's Mr. Bean impression. Karen regarded her friend. "I'm just eating lunch."

"Why are you eating with *them*? Come on, we've barely seen you over the past few weeks."

"She's been with her girlfriend." Tasha and Emma cracked up like it was a massive joke. Olivia glared at them, then back at us. "Look, Karen, if you want to be gay be gay, whatever. Just not with *her*."

I stood up. "First of all, you don't decide to be gay. It's a naturally occurring phenomena just like being straight or black. Second, you can't g-go around telling people who they can and can't be with."

"Right, I've had enough of you." Olivia started walking around to me, but I came over to her. A few people at other tables were starting to quiet and watch.

"You come stuttering here with your posh all-fucking-knowing accent and act like you're the shit. You suck up to all the teachers, practically lick Mr. Oseni's balls in English, all those times you stay back after class and have your long fucking chats, then you come here tryna get rude with me and my friends, and now you're tryna turn Karen against me. Very fucking stupid. I've tried to be nice, but I am *this* close to giving you a slap in the face."

"You had your chance to slap me once before," I said. "I g-grew up in a violent household. People hitting each other isn't alien to me."

I heard Simone whimper behind me. Emma and Tasha stopped laughing and looked scared. Even Olivia was taken aback. I wasn't shying away from her; I was standing right in front of her, my expression hard.

"Karen is not your friend," I said, speaking very slowly. "She's just someone you use and take advantage of to bulk up your numbers. None of you people know anything about real friendship. Your entire group is based on lies and false appearances." I walked over to her table where Kim, Amelia, Jacinta, and a bunch of rowdy boys — some of whom Simone described as "roadmen" — were sitting.

"You walk around the halls, trying to threaten and intimidate everyone else and put down those who don't c-conform to whatever standards of 'coolness' you decide are acceptable. But there's nothing special or cool about any of you — you just use one another to keep a sense of autonomy that somehow surpasses the other cliques and evokes fear and dread into anyone who dares to c-cross you.

"You use all the standard tactics — name-calling, g-ganging up on those too afraid to stand up to you, and false senses of charm — to keep the teachers and staff members in your good books. But it's all a l-load of — of horse-shit!" I picked up one of the plates on their table and threw it on the ground. Kim stood up, yelling in protest, but Olivia motioned for her to sit down.

By now, most of the upper third and fourth formers in the hall had gone quiet and were watching us.

"All right, you dykey coconut, you've said your shit and used your big fancy words. Now, it's my turn."

I should have ran for it, but I stayed where I was. Her hand connected with my face; I stepped back, and she stumbled, her attempted punch becoming a slap.

A teacher shouted something and started towards us. Someone from my table — Melvin, I think — picked up scraps of food from his plate and threw them at Canel, yelling, "FOOD FIGHT!" She spluttered and threw potatoes at him, and then food was flying over my table. I ducked my head, trying not to get hit as everyone around us tossed edibles at one another, even Olivia's friends. I took this as an opportunity to run, but Olivia caught up with me and got ready to whack me again. Mr. Mittles and Mr. Oseni intervened.

Mr. Oseni caught me gently, but firmly, by the shoulder, and Mr. Mittles did the same to Olivia. I observed the rest of the hall. It was like some Nickelodeon teen show — everyone was hurling remainders of their lunch at their friends and laughing and shrieking. Some looked appalled and were rushing out of the hall as fast as they could. I closed my eyes, wondering if I was dreaming. I opened them and the hall was still a frenzy of chips, fish fingers, lettuce, and lemonade.

Olivia and I were escorted to Mr. Mittles' office. His office was small and neat, the sound of a dehumidifier hissing in the background.

He positioned himself on the chair in front of his office desk and motioned for Olivia and me to sit on the sofa at the side. Mr. Oseni sat on a chair opposite us, clasping his hands together.

"So, girls, what's been going on today?" asked Mr. Mittles. Olivia's arms were folded, and mine were in my lap. Neither of us acknowledged one another.

"I know there's been a bit of tension between the two of you in my lessons," said Mr. Oseni in his lovely relaxed voice. "Anne, I know you're new here, and, Olivia, there have been a few problems in the past with other students."

Olivia scoffed and kissed her teeth.

"But needless to say, you're both very bright girls and I would hate to see that talent wasted on something as petty as fighting."

"It wasn't my fucking fault," said Olivia.

"Language, please," said Mr. Mittles. Olivia rolled her eyes again, then mumbled an apology.

"Look, everything was fine until she showed up and started acting all entitled and shit just because she thinks she's so much smarter than us." Olivia glared at me.

Mr. Oseni raised his eyebrows. "That's quite a big statement to make," he said.

"Yes, and I don't think it's a g-good enough reason to go around h-hitting people," I said. Olivia threw me another scowl. I shuffled away from her on the sofa.

"Violence towards other students is not tolerated, as the pair of you know. That's why I'm going to have to suspend you until the end of term, Olivia, and you will not be allowed to attend the Key Stage 3 Christmas Party."

Her mouth fell open. I tried not to appear gleeful or relieved.

"But, sir, that is *so* unfair! What about her?" She pointed to me. "How come I'm the one who gets in trouble?"

"Anne, did you physically attack Olivia in any way?" asked Mr. Oseni. I shook my head. He regarded Olivia. "Is she telling the truth?"

"Oh, come on, she couldn't hit a fucking eight-year-old."

"Stop cursing please," Mr. Mittles said in a harsher, firmer tone that made Olivia gulp and sit up. "I think all of us are aware here Anne was a victim in this incident."

"Oh, for—" Olivia shut her mouth when Mr. Mittles threw her an angry look. She folded her arms again.

"However, there are always two people involved in any kind of incident and provoking other students by throwing their plate on the floor is not acceptable behaviour either. Anne, I think one week's detention with Mr. Oseni starting today should do it."

Olivia smirked. I nodded at my English teacher with relief.

Olivia was told to go straight to her dorm and start packing while Mr. Mittles phoned her parents to pick her up. My detention wasn't until after my final lesson, but Mr. Oseni beckoned me to come to his office.

He motioned for me to sit down on the sofa. "I just wanted to make sure you were all right," he said. I felt like bursting into tears.

"W-Why does she hate me so much? I d-didn't d-do anything to her. I don't think I'm entitled, or whatever she seems to th-think. I can't *help* b-being clever, or whatever she s-says."

He smiled softly at me. "I've been teaching for over ten years and I've been here for five. Working in a boarding school is different from a day school. You get to know students a lot more in deeper contexts because you see them outside of class. I saw what you said to Olivia in the canteen, and that was very brave."

I shuffled in my seat. "It w-was nothing. I mean, someone had to st-stand up to them."

"And you did," he said. "That's very admirable. Few other students would have the guts to do that."

"I just don't see why they should be allowed to treat everyone else the way they do and p-put them into little boxes. And the way e-everyone watches them, like they're afraid of them. They shouldn't be allowed to intimidate people like they do. So, why do they?"

He gave me a sad smile. "At your age, people don't always know how to explain or express certain things. It can be tough when someone comes along and seems like they're in competition with you—"

"C-Competition?"

He laughed. "I'm not sure how to explain it. Sometimes, when things have been a certain way and someone comes along and disrupts the original sense of order, things almost fall apart." He nodded at the pile of books on his desk next to the unmarked papers and pulled one of the books from the middle out. The rest all tumbled down. My eyebrow raised.

"What's your last lesson?" he asked me.

"D-Drama." He smiled. I shuddered. "I hate drama. I'm rubbish at it."

"Really? Maybe see it as a break from being so in your head. That's what I do. I try to go swimming once a week. My wife is always telling me I spend too much time in my head, so I try to get out of it." He rubbed his fingers against his temples. I blinked, trying to imagine him with a wife. I wondered if they had children. What would my life have been like if I'd had a father like him — someone who was kind and patient and never raised their voice or lounged drunk all over the sofa?

"I'd better go g-get my things," I said, getting up. I had a feeling most of my year group would be in trouble anyway.

Chapter Twenty-Four: Bohemian Rhapsody

I was right. Most of Key Stage 3s last lessons were cancelled because everyone was told to go clean up after Mrs. Saydes gave everyone a massive lecture in the canteen. Mr. Mittles had also come back down, along with Mr. Stanford, the deputy headteacher. The dinner ladies were cleaning up everything, and I hoped they were getting paid extra to do so. My bag and coat weren't there, but I guessed Simone must have taken them back up to our dorm. As I made my way back, I passed Karen, who was grimacing and pulling bits of spaghetti out of her hair.

"God, that was crazy," she said to me. She leaned in to hug me, then stared down at her clothes, patted me on the arms, and kissed my cheek. "You're lucky you missed it. I honestly can't believe that happened."

"Olivia's being suspended 'til the end of t-term."

Karen's eyes widened. "Seriously? Wow, she should be after the way she treated you. Are you okay?" Her hands stroked my arms, and I felt like I was in a park surrounded by snow on a December evening.

"I'm fine. I have a w-week's detention, though."

Her face tensed. "What! That is so unfair. You did nothing wrong."

"They couldn't make it seem like I was getting f-favoured over Olivia, I guess. Plus, I did throw Kim's plate onto the ground."

"That was amazing. You're amazing." She leaned in to kiss me again — on the lips. A few people sniggered as they walked past, but I didn't care.

"Well, I don't know about th-that," I said, examining the floor. "Guess we're all missing last lesson anyway, so I may as well go st-straight to Mr. Oseni's office."

"Ah, detention with him for a week! Now I get it." She tugged my dress sleeve. "Teacher's pet."

"Shut up. What lesson do you have?"

"English, funnily enough. And you?"

"Drama."

"Oh, crap!" Karen's fist smacked the air. She loved drama. I reminisced one evening where we were curled up in my room, and she told me her dream had always been to be an actress:

"Like, sometimes I'd look around my shitty council estate and think to myself, imagine if I could make it out of here and onto some West End musical or one of those TV soaps." We were laying on my bed facing one another with our hands clasped together. I could have laid with her until the ice caps melted.

"I'm r-rubbish at acting," I said. "I get all shy and awkward, and I hate having people l-look at me."

"Nah, I feel way less awkward on a stage than around people." She grinned, showing her slightly crooked front teeth, the imperfections making her more beautiful. "I used to play at pretending to be different people all the time when I was younger. At times it drove my mum mad. I'd be like, 'I'm not Karen, I'm Lady Potts from Windsor, and I don't go to bed until I've watched the ten-o clock news,' and she'd get all annoyed. My brother and I often played daft games as well and made up different characters. We were quite close when we were younger, before he got into the drugs and shit."

"I used to wish I had a sibling. Being an only child get so lonely. But Mum and I did l-loads of stuff together." I felt my chest tighten. Karen gripped my hand and leaned forward to kiss my forehead.

I showed her the pictures. I'd only shown Zoe, Luke, and Simone up until that point. They were kept in their little photo file in the bottom drawer of my bedside table. Karen flicked through them, stroking the glossy images. Like the others, she commented on how beautiful my mum was.

"You look alike," she said.

"No we don't. I f-favour my dad. I got his shit genes."

She brushed my cheek with her fingers. "You've got lovely genes," she said. Her eyes seemed to burn right through me, and I felt myself move away from her, as if her gaze had undressed me.

"Want to listen to one of my monologues?" She bounced up. "I used to do acting classes after school with this company called John Robert Powers, or JRP for short. That was so fun. And I tried writing a few monologues. Though, I'm shit at writing, so I just recorded it on my phone and memorised it." She stood up and cleared her throat, then her face fell into deep despair, her hands lifted to her waist, and her eyes became downcast. She started reciting something in the voice of a woman who had lost her husband in the second world war. I watched her, mesmerized, falling even more deeply for her as she performed in front of me. When she finished, I applauded.

"That was so good. It's like you became a different person."

"Well, that is what acting tends to be." She sat down next to me. "I'm just glad you didn't hate it."

"I could n-never hate anything about you," I said, kissing her on the mouth.

When I went back into my dorm to collect my things after the food fight, Simone was lying on her bed giggling at her phone screen. She had her dressing gown on, and her hair hung damply around her head. I cleared my throat.

"Aaanne," she said in a strange voice. I stared at her. Her eyes were glazed, and her smile was too bright and toothy. "Hooow goes it?"

"You're drunk," I said. "W-Why are you drunk?"

She shrugged her shoulders slowly, like a character in a *Loony Tunes* cartoon. "Me no no."

I walked up to her and crouched in front of her. "I ha-have to go to Mr. Oseni's for detention, but if you need any help, maybe I can get someone—"

"Sssshhh." She put a finger to my lips. I pushed her hand away, and she giggled. "I'm fiiine."

"This is ridiculous." I had no idea what to do. "I th-think you should talk to somebody…"

"I am talking to somebody." She flashed her phone screen at me. "I'm talking to Toby."

"Who's Toby?" I said, tapping my hand against my knee. Her face went all dreamy. "That guy…back when I played you my song in the music room, and Olive-bitch-face and them were there, and *he* was there with Gus…"

I racked my brain, and the memory swooped back. "Yeah, th-there were those two guys. Okay, so you're drunk and messaging him. Isn't he like sixteen?"

"Fifteen. He's in the upper fiiifth," she said. She started giggling, lisping the latter part of the word. I smacked my hand against my head. "J-Jesus, Simone, it's like quarter to three in the afternoon. Why are you...?"

"Any time is drinkey-time, Annie baby." She swayed on the bed. "I likey to drinkey wheneverrrr."

"What...h-how much have you had?"

She did that stupid cartoon shrug again. I sat on my floor. I was back in Richmond with my dad, who was sitting on the sofa laughing at *The Jeremy Kyle Show.*

"Look, I th-think you should call your parents and get them to talk to you or something."

"My parents?" She roared with laughter. "My parents don't care or know *shit* about me. They just care about the house, and their stupid jobs, and us going to Aunt Maggie's for Christmas, although I'd rather not fucking go because my whole family *hates* me except Uncle Lucas, but then, I hardly see him because he lives in Holland..."

"I'm sure your family d-doesn't hate you." I shook my head. She patted me on the head, and I pushed her arm away, glaring at her. Saliva escaped her mouth and she wiped it away like a deranged cayote.

"You know *nothing,* Annie-Pannie," she said. "You don't know me. Nobody knows. Mum and Dad tried to take me to Doctor Phillips, but he could do *nothing.* His solution: medication! Haha! But I was only eleven. Parents thought wasn't good. Was too bad. Too bad, too bad. Oooh!" She squealed at her phone screen. "Toby thinks I'm cute. He's *sooo* nice."

"Shall I get Matron?"

"I'm just a *poor little rich girl,* and I *don't need any sympathyyy from anybodyyy.*"

She was starting to shriek, and I was worried someone was going to come in. I gazed at her and saw who was really there: a lonely thirteen-year-old girl who felt like she had no one. I was frustrated, but I felt sorry for her, and I had grown to care for her in an unexpected way. I stood up and walked down the corridor. Canel walked out of her room and smile, then frown at me. "You all right? Are you coming to the assembly later?"

"What assembly?" I said, folding my arms and tapping my foot quickly.

"You know, everyone in the lower and upper fourth has to go to this assembly for some pointless lecture about throwing food, then we all have to go prep for like two hours and get this report card signed, otherwise we won't be allowed to go to the Christmas Party." She rolled her eyes. "Sooo fucking long. You all right?"

"Yeah, fine." I moved past her. "Is Simone coming?" she called.

I hesitated. "Sh-She's not feeling v-very well. I'm just going to get Matron. I ha-have this detention with Mr. Oseni I'm meant to go to in like ten minutes."

"Oh, shit, that's bare annoying, but then, he is blessed, so should be kind of calm still. Should I check on Simone?"

"N-N-No, it's nothing. I think she just n-needs to r-rest for a moment." I didn't know if anyone else knew about her drinking, and I thought it would be unwise to freak the others out.

I rushed downstairs to get Matron and we came back to my room, and there Simone was, lolling around on her bed, playing her guitar and singing *Bohemian Rhapsody.* She turned to us and nearly fell off the bed when she saw Matron.

"What's going on? Why...huh?"

Matron crouched down and gazed at my drunken friend. "Your roommate here is a bit worried about you. Do we need to call anyone at home?"

"There's nothing wwr*rong*," she slurred. "I am just chillin' and hangin' like a little bang-bangin' something. Erm…" she squinted her eyes, "that — that came out wrong."

"Has this kind of thing happened before?" Matron asked me. Simone shook her head wildly. "No! Not at all. Just this once. Just one time, food fight made me a little nuts, everyone throwing stuff, out of control, chaos and all that."

"Simone, that's n-not true," I said.

Matron scanned her head from me to her. Simone smiled and cocked her head like a dalmatian puppy.

"I. Am. Great. I just felt like I needed something. Was an accident. Won't happen again, I swear." She considered me, then Matron. "I'll be back to normal tomorrow. Right as rain," she promised. "And I'm a bit stressed out, what with the Christmas Party coming up, and my band performing, and yeah…" She giggled, then began to cry. "Oooh, I feel so stuuupid…"

"If you have to go to your detention, then you can go. I'll stay with her," said Matron. I nodded and glanced at my friend, giving her a little wave before leaving.

I tried to concentrate as I poured through my notes on *Native Son* with Mr. Oseni. All I could think about was Simone drinking, my dad drinking, and the parallels that seemed to bounce back and forth within my life. From one broken soul to the next, one tirade of pain to tide the other over. Was there no end?

"Anne?" Mr. Oseni waved his hand at me. "Is everything all right?"

It was like Michael Jackson was singing 'Smooth Criminal' to me on a loop.

Is Annie okay today?

Feeling okay, little Annie?

What's up Annie, are you okay?

"No, sir. Th-Things aren't all right. My friend...my mum...I-I don't know what to do." I began to break down in tears. "It all j-just f-feels like t-too much, and..." I bent forward and put my head in my hands. Mr. Oseni walked around and gently put his arm around my shoulder. "It's all going to be alright."

"No, it isn't," I wailed. "Sir, I'm s-so scared. S-Simone...she drinks, by herself in her room, and..." I sobbed harder. "M-My mum...sir, I h-haven't seen her...she went missing...I don't know where she *is*!"

"What do you mean?" He remained level-headed; a safe confidante.

"She w-went m-missing...two years ago...she and my d-dad...I don't know w-where she is and my d-dad...I haven't spoken to him and I *don't want to,* I hate him, h-he's a m-monster, but he's still my d-dad, and I'm so glad he s-sent me to live with Aunt Colette and Uncle Brian because I'm s-so much happier, but I'm still so *confused,* and I d-don't know what to do — it's all too much!" I wept and wept, letting my English teacher soothe me.

"Have you contacted the authorities?"

"I can't, sir. I c-can't..." Words stuck in my throat. He didn't persist, allowing me to pour my darkest fears into his ears.

Chapter Twenty-Five: Radio Silence

Simone insisted she was fine, everything was fine, no one needed to worry about a thing. She kept up her work as we approached the end of term, and went to her rehearsals, and spent a lot of time on her phone messaging Toby. I had a horrible feeling about all of it, but maybe I was just paranoid.

I tried not to think too much about her and enjoy being with Karen. With Olivia gone and the teachers watching closely, her friends began to keep a distance. She and I would go to the library together and I'd select different books, moving through them with her.

She was slower than I had imagined. I had thought she may stumble upon longer words and mix up tenses or words like "there," "their," and "they're." Instead, she took about three-to-four seconds to read each word, and longer if it had several syllables. I pointed to the words she had more trouble with, saying them aloud, then letting her repeat it.

"'Tara laughed,'" I said, pointing to the sentence.

Karen blinked at it. "See, that's so stupid. Why is 'laughed' spelt like that? Why can't things just be spelt the way they sound?"

"Phonetics," I said. "English isn't a phonetic language. Words don't s-sound the way they are spelled. You can pronounce the letters o-u-g-h differently d-depending on the word, like 'slough' or 'borough.' That's what makes it confusing."

"It's stupid," she grumbled.

I smiled and patted her arm. "You'll get used to it. Spanish is a phonetic language. If you write out a sentence, it's generally pronounced how it's written."

"I should have been born in Spain." The book we were reading was for ten-to-eleven-year-olds about some kids who discovered buried treasure in their back garden. Karen picked it up and puffed air out of her cheeks. "I'm so stupid."

"You're not stupid." I took her hand. "Loads of p-people are dyslexic, and it's not like it's your fault or anything. Like my stutter — it only ap-appeared after I moved in with my aunt and uncle."

"Yeah, but it just gets me down. Like, you're so smart and you read so much, and I wish I could be more like that." She slumped down in her chair. "This is why I love acting. You don't need to be good at reading and writing. It's all about expressing yourself."

"But you still have to learn lines," I said.

"Exactly! That's why I got used to memorizing stuff. I tape things on my phone or watch them on YouTube and memorize them. Like Caliban's monologue in *The Tempest* by Shakespeare. We had to learn that a few years back when I was with JRP, and I just listened to everyone else read it out, then kept repeating the words to myself." She started reciting it with full expression, peering deeply at me, her eyes wide. She then smiled and stuck her tongue out, and the two of us burst out laughing.

Later in my room, we snuggled on my bed, the two of us kissing and curling our palms together. She moved her lips down my chin, then cupped her hand around my breast. I did the same to her, our hands dancing in synchronised harmony over each other's clothes. Her hands slowly trailed up my tights and under my dress.

I stopped kissing her, edging back. Sweating.

"Are you all right? Sorry if it's too much," she said.

I shook my head. "No, it's f-fine, just...I'm n-nervous. I've n-never really d-done...l-like, anything w-with a girl. Or a guy."

"I haven't really either. I mean, me and my ex kissed, but we were, like, twelve."

"I'm fourteen," I said. Karen giggled. "I know." She would be fourteen in March.

"We don't have to do anything if you're not comfortable," she said. "I just really like you."

"I do too," I said, stroking back her hair from her eyes. "In fact, I th-think I'm falling in love with you."

She smiled and bent down to kiss my hand. "I feel the same."

We kissed again, stronger, and I shifted her hand so it was between my legs. I began to pull my tights down, then my underwear. I did the same to her jeans, the two of us reaching in and gasping in joy as our fingers caressed pink buttons.

Later that night, I felt a warm glow run through me. It had been weeks since I'd had any nightmares or real thoughts about my mum. I simply lay in my bed, half-dreaming of Karen and the smell of her clothes. I barely heard Simone stumble in, then looked up when I realised she was there.

"Hey," I said, switching on my bedside light. She nodded at me, flopping down onto her bed. I sat up. "You been rehearsing today?"

"Mmm. Can't wait for the performance. Just a few more days." She put her palms together in front of her face. "I feel a bit weird about going back home for Christmas. Like, to my aunt and uncle's house. I don't know if I want to."

"Have you told your parents?" I asked. She shook her head. "They'd just tell me to do what I want. Or they'd get all annoyed and say it's been arranged and it's a family gathering, blah, blah, blah."

"Christmas is meant to be a time f-for families," I said.

Simone put her palms down and swung her legs. "It would definitely be more shit if it was just the three of us. We'd have to pretend to really care about each another, and it would be more intense. At least with my cousins and that around I get some space." She blew a raspberry. "I know Mum and Dad are getting a divorce soon, I just don't know when. They're probably just waiting for me to finish school first so I'm out of the way."

A thought occurred. "What if you came to stay with me for a f-few days? Wouldn't have to be for the whole holiday, just maybe three nights or something? Just t-to break things up."

Her eyes widened. "Would I be allowed?"

"I'm sure you would. My aunt and uncle are lovely, and we've got loads of space. They'd be more th-than happy to accommodate you. And you'd g-get to see Zoe again, for longer."

"Okay," she said, shrugging like it was no big deal, but her face was hopeful. "Maybe I could go to yours first, then to my aunt's? I could let my parents know, and they could pick me up."

"Yeah, th-that would be great."

I called my aunt the next day asking about Simone coming to stay for a bit. She said that was no problem if her parents didn't mind. Simone seemed insistent they wouldn't care if she was back in time for Christmas. This made me uncomfortable, but I didn't show it. Instead, I smiled at the prospect of her coming to stay. I was also happy about seeing Luke again, who I did see once during the half-term week.

The Christmas Party approached, and I was beyond relieved Olivia wouldn't be showing her smug face. Her cronies were still among us, but they had been more cautious after the food fight.

Canel, Simone, Karen, and I were getting changed in our dorm. Canel insisted upon doing my makeup. I glanced at Karen, feeling self-conscious as Canel dabbed powder and brushed a thick black wand in my eyes.

"Stay *still*," she instructed as I blinked. I glanced at Karen. Canel turned around. "Oi, you, don't stare — you'll put the girl off."

"I'm just admiring the view," said Karen, smiling. She took off her jeans and jumper, and my heart thumped faster. I stared upwards as Canel swiped a brush underneath my eyelids.

I was wearing a long-sleeved purple dress Zoe had insisted I buy when we visited Lakeland Shopping Mall with my aunt. The two of us spent ages trying on random clothes, and I told her at the end of term there was always a party and some of the student bands played live music. "Then you *have* to wear something nice!" she yelled, clapping her hands. "You need variety. Plus, your girl will love it."

Zoe had also insisted I get some strappy mauve heeled shoes to match the dress. I put them on and imagined myself with purple eyeshadow and mascara and lip-gloss and felt like a whole new person. Nearly as pretty as Mum.

"You look beautiful, Anne," said Karen as Canel finished swirling dusky pink blusher on my cheeks. I stood up and surveyed the mirror. I had taken my bun out and left my hair cane-rolled on top. The rest fluffed around my head. I wore my sapphire-crystal earrings and my new dress and shoes.

Simone wolf-whistled. Karen mock-slapped her. "Leave off. She's taken." She was lovely in a short-sleeved flowery blue dress with her hair hanging down over her shoulders. She came and stood next to me in the mirror, putting her arm around me. Canel picked up her phone.

"Say cheese," she said.

I ducked my head. "N-No. I hate pictures."

"Fuck that. I need a pic of the cute couple," said Canel, sticking her tongue at me. Karen kissed my forehead. She had one arm over my shoulder and the other held my hand stretched across my waist. She stroked my palm with her fingers.

Simone blew us a kiss. "So cute," she said. "You should put it on Instagram."

I glared at her. She came over and stood next to me, putting her arm around me. Her eyes were made up with heavy black eyeliner and mascara, her lips were painted rosy-red, and she wore a tiny black skirt and a silvery off-the-shoulder top and black heels. She was thirteen going on seventeen.

Canel came and took a selfie of the four of us before Simone rushed down to the main hall with the other bands to get ready. We played some music in my room and danced around a bit before getting our bags and heading downstairs. "What do you think the boys will be wearing?" asked Karen.

"Whatever it is, it'll be better than the crap they usually throw on," said Canel. She and Karen giggled while I shook my head.

The main hall had been transformed. Coloured lights dangled from the ceiling, and balloons were placed liberally around the floor and tied to the doors. Glittery red and green cloths decorated the tables and chairs, and fake flowers were placed on the centre of each table. There was a long table away from all the chairs heaping with plates of food covered in foil and cups and bottles of juice and fizzy drinks beside it. The stage also sparkled with glitter around it and musical equipment set up for the bands to play. Simone had said the bands would play while we sat and ate, then the tables would be cleared while the DJ came to set up.

Other people in the upper third and fourth forms poured in. Canel waved at Steve, Roger, and Melvin, who were at the other end of the hall. Roger was as well-dressed as usual — his hair perfectly gelled, his glasses polished, his white shirt tucked in to his sleek black trousers. Steve was surprisingly tidy. His hair was washed and un-greasy, and he wore a long-sleeved navy shirt and skinny jeans. Melvin wore in a purple shirt with a black jacket and blue flared trousers with swirly patterns. Canel and Melvin both hugged each other, then there were hugs all round.

"You look nice, Anne," Melvin said to me, which made me stare at the ground. "Erm, th-thanks," I said, wishing I wasn't so awkward. Karen put her arm around me and kissed my cheek, staining it with her lip-gloss.

"Can't wait to see Simone play," said Roger, clasping his hands together. I couldn't help smiling at him.

As everyone else entered, we got some food, and sat at various tables. I observed the hall, but there was no sign of Olivia, so I guessed she wasn't breaking her expulsion. Her friends were seated far from where my friends and I were. Mr.

Mittles, Ms. Handells, and some other teachers started talking about how well we had done this term and congratulating the new students for settling in. The musical acts started.

Simone's band was third. They came onto the stage — drummer, bass player, lead guitarist, and Simone centre stage, facing away from the audience. The drummer tapped his sticks four times, Simone jumped around, walked up to the microphone, and yelled, "You guys ready!" We all applauded and cheered. The bass player hammered out a riff while the guitarist played some accompanying chords. Simone clapped her hands, announcing "We are Radio Silence, and we're anything *but* silent!" She flicked her hair out of her face, played something on her guitar and launched into a strong punk-flavoured vocal number.

It was great. We all waved our arms and chorused along. "She's got so much confidence!" said Karen. "I wish I could be like that."

Roger was watching Simone the way I had watched Karen when she acted out her monologue to me. I wondered if there was some way I could get Simone to see him.

As the band's third and final song came into play, Olivia's friends got up, saying things to one another. Kim, Tasha, and Emma stood up one by one and walked past the stage. My eyes followed them. They put their hands in their bags. Two boys from their table also followed them.

I stood up, hurrying to alert a teacher, but it was too late. The girls threw fruit and eggs at the stage, while the boys squirted water guns at them. Simone gasped, screaming as fruit hit her guitar. The bass player and guitarist stopped, horrified. The drummer angrily stood up and came to the front of the stage, but then ducked his head as he got sprayed by a water gun.

Several of the other students laughed. Karen and Canel had their hands clasped over their mouths while the boys held their hands to shaking heads. Some people sniggered, while others watched in horror and humiliation.

Mr. Mittles, Ms. Handells, and Mr Stanford clamped their hands on the shoulders of the populars and escorted them out of the hall. But it didn't matter. The girls high-fived one another while the boys made stupid faces and hand gestures as they walked past. The term was over. Half of Key Stage 3 was laughing while Simone and her band-mates still stood on stage, frozen and soaked in water and wet food.

Chapter Twenty-Six: Dance with Me

"You guys killed it, honestly," Canel kept insisting to Simone. We were in the girls' toilets, Karen, Simone, Canel, and I. Simone had managed to stop crying, but she didn't want to go outside. I was sitting next to her on the floor with my arm over her, while Canel and Karen crouched by us.

"Those fuckers," said Karen. "Liv must have put them up to it. I can't believe they did that. They've done some shit, but that's a real low."

"And they knew they could cos it's end of term innit," said Canel. "I mean, they'll be in trouble, but what can the teachers do? They're gonna go back home anyway."

Simone shook her head, rubbing her red eyes. "I dunno. Maybe my music's just shit."

"No!" the three of us gasped. "You were brilliant," I said. "Th-they were probably just jealous because they wouldn't be brave enough to go up on stage like that."

"I wish I had that much confidence," said Karen. "And your energy, oh my God."

"Yeah, it's brave of anyone to go up on stage and perform," said Canel.

Simone shook her head. "I'm never performing again. Only place I should sing is in my bedroom."

"You can't let those bitches ruin it for you," said Canel. "You were amazing. I was all there like, 'Go, Simone! That's my girl!' Watch, when you're famous, you'll be able to laugh at those idiots who'll probably be stuck working at McDonald's."

Simone sniffed and managed a weak smile. I put my head on her shoulder.

"I think I'm just going to go back to our room and finish packing. I can't face people," said Simone. Canel, Karen, and I threw glances at one another. "Shall I c-come with you?" I offered. Simone shook her head. "I think I need to be alone." She stood up and looked at herself in the mirror. We'd managed to help her get most of the fruit off her clothes and out of her hair.

We walked out of the girls' toilets in the downstairs main building. Roger, Melvin, and Steve were waiting for us by the back entrance to the hall. Roger threw his arms around Simone when he saw her. We all stepped back.

"You were amazing, fuck what those guys did," said Roger. Simone nodded, staring at the floor. "Come on, let's get something to eat."

"I think I need to be alone. I was gonna head up to my room," she said. "Shall I walk you up there?" asked Roger. She shrugged and mumbled that she didn't mind. Roger considered the rest of us, then began to walk Simone to the girls' dormitories.

"I can't fucking believe that," said Melvin, shaking his head. "I know," said Canel. "Did you see any of the others who were playing with her?"

"I think they all left," said Steve. He was biting the skin of his thumb.

"It was cos of the food fight," said Melvin. "They were getting back at us for that."

"Getting back at her, you mean," said Karen. She sighed. "What the hell are we gonna do next term?"

"At least they've all been sent home," I said. "Sh-Should we go out and still try to have a good time? It is the Christmas Party, after all."

They all ogled me. It wasn't like me to sound so optimistic. But Melvin nodded. "Anne's right. We can still try to have fun."

We went back out to the hall. Most people had moved on already. They were dancing and chatting and enjoying the atmosphere. Such is the way when things don't personally affect you. Some girl with brightly dyed red hair came running up to me.

"Anne, right? You're Simone's roommate?" The girl wore a black sleeveless dress and heels too high for her. Her eyes were ringed heavily with black eyeliner.

I nodded at her. "I'm Cerys. I'm in Simone's music class. I played drums with her band for a bit around the start of term. Is she okay? I wanted to speak to her, but I can't see her anywhere."

"Sh-She's gone back to her room," I said.

Cerys ran a hand through her hair. "I don't blame her. That was the most awful thing I've seen. Someone filmed it and put it on Facebook. I don't know why they would do something like that."

"Yeah…well, the world's a c-crazy place," I said, shrugging.

"People can just be dickheads, man. But, seriously, I felt so bad for them. I wanted to run and give Tasha and the lot of them a massive slap. I hate the way they think they can just do what they want." She smiled. "I loved you for standing up to them that day back in the canteen. Thought that was proper brave."

"Thanks. Though, d-didn't seem to do much good."

"Trust me, that whole group needs to be taken down a peg. I hope next term someone messes shit up for them."

"Mmm." I felt worn out, as if I'd just spent ages searching in the shops for something only to find it was all sold out. I wanted my mum, and I felt worried I might have a panic attack. I looked behind me, wondering if there was anywhere I could sit down.

"Hey." Karen came to me, her touch familiar and kind. "Are you okay?"

"No," I said. "I think I n-need a drink."

"Come, let's get some." We moved past the people dancing in their groups and went to the drink table. Karen poured out some coke for herself and apple juice for me.

"Why do people have to be so horrible?" I asked, half to myself. "W-Why do people have to hurt those deemed more vulnerable or less able to defend themselves? Why can't people j-just be kind? Is it really so hard?"

"The world is full of awful people," said Karen. "But then, there's good in it as well."

"I just don't…cruelty for cruelty's sake. Why do people *do* that? Just be mean to people for the s-sake of it? They get some stupid kick out of it?"

"It makes no sense. But we're not all like that." Karen bent her head close to mine. I faced the floor. She stroked my chin with her hand.

"Someone might say s-something stupid," I said.

She shrugged. "Let them. I don't care what people think. Just look at me." She peered into my eyes, then bent her head forward and kissed me. I forgot the world and felt nothing but her lips pressed against mine and her arms around me. I put my arms around her, the two of us embracing. A song I hadn't heard in a while came on. It was "Ain't Nobody" by Chaka Khan.

"Wow, my parents used to play this song when I w-was younger," I said, blinking as memories flooded my subconscious.

Karen took my hand. "Come on, we're dancing." She led me away from the drinks, then took my hands into hers as the vocalist began to sing. She smiled at me, and I smiled back, giggling. "See, music — that's a nice thing about the world."

"I guess." I began to sing along, taking in Karen and how wonderful it was being there with her. "I know most of the words," I said. She smiled, not taking her eyes off me. I suddenly felt exposed, excited and scared all at once. She was gazing at me in that way again, like I was all she wanted to see. I stared back at her, unable to bring my eyes away. I stroked her fingers in mine as we moved to the music, the two of us gazing at one another. I ached for her to kiss me again.

"I love you, Karen," I said, my diction clear.

She smiled. "I love you too."

I reached up and kissed her on the cheek. Never had a person seemed so wonderful to me. When I look back on my life, that moment is one of the most beautiful and most sad. It's those kinds of moments that never last.

Chapter Twenty-Seven: Revelations

It was a relief to see Aunt Colette and Zoe waving at Simone and I as we stood outside the Lakeland gates. Simone was wearing dark glasses even though it was cloudy. Both of us had a suitcase and bag, and Simone had her guitar slung over her back. Patrice was staying at his girlfriend's house for a few days before coming back to my aunt's.

Zoe gave me and Simone massive hugs when she saw us. I had told her about the incident at the Christmas Party and mentioned it was best not to bring it up. Simone had barely spoken a word. People had begun to leave the day after the party, and she had muttered quick goodbyes to our friends who were going back home.

Karen was going to Wales for Christmas with her parents to stay with her mum's sister and their two dogs. *"Aunt Lisa gets really lonely around Christmas, so we always go there."*

We'd promised to WhatsApp video-chat one another as much as possible. Already, the feeling of her being away from me left something hollow. Zoe babbled on: "School has been *crazy* stressful lately what with choosing our GCSE Options. Oh, last week at Jessica's party I kissed this *really* cute boy during 'Spin the Bottle', but he hasn't responded to my Facebook messages." She groaned. "I'm worried he likes this other girl."

Simone stared out the window, occasionally glancing at her phone. I sat on the other side, making a few comments as Zoe chattered. I peered at Simone, wondering if I should say something to her. Aunt Colette broke that for me.

"So, Simone, Anne told me you play guitar in a band? That's really impressive!"

It was the wrong thing to say. I expected Simone to just murmur or clam up, but she turned her face to the front and smiled. "Yeah, we're called Radio Silence."

"That's a really cool name! What style of music?"

"Indie-punk, bit of alt-rock in there. Really loud, upbeat stuff." She chuckled, but I couldn't tell if it was genuine. "I dunno if you'd like it."

"I like most styles of music as long as it has a good rhythm," said my aunt. "Have you played live yet?"

My phone buzzed. Zoe had texted me saying *Should I get her to stop?* I regarded her and shrugged. Simone took off her dark glasses. Her eyes were pale underneath, but she didn't seem upset.

"Yes, we played at the Key Stage 3 Christmas Party, and hopefully we'll play some more next term."

"And do you write your own songs?"

"Oh, Mum, what's with all the questions?" asked Zoe.

Aunt Colette laughed. "I'm just intrigued and trying to get to know the friend of my niece, especially as she's staying with us! But of course, Simone, if this is a bit much, you don't have to answer."

"It's fine," said Simone, flashing a tired smile. "Yeah, I write my own stuff. We've written some stuff together as a band — mainly me and the bass player."

"That sounds wonderful," said Aunt Colette. I was worried she might continue, but she switched on the radio and began humming to the music. Zoe turned and gave me a look of knowing relief.

I hadn't been back to my aunt's house since the half-term week, which had been two months ago. I hoped the change of scenery would be nice for Simone. Agatha came to help us with our bags. Simone leaned her hand against the shiny brown bannister and marvelled in wonder. Her eyes followed the swirling staircase, the Salvador Dali paintings, and the creamy white sofa and glossy magazines stacked neatly in a pile on the floor next to the new zebra-striped rugs. She walked into the living room, stroked her hands over the cushions, and smiled at the fifty-inch television.

"You have a lovely house," she said politely to my aunt. I was a little surprised by her reaction. She came from a wealthy background too. I had seen pictures of her home, and it was just as lavish. But then, I suppose whenever you enter an unfamiliar environment, everything can become fascinating.

She admired the paintings, saying the one with the clocks by Dali was her favourite. "My mum has some Picassos. I don't like his as much. Think it's a bit weird."

My aunt chuckled. The two continued to explore the downstairs area whilst Zoe and I went upstairs. I went into my room where Agatha had taken up my suitcase, and Zoe flounced herself onto my bed while I began to unpack.

"She seems okay," Zoe said, tapping her fingers on my fresh sheets. "Maybe she's feeling better."

"I hope she is." I took out my clothes and folded them away. "I thought it might be nice ha-having her around for a few days."

"So, how have things been with Karen?" she asked eagerly. I smiled. "It's all wonderful." I was set to tell her all about it, but my aunt knocked on my door.

"Hey, girls, I hope I'm not interrupting," she said. Zoe sat up.

"Nah, Anne was just telling me about her girlfriend."

I shuffled my gaze to the floor. Aunt Colette beamed. "That sounds lovely! But, Zoe, I need to speak to Anne on her own for a few minutes if that's all right with you. Maybe go see if Simone needs a hand unpacking."

Zoe bounced up and out of my room, closing the door behind her. Something ominous alerted me, and I felt my throat go dry. My aunt came and sat down on my bed.

"I think you should maybe sit too," she said gently.

I smoothed my skirt and sat beside her. "I-Is it about my dad?"

"I know we haven't spoken much about him," she said, stroking her braid. "As I told you, he sends money every month to help with you, and he's also helped us out with Zoe and the boys over the years. I don't suppose he's tried to get into contact with you?"

"I d-deleted and blocked his number. He tried a f-few times ages ago, but I don't think he has since. I don't have a F-Facebook account, so he can't try to talk to me on that."

She nodded. "I don't know exactly what went on between him and your mum. I completely understand if you don't want to talk about it, but I do know my brother. He's been through some rough patches — losing his first wife, the miscarriages—"

"There was only one miscarriage with m-my mum," I said.

She shook her head. "His first wife had a miscarriage as well. It's partly why they split up."

"Oh." I hadn't known.

"And then his work — he places so much pressure on himself and ends up taking on far more than he needs to. He's always been like that — like when we were growing up." She sighed. I felt my body stiffening.

"That doesn't excuse what he did to her. That d-doesn't excuse being a crap father." I expected her to be worried, but she just gave me a sad smile.

"Of course it doesn't. I'm just trying to contextualize it all. He is still your father."

I stood up. "Why are you defending him? You don't know what it was like growing up with a dad who didn't care, ha-having to listen to the way he treated Mum for all those years. He was a monster. No one deserves to be treated like that."

"I'm not saying—"

"I don't *care* what he has to say to me. I don't want to listen to his r-rubbish excuses. He's the one who sent me away — who told me to come live here. Moving here has been the best thing that's ever happened to me. I don't know where Mum is, I don't know if she's dead, alive, and maybe I'll never know. I can't talk to anyone, I can't contact anyone. I don't even—"

"Anne, he has prostate cancer," she said.

My arms fell to my sides. "What?"

"He was diagnosed two years ago, shortly before asking me if you could stay here. Stage three. He received treatment for it and was in partial remission, but it came back. Now it's worse."

My heart raced like a sprinting cheetah. "Two...years...pr-prostate...a-are you sure?"

"I'm not denying the way he treated your mum was disgusting. He's always been a difficult man and had a bad temper. It's partly why we don't speak much and why I've never allowed him near my children. But he's been sick for years. The drinking, the smoking, the over-working, and his depressive episodes—"

"My dad has depression?" I didn't know why I was surprised.

"He's had it for many years. We grew up poor. He had to take care of us — me and our two brothers — and our mum worked a lot for rubbish pay. All he wanted was to give you and Martinique what he never had. He just made a horrible mess of it in the process."

"So, where's Mum?" My voice shook. "Do you know what happened to her? Do you know what he did?"

She sighed again. "She's been in Charing Cross Hospital for the past year and a half in an intensive care unit."

My body sank into the bed. "Sh — She's alive?"

"On the night your parents went out, your father was driving drunk and crashed his car. Your mother was already hurt from…" She swallowed. "He had already beaten her badly, and the accident didn't help. She was severely injured, and she wasn't wearing a seat-belt."

Oh, God — so he hadn't killed her or attacked her…they'd been in a car accident. Had he bought a new car? I hadn't even noticed. It was the night of the Olympic Games. London was heaving. People would have been all over the place.

"W-When did he realise he had cancer?" I asked. "Was it before or after what happened to Mum?"

"It was around the same time. The doctors were obviously worried about you, what with him being ill and your mother's injuries. He thought it would be better for you here, being with us. We signed the documents months before you came here, listing your uncle and I as your legal guardians."

I rubbed my cheeks with my hands, trying to make sense of it all. "So, my dad knew he was sick…Mum…" I started crying. Aunt Colette leaned over and pulled me towards her massive bosom, rubbing my shoulder while I sobbed.

"I want to see her," I said. "I have to see her. Why didn't you tell me?"

"We didn't know if she was going to recover. She'd suffered severe brain damage and head trauma. She was in an ITU in West Middlesex Hospital before being transferred to Charing Cross. She's been on life support for over a year, until she started getting better around the summer."

"So, all this time…you *knew* she was alive?"

"We didn't want you to go through any more pain," she said gently. "Your father insisted it was better you didn't know until we knew for sure whether your mum was going to survive. Your uncle was furious. He said you had a right to know, but I didn't want you to suffer any more after everything. I just wanted you to have a regular childhood spending time with Zoe and not having to worry for a change." She sighed. "I kept wondering if we'd done the right thing. I know it's been so horrible for you with everything that's happened. Because her injuries were so bad, her chances of recovery were extremely low. It's only in the past few weeks she's started to become able to talk, although it's very difficult for her."

They had seen her. They had been to see her, and they hadn't told me.

"We will take you to see her soon, I promise. We just wanted to make sure she began healing a bit more."

I was shaking. *Mum is alive.* I nodded, wiping the tears from my eyes.

"Your dad also wanted to talk to you," she said. "I know he's done some unspeakably horrible things over the years — things I hope, if there's any sort of afterlife, he'll be forgiven for — but deep down, he does love you, Anne. He always has."

"I'll b-believe that w-when I see it." I sniffled. It was the same thing I'd said to Karen when she told me her friends weren't all bad.

"He started going to Alcoholics Anonymous over the summer, when your mother began to wake up. He's been sober for five months, as far as I'm aware."

"Good f-for him," I muttered. She patted me on the shoulder, then twisted her wedding ring around her finger.

"You know, before he left us, our father — your dad's dad — used to hit your dad," she said quietly. "Your dad was the eldest of the four of us. Our father beat him from a young age, from when he was about two until he was five."

"Oh."

"He's been going to psychotherapy as well while treating his cancer. I'm not trying to excuse him, Anne. But men can have a lot of pressure thrust upon them. All his life, he'd been taught to hold his feelings in, and to be emotionally repressed and 'strong.' Having to care for all of us. And for young black men, it can be especially hard. Showing vulnerability is a sign of weakness. I know he tried to seek solace within the church, but that doesn't always work." She sighed again. "And then, losing a child…he wanted to make things right with you and your mum, but he turned to drinking because he couldn't cope."

"I still hate him," I muttered.

She nodded. "I understand. But he is my brother, Anne."

"Why are you m-making excuses for him? Brother, no br-brother — all the p-pain he's c-caused me…"

"Because blood is thicker than water. You can't choose your family. When he dies, we'll be the ones sorting out his funeral arrangements and his will. I hate what he did to you and your mother, and the poor treatment he's inflicted upon other women over the years. But he's my blood. He's the father of my niece." She looked at me. "He asked me to take care of you because he knew I would take you in. We're family, Anne. Families have to stick together, even when times are hard. Blood matters."

Chapter Twenty-Eight: Papa

Aunt Colette left me her phone and said my dad had said to call any time that day. She'd already spoken to him. I could faintly hear Zoe and Simone laughing and chattering out in the corridor. Marcus would be back soon; he'd stayed over a friend's house the night before. I clutched the slim iPhone in my hand, blinking and allowing my mind to flash back to the night Mum had vanished. She and Dad had been arguing. He'd hit her. She'd cried. They'd left. He'd returned and sat, solemn and drinking. Several months later, he had wanted me gone.

I couldn't make sense of any of it. I held the phone away from me like it was a snake about to spit venom in my eye. Sighing heavily, I tapped the number my aunt had given me and put the phone to my ear.

He picked up on the third ring. His voice sounded gruff, but it wasn't slurred.

"Hello?"

"It's me, Dad. Anne." Clear diction. No stuttering.

"Anne." He sounded relieved, but also forlorn and grave. "How are you?"

It had been so long since I'd heard that voice, I wasn't sure what to say. How could I condense everything into a few words?

"I'm fine. Everything's fine."

"That's good." He coughed, and I wondered if he was still smoking those fat cigars. "So, everything has been good with your aunt and uncle? She told me you're at boarding school now."

"Mmm." I began to tap my knee with my fingers.

"It's all going good? I bet your grades are wonderful. You've always been such an intelligent girl."

"Mmm, yeah. Dad, what do you want?"

"Sorry?"

"Aunt Colette told me about Mum. Why did you want to talk to me?"

"I can't explain everything right now. But your aunt told you I'm unwell?"

"Prostate cancer," I mumbled.

"I thought it would be easier if you were away. Things have been difficult for me." He coughed again. "I know I haven't been the best father, and I'm sorry. But you're my daughter and you have to know I care about you. All I ever wanted was for you to have the chances I never had."

I blinked. "Okay."

He chuckled nervously. "I know things haven't been exactly perfect—"

"I don't want to hear it, Dad," I said. "I'm sorry you have cancer, but I don't know what you expect me to say to you."

"Anne, please listen—"

"No, *you* listen." I clenched my fists. "You're a p-pathetic alcoholic liar and if I ever have children, I hope they don't turn out like you. You failed as a husband, and you've failed as a father. I hope your precious business doesn't fail — it's the only thing you have left." Ending the call, I put the phone down on the bed, then picked up a pillow and screamed into it.

There was a knock at my door. I looked up. Simone peeked her head around.

"Is everything all right?"

I shook my head. She came in and sat down next to me. "I just thought I'd check on you. Your aunt said she was talking to you about something…to do with your dad?"

"I just got off the phone to him." I hugged the pillow to my chest and stared at the carpeted floor. "I haven't spoken to him in almost two years, s-since he dropped me off here."

Simone nodded.

"He has prostate cancer."

"Fuck," she responded.

"Yeah, it's shit, but there's a part of me that d-doesn't care." I turned to her. "Does that make me a bad person? My dad ha-has a terminal illness and I basically told him to get lost. What kind of person talks to their own dad like that?"

"You're not a bad person," she said, stroking my shoulder. "You're one of the best people I know. You're kind, intelligent, loyal, and really fucking brave. The shit you've been through…someone else would crawl in a hole in the ground. I'm pretty sure I'd have killed myself by now." She laughed. I smiled, although my stomach twisted at her choice of words.

"And you were angry. We all say crazy shit we don't mean when we're angry. Everything we feel gets distorted and builds up and comes out all messed up. On the one hand, you hate him because of everything he's put you through and did to your mum. But you still love him because he's your dad. That's the thing with people we love — they can rip us apart, but we still end up forgiving them. Because they're the ones who care for us the most, deep down."

"I don't know what to do." I pictured my mum, lying in the hospital, comatose, on a life support machine. I tried to visualize her face and her battered body, broken beyond repair. "My mum's been in hospital for the past couple years.

She and my dad were in an accident. He crashed the car while drunk-driving."

"Oh, shit. I'm so sorry, Anne. Why didn't anyone tell you?"

"They thought it would be too much. My aunt said she wanted me to have a chance at a 'normal childhood.' I guess after growing up seeing ev-everything my dad did to Mum, th-the pain he inflicted…" I closed my eyes and put my head in my hands. "It's all just one big *fucking* mess. I'm fourteen years old. W-Why do I feel like the world's crashing down on me? It's not fair."

"Life's a bitch, then you die," she said darkly. "Makes me wonder what the point is."

"Maybe the point is to make things as less sh-shit as you can." I sighed. "There's good stuff as well."

"Is there?" I glanced at her. Her eyes glazed into a faraway void. I suddenly felt afraid. "Of course there is. Despite everything, things get better. You can't have bad without good."

"But is it worth it?" She faced me. "All this pain? I mean, look at us — we're so young, yet we're having to deal with so much crap. And people see people like you and me and think we're oh-so-privileged because our families have money and we're smart and live in the fucking UK where there's free healthcare. My parents don't give a shit about me."

"Karen's parents are great," I said, thinking back to her telling me about her dad. "Her dad talks to her loads and c-cares for her and supports her acting. That's how a dad *should* be. And she doesn't come from a rich background."

"But she has a family who gives a shit," said Simone. "I could bet you anything she wouldn't trade them for some big house in Kensington or Richmond."

"But I d-do have family who cares. If my dad hadn't sent me away, I wouldn't have come here, and I wouldn't have g-gone to Lakeland and met Karen, or you. So, everything has good and bad sides."

"But at what cost?"

But…but…but…

"Simone, why are you talking like this? You're here, aren't you? With me?"

"Mmm, yeah. Sorry." She smiled, but there was no light behind it. "I've just been a bit down about this guy, Toby. The one in the upper fifth. I mean, he said he'd come watch us play at the Christmas Party — but…probably better he didn't after what happened!" She giggled, putting her hand to her mouth, though her eyes filled with tears. I put my head on her shoulder and my arms around her.

"Jesus," she said, wiping her eyes. "Why are guys so confusing? I was complaining about the whole thing to Zoe."

"She's nice, isn't she?"

"Oh, God, she's lovely. So fucking happy and cheerful. God, I wish I was like that."

"You can be," I said.

She shook her head. "Nah, not really. But oh well." She shrugged and swung her legs, as if she no longer cared what happened to her.

Chapter Twenty-Nine: Hard Choices

We had a great next few days. Simone, Zoe, and I went up to London and had a day out at Winter Wonderland, ice-skating and riding on the carousel and checking out the Christmas market. Zoe bought a fluffy toy penguin and some pretty silver earrings. Simone got a cute little ornament of an electric guitar. I got a purple candle and some hand cream and perfumed oil for Karen.

The two of us had video-chatted, and she'd shown me some pictures of where she was in Ireland. It looked nice, but my mind was so occupied with my dad and mum and Simone, I'd barely been able to concentrate. A fear had begun to dawn on me about what might happen after Christmas. Would I be able to still see her? Or would I be too concerned with what was going on with my family? I loved her, but already, thoughts of her had begun to slip from my grasp.

I didn't know if Simone was still secretly drinking or not. She seemed fine with my family — cracking jokes with my uncle, bantering with Marcus and Patrice, and getting on great with Zoe. She ended up staying right up until December 23rd, clearly reluctant to leave. My aunt dropped her off at the train station.

Meanwhile, being back in Copperwood meant I could see Luke again. He was jovial and in good spirits and had been thrilled to hear about my relationship with Karen. I didn't mention the doubts I was having about being with her. We strolled down the park, the pair of us shivering in the December winds. Luke said school had gotten a bit better now that he had a solid group of friends to hang out with. "Yeah, they're nice," he said. "Sometimes I talk to your cousin as well."

"Zoe told me." She'd revised her definition of Luke being "weird." I stuffed my gloved hands in my pockets. "I much p-prefer it at Lakeland."

"You seem happier there. It's always good to find somewhere you feel comfortable."

"I spoke to my dad recently."

"Oh yeah?" He peered at me, brushing his tawny blond hair out of his face. "How was that? It's been a while, hasn't it?"

"Almost two years." Flashback to December 2013 — the last Christmas I had spent with my father. I told Luke what I had told Simone, and he hugged me tight. We stopped walking and sat on a bench, observing the twisted branches of the naked trees. I kicked my legs in their grey woolly tights out in front of me.

"I s-said some harsh things to him. Things I maybe shouldn't have…" My shoulders sagged. It was all so exhausting.

"Anne, if you don't feel comfortable about getting in touch with him, then you don't have to."

"But he *is* my dad. And I don't know how l-long he has left."

"Are you his only child?" he asked me.

I nodded. "As far as I'm aware."

"Maybe he left you a bunch of money in his will? And his business to inherit? I mean, what's gonna happen to it when he's…well, gone?" He shuffled and shook his shoulders.

"I don't want his business. I don't want anything to do with him. But…" I didn't want him to die. Heavens, I didn't want anybody to die. I wanted him to love me and care for me like a real dad. I wanted him to take an interest in me and be patient and caring, like Mr. Oseni.

"He might not die," said Luke. "Loads of people survive cancer."

"But he's had it before. And it was stage three. I think it's stage four this time. It's worse."

I had researched online to see if drinking too much alcohol could cause prostate cancer. I knew it messed up your liver. I didn't find anything on that, but it did say men of African or Caribbean descent in their fifties had a higher risk of getting prostate cancer. My dad was in his late forties.

Still, there was nothing I could really do. I decided to wait until my head was clearer. Maybe once the school year was over.

Christmas and Zoe's fourteenth birthday came and went, followed by the New Year, and we entered 2015. There was to be another UK General Election in May — there had been talk in the news about some far-right party called UKIP, and how there would be several parties competing for the majority. There was also talk about Britain leaving the European Union.

"David Cameron says that if the Conservatives win in May, he'll vote for us to leave the EU," said my uncle as we sat in front of the TV one evening. Zoe blew a raspberry. "David Cameron is boring. I hope we get a new Prime Minister."

"Well, let's hope Labour win," said my aunt. Unlike my dad, she and my uncle didn't vote for the Conservative Party.

Shortly before I returned to Lakeland, something horrible happened in Paris. Islamic terrorists slaughtered a bunch of French cartoonists.

"Everywhere on Twitter and Instagram #jesuischarlie is trending!" cried Zoe, showing me on her phone. I did see. It was everywhere; online and on the streets. When I returned to Lakeland, it was one of the first things Simone said to me:

"Did you hear about the Charlie Hebdo thing?" asked Simone as I unpacked my suitcase.

"It was three days ago. I'd have to have been l-living under a rock not to have heard about it."

She shook her head. "These fucking terrorist attacks are scary. What if someone bombed our school?"

I laughed. "It's in the middle of nowhere. I doubt that would happen."

"Still, my older cousin said we all need to be really careful," she said. "It's getting crazier now with all these terror attacks."

My life is a terror attack, I wanted to say. Instead, I nodded and put away my things.

It was nice to see our mates again. Canel and Melvin were now dating, which wasn't a massive surprise. They'd cosied up together at the Christmas Party. And Karen was super happy to see me again. We met up outside the library, and she kissed me deeply.

"I've missed you so much," she said, running her fingers over my cheek. "Did you have a good Christmas?"

"Y-Yeah, it was nice." I took a deep breath. "Is it okay if we m-maybe go to my room, or yours, just to talk for a bit?"

She nodded, her face flushing with excitement. "That would be great. I've missed talking face-to-face."

I felt awful as we walked to my room. Simone was hanging with her musical friends, showing off the new guitar she'd gotten as a Christmas present. I was glad she had something to make her happy.

I sat next to Karen on my bed. She leaned in to kiss me, but I gently pushed her back. "Listen, this has b-been amazing, and you're a lovely person, but I don't think I can be in a relationship right now."

She blinked at me, and her hands recoiled. I swallowed. "Well…that was unexpected," she said, her voice shaking. "You're…breaking up with me?"

"It's nothing personal," I urged. "You're a g-great girl. It's just that stuff has come up with my f-family and I don't think I'm in the right frame of mind—"

She burst into tears. I leaned over and put my arms around her, trying not to weep myself. "I'm so sorry, Karen. The last thing I w-wanted to do was hurt you."

"But — I'm here! I don't mind — if you need — I support you — I can be here for you! I won't get in the way."

"I know you won't. But this isn't about you. My d-dad is sick, and I've found out…things are complicated. I c-can't take on too much now."

"But I wanted you to meet my parents," she said, wiping her eyes and sniffing. She resumed crying loudly, then tears began to spill down my face. "Don't you…don't you feel that way about me anymore?" she asked, pulling back and gazing pleadingly at me. I ran my fingers through her beautiful red hair.

"Of course I do. It's not like it vanishes overnight. But I c-can't have a girlfriend right now. I'm not in a good position emotionally."

She gulped. "You sound like you're twenty-five, not fourteen," she said. I smiled. Then she started sobbing again. "Oh, God, am I too immature for you?"

"Don't be ridiculous. You're a lovely girl, and you've made me so happy." I leaned forward to hug her again, but she stood up. "Karen, p-please don't go. We can still be friends—"

"I need to be alone right now," she said, going to the door. She sniffed. "I thought we'd be together for ages."

"Well, I mean, you can't really p-plan these things."

She shook her head at me and flung the door open, slamming it behind her. I put my head in my hands and wept. Part of me wanted to run after her and tell her I'd made a terrible mistake, that I loved her, that I was just being scared. But most of me knew I'd done the right thing.

Chapter Thirty: Puppy Love

The following day, I sat with my friends in the canteen at lunch, hoping to see Karen. I wasn't sure if she'd want to sit with us or not, but I wanted her to know nothing had changed.

Melvin had his arm around Canel and was feeding her chips from his fork while giggling. Steve made vomit noises. "Get a room, you two," he said. "You're worse than Karen and Anne."

"Where is Karen?" Roger asked me. Simone shook her head at him.

"Oh, shit, did you guys break up?" asked Steve.

"Steven!" said Melvin, shaking his head while Canel nuzzled against his shoulder. "Can't you take the hint?"

"She's over there," said Roger, nodding straight ahead. Everyone's head turned except Melvin's. "Guys, don't all stare at once. You'll make it more awkward than it needs to be."

Unfortunately, she spied us. Her hair was pulled back and she wore a woollen grey jumper and jeans. Her eyes were red and her face was sunken like she hadn't slept. She was carrying her tray. She glanced over, then walked away. I hoped she wasn't going to sit with Olivia and her crew, but she went to sit with a couple other girls I didn't recognise.

The populars noticed, of course. They peered over at our table, then at Karen, putting two-and-two together. Simone gulped.

"My God, c-can't we catch a break?" I groaned as Tasha, Kim, and Olivia walked over to us. They paused, seeing Mr. Mittles and another teacher on the other side of the room watching them. Olivia smiled at me. I glared back.

"I just wanted to clear things up about last term," she called, standing several paces away. "I don't want any trouble."

"Just l-leave us alone," I said, shaking my head. "Last thing we need is your bullshit."

"Karen isn't sitting with you," said Tasha, flicking her curly hair. "Did you two break up or something?"

I stood up. "You can't come over here and antagonize us, especially after what you did to Simone at the Christmas Party. That was a v-v-vile thing to do."

Kim smirked and Tasha giggled while Olivia blinked innocently. "I dunno what you're talking about. I had nothing to do with that. I wasn't there, remember?"

"Just g-go *away,* Olivia," I snapped. She glared at me, but the teachers were watching, so they made a move. I sat back down.

"I need to get going as well," said Simone, getting up. "I'm meeting Toby."

"Who's Toby?" asked Roger. Melvin and I glanced at one another.

"He's her new boyfriend," said Steve in a silly voice. Roger studied the table, then faced up again. "Didn't know you had a new boyfriend," he said.

"He's that guy she's been texting in the upper fifth," said Canel. "He looks like a wanker, to be honest. I always see him outside smoking and drinking beer."

"He's really nice. He's funny," said Simone. There was a strange glow in her face. "Anyway, I'll see you guys later."

She stood up to walk away. Melvin patted Roger on the arm. "I bet he's full of shit," he said.

"She seems proper into him, though," said Steve. Canel shook her head at him.

"Steven, why are you so fucking oblivious?" said Melvin. Steve blinked at us quizzically, shuffling a hand through his greasy hair. "What are you guys on about?"

"Come on, have you not noticed?" said Canel. "Everyone else has clocked."

"Clocked *what?* I'm so confused."

"Mate, have you not seen how I am around her?" said Roger. "I've liked her for months."

"Simone? You like *Simone?*"

"Shhh!" I said. "We don't want the w-whole of Key Stage 3 to hear."

"Oh, really? Because I was just taking the piss all those times, but I didn't — oh, so you actually like her?" asked Steve. Roger took off his glasses and began wiping them on his shirt. Steve smiled, then appeared sad. "Aw, man, I'm sorry. Being friend-zoned sucks."

"He's not in the friend-zone," said Canel. "Simone just ain't noticed yet."

"M-Maybe you should just tell her?" I said.

Roger shook his head. "No way. She likes that other guy. He's older and all that. She won't go for me."

"But you guys are friends," said Melvin. "She's known you way longer."

While they were talking, I noticed Karen walking past with the two other girls. I stood up, hanging back as they left the canteen, then ran up to her.

"Karen?"

She turned around, flinching. "Hey," she said, as if I was some random person she barely spoke to.

"How are you?"

"Look, Anne, no offence, but I can't really talk to you right now," she said.

My heart sank. "B-B-But—"

"I can't be 'just friends' with someone I still have loads of feelings for. I'm not trying to sound like a bitch, but I need distance from you right now. Is that all right?"

"Oh, of c-course." I wanted to thrust my arms around her and hold her tight. "If you ever n-need to talk or anything, please know I'm here for you. I d-do care about you. You must know that. Ending things w-wasn't easy."

She nodded. "I get it. But let's just have some space for now so I can move on. I probably won't be hanging out with you guys for a while."

"I understand." I watched her walk away. What's that old saying? If you love someone — even if it's teenage puppy love — you have to let them go.

Over the next week, I tried to get on with things. Mr. Oseni assigned me a new book to read, *Half of a Yellow Sun*.

"Chimamanda Ngozi Adichie is one of my favourite writers," he said. "This one won the Orange Prize for Fiction in 2007, among a few others. *Purple Hibiscus* was her first one. It was brilliant."

"What's this one about?" I picked it up and examined it.

"In short, it's about the fight for Nigerian independence. It's set around the sixties when colonialism in Africa was ending. I related to it a lot, especially because my family are Nigerian and both my parents grew up around that time. The characters are great and it's beautifully written." He considered me. "How have you been?"

I shrugged. "U-Up and down I guess."

"You know I'm here if you ever need to talk about anything."

I sighed. "It's just…during the holidays, I s-spoke to my dad, and he's very sick. He has c-cancer."

"I'm so sorry to hear that."

"But part of me feels nothing. And my mum…" I shook my head. "Sorry, sir, it's just a bit t-tough talking about it."

"I understand. How is Simone?"

Simone was barely around. She seemed to be spending all her time with Toby. I saw them together out in the gardens, smoking and giggling. I was reading my new book and heard laughter somewhere, and curiously got up to investigate. Maybe part of me knew it would be Simone. She hadn't been around at lunch and said she'd be hanging out with him after lessons.

The smell was strong. It wasn't just cigarettes they were smoking.

Cerys had also come up to me and said Simone wasn't turning up to her music lessons and her bandmates were worried about her. "I think that whole incident really messed them all up, but they wanted to keep playing together," she said. "Especially since she got that cool new guitar. We thought maybe after Christmas she'd want to get back into it."

I didn't like the look of Toby, with his ragged grey and black clothes, spiky gelled hair, and a tattoo on his upper bicep saying "ACAB." I wondered if that was a band.

She wouldn't introduce him to us either. She claimed he was "shy" and "insecure." As I peered at them in the gardens, a cat moved past me. I could have sworn it had glowing green eyes, but I wasn't sure. I got momentarily distracted, wanting to follow the cat. It sensed me, then directly inspected me, as if it knew me. Then it disappeared and ran up a tree.

Simone had also noticed the cat, because I heard her call out to me. "Anne!" She giggled. Her voice was wobbly and mushy. "Did you see that cat? I swear it had glowing green eyes."

"I think you're a bit stoned and seeing things," said Toby, kissing Simone on her forehead. His arm curled around her thin shoulders like a boa constrictor. He looked me up and down.

"What you doing out here anyway?" she asked me.

I blinked a few times. "I-I was j-just reading this new b-book Mr. Oseni a-assigned me." I scrutinized Toby. Something about his expression scared me. It reminded me of the way my dad used to watch my mum — hard and empty, like if you cracked him open, you'd find nothing inside.

"Anne's really smart. She loves to read," she said, giggling.

I observed the two of them. "Have you had band practice recently? Cerys was asking about you."

"Cerys! Cerys doesn't play with us anymore. She *abandoned* us."

Toby's hand slid down behind her, and she squealed, then burst out laughing. I felt sick.

"Don't pinch my bum in front of Anne! Behave yourself." Her whole body was shaking with hysteric laughter. Toby smiled, but his eyes remained a dark void.

"W-Why don't you come ha-hang out with m-me and th-the others?" I stammered. "Canel said we should all st-start watching this show called *Jane the Virgin*. It's m-meant to be really funny. We've m-missed the first few episodes, b-but she's going to st-stream it online."

Simone was barely listening. I watched her and Toby together, and realised my best friend was being pulled away from me into a crevice.

Chapter Thirty-One: To Sex or Not to Sex

"You know…you and Karen, did you ever, like, do stuff?" Simone asked me. It was coming to the end of January. I was lying on my bed in my nightgown, a few chapters in to *Half of the Yellow Sun.*

"What do you mean?" Our light was off, but both of our lamps were on.

"You *know.* Sexual stuff."

I snapped my book shut. "That's kind of a p-personal question."

"Aw, you can tell me." She walked over and flopped onto my bed. "Plus, I've always been curious. I've kissed girls, but I've never done sexual stuff with them."

"What about with guys?"

She giggled. "You flipped the question!"

"Yeah, Karen and I…" My skin grew hot. "F-Felt each other up, t-touched each other…erm, *downstairs.*"

"Fingered each other?"

I picked up my pillow and smacked it over her head. She moved out the way, squealing. "Come on, don't be embarrassed!"

"I haven't discussed this with anyone, not even Zoe."

"It's cool, I won't judge. It's your business."

"W-Why are you asking anyway?"

"Toby wants to have sex with me." She said it so casually, she may as well have said, *he wants to go to the cinema with me.*

"I've sent him, like, pictures of myself," she said. "Over the holidays. He asked me to."

"P-Pictures?"

"Yeah, just in my bra and knickers." She rubbed her lips together.

I regarded her. "Okay."

"I mean, loads of girls do it."

"Yeah," I said. "As l-long as you're comfortable with it."

"Well, I didn't want him to get annoyed. Other girls he's been with have, and they're a bit older than me...I didn't want him to think of me as like a little kid."

"Mmm." A gnawing feeling grew in my gut. I knew where this was going.

"We've done a few things. I know I've talked about me doing stuff with other guys, but it was all a lie. I mean, a few wanted to, but I didn't, and he's older than me, so I thought, I dunno, I should. He's the first guy I've done anything sexual with."

"B-But it's because you w-wanted to, right? He didn't p-push you into it?"

"Of course!" she said, too quickly. "He would never...I mean, he has said about wanting to do more. Because he's sixteen, and I'm not even fourteen yet."

"Isn't that..." something flashed in my mind, "the age of consent? If someone aged sixteen or over ha-has sex with someone underage..."

"I'm not a little kid — and anyway, I think it's stupid if you consent to it and the other person still gets into trouble. Thirteen, sixteen — they're just numbers."

"Mmm."

"You and Karen did stuff. And you're older than her."

"By a few months. And that was different."

"What are you getting at?" She glared at me. I pondered her, sitting up. "I'm not getting at anything. I just w-want you to be careful."

"Look, Toby said he loves me…and he's had sex before. And if I really liked him, then I'd do it too. I need to show I trust him."

"Did he put those w-words in your mouth?"

"Fuck this." She stood up and walked over to her bedside drawer, taking out a glass bottle.

I swallowed. "I don't know why you're getting annoyed at me when you're the one who b-brought this up," I said.

She unscrewed the top and took a swig, grimacing. "I just don't like the way you're being all judgemental, like you think I'm only doing it because he wants me to and I'm trying to 'prove' something, like I'm cool or whatever."

"Well, you're the one who said that, not me. You're p-projecting onto me."

"Shut up."

"What the hell!" I snapped off my light and turned over. "I'm going to sleep."

"Anne, I'm sorry." She walked over to me and tapped my bedsheets. I pulled away from her. "I'm sorry, please don't be annoyed. I'm just worried."

"Look, I can't tell you what to do. I'm n-not your mum." I suddenly, achingly, wanted my own mum. I wanted someone to come along and make everything all right, rather than me having to fix everything all the time.

"I can't ask my mum for advice on this. She wouldn't know what to say and she wouldn't care anyway. Please, Anne. I'm scared."

"Have you discussed this with him?" I rolled over, switching my light back on. "If you're so nervous, why don't you just t-tell him you're not sure?"

"Because I'm not sure if I'm not sure."

Sighing, I sat up again. "Sex is weird for girls. We're not supposed to talk about it or even really want it, and if we do, then we don't know w-what to do or what the guy's going to think of us. I guess because I'm gay it felt easier because I was w-with another girl. But I'm not going to tell you what you should or sh-shouldn't do because that's not my place. Yeah, thirteen is young to have sex, but if you really like him and feel comfortable, then do it."

"I do…I think I love him."

"But also, if he cares for you, he sh-should respect you and not make you feel like you *have* to do stuff." *Roger wouldn't make you feel like that,* I wanted to say. And it wasn't because his sex drive was lower or he was less experienced — it was because he really did respect and care for her. But I didn't say that.

"And guys…I dunno, they have p-pressure put on them from other guys to have sex with as many people as possible, even if they don't want to. It's a bit shit for both genders."

"I'm scared it will hurt," she said. I shuffled over so she could sit next to me, stretching her legs out on my duvet. "Toby said it will and he can't do anything about it. He said it hurts for all girls on their first time."

"He doesn't sound like he's t-trying to ease your worries," I said.

"He's just being honest. It's *supposed* to hurt, because they break the hymen or whatever." She started twiddling her thumbs in her lap. "I was thinking maybe I could drink beforehand so I'm less scared."

"Simone, do you really w-w-*want* to do this?" I stared hard at her. "You can tell someone. Or just tell him you're n-not ready to have sex with him. Or—"

"But I *am*. And what if he breaks up with me?"

Good riddance. "If a guy makes you feel like he's g-going to break up with you if you don't have sex with him, then he doesn't sound like a very nice guy."

"But...he has needs," she mumbled. "He turned sixteen two weeks ago."

"So what? Then he should f-find a girl his own age who's more experienced. Anyway, you said you've been...erm, 'satisfying' him in other ways?"

"I gave him head. I didn't really want to, but he asked me to. I was just using my hand before, but then he kind of pushed my head down, and I felt like I was going to throw up." My eyes widened. "But then it was fine," she added quickly. "I got really into it. It was kind of fun."

"Mmm."

"Apparently guys like virgins as well. We're...tighter or something." She giggled, but it sounded more like crying.

"That's just more r-rubbish, isn't it? He wants a virgin but also wants a girl to p-put out. If she doesn't do it, he's annoyed, but if she does, she's s-soiled." I thought of my dad and his drunken rants about sexual purity and wives "submitting" to their husbands.

"Girls basically can't win either way," she said.

"That's why we should just be gay," I joked. We both laughed.

"Or we could just kill ourselves," she said.

"That won't h-help anything."

"Why are guys so confusing?" She blew upwards on her long black hair.

"Careful. Now you sound like Zoe." Although...Zoe's innocence surpassed Simone's lack thereof. "There are g-good guys out there. And there are shit girls. There are simply good and bad people — doesn't matter if they're a guy or a girl or a jellyfish. We just have to s-s-sift the shit from the gold."

"You should be a writer. You're so good with words."

"I certainly ha-have some stories to tell," I said. She got up, going back to her own bed. One more thought occurred to me. "What's 'ACAB'?"

"Sorry?"

"On Toby's arm, I s-saw a tattoo. 'ACAB.' What does that mean?"

"Oh, that! 'All cops are bastards.' Something to do with this organisation he's part of."

"Hm." Police officers were trained to protect and care for citizens. Anyone referring to them as bastards had likely been unfairly wronged by the system or treated poorly by officers.

Unless they were a danger to the public and hated the police for supplying security. I hoped Toby was the former and not the latter.

Chapter Thirty-Two: Blood

I picked up my phone, staring at the number to call my dad. I had gotten it from Aunt Colette before she had dropped me back at Lakeland. Did I ring him or not? The thought came to mind, and then I closed my eyes and put the phone down. Instead, I reached into my drawers, taking out the pictures of my mum and me. *See you soon,* I whispered, kissing her smiling face.

I put my head in my hands and lay back on my bed for I'm not sure how long. Eventually, Simone burst into our room. She was weeping. I didn't notice until I sat up and saw her take a bottle from her bedside table.

"Simone?"

She took large gulps from the vodka while tears spilled down her face.

"W-What's the matter? Did something happen?"

"Toby," she said, sobbing. She rubbed her eyes. "We...he..."

"What ha-has he d-done to you?" I walked over to her, pulling the chair from the corner and sitting in front of her. I placed my hand on her knee. "Tell me everything."

"We tried to have sex...I mean, I told him I was ready and I wanted to, and we were kissing, then undressed and all that, and he started to put it in...he said he'd be gentle, but it *hurt,* Anne — really *hurt*. I started screaming, and he told me to be quiet and said there was nothing he could do about the pain, that it was going to hurt and I had to just deal with it. He tried again, and I was yelling so he put his hand over my mouth and tried to keep going, but then I kicked him off me—"

"I'm going to kill him." I stood up, ready to leave the room and go after him.

Simone grabbed my arm. "No, Anne, DON'T! Please, you can't tell anyone. It was all my fault—"

"Your f-fault?" My entire body was shaking. I felt like a volcano ready to explode. "How w-was this your fault?"

"I told him I was sorry, I did, I told him I was just—"

"SORRY? He made you say SORRY?!"

"*Stop shouting!*" she wailed. "Please, just sit back down. I shouldn't have said anything!"

"This guy is not right! He's completely t-taken advantage of you! We have to tell somebody — Ms. Handells, or M-Mr. Oseni—"

"I can't! I can't tell anyone. It's too embarrassing. What if no one believes me? He'll say I exaggerated or something."

"Simone, what your describing s-s-sounds l-like...I can't even say it."

"I consented," she said, wiping her face. "He didn't force me. Look, he stopped."

"Yeah, when you f-fucking kicked him off you!"

"He was just annoyed because he wanted to do it and I was being a baby...an inexperienced virgin. It was just sex, for God's sake, everyone does it and everyone's going to do it, and why do people make such a big deal about the first time anyway? Like it's some big 'special' moment that is going to magically change your life and define you? Like a guy's dick is oh-so-magical, it will transform you from some little girl into a grown woman?" Her words were slurring badly now. I felt sick to my stomach.

"You c-c-can't see him again," I said.

"I was only crying because I was in pain. It kind of hurts to sit down. I was bleeding a lot, and I got blood all over his sheets. He was really irritated and said it would be better if I left. I tried to contact him, but he hasn't gotten back to me, and I'm scared he's going to go off with some other girl."

"I think we should g-go to Matron. Good God, did he at least use a c-condom?"

"Of course, though he said it's usually better without."

I folded my arms across my chest and began to tap my feet. "This is fucked up! I — we — h-he's a bad person, Simone. I knew it w-when I saw him. Those eyes."

The eyes of a man with no soul.

"Maybe we should t-tell the police—"

"NO!" she screamed so loudly, I was sure they could hear us in the next dorms. "There's been no crime! People will just say it was my own stupid fault for being all vulnerable! I'll be humiliated! And his life will be ruined even though what happened technically *wasn't* a crime, because I *did* consent—"

"But you're underage," I said slowly. "He's sixteen. You're thirteen. It can be c-classed as statutory rape."

"Don't, Anne," she said, weeping again and reaching for the bottle of poison. "Please don't use that word."

I was eight years old again, listening to my mum weep and plead and insist I didn't call the police or tell the ambulance what had happened. Listening to her stick up for a man who used and abused her, all to protect him but also…*to protect herself?*

My dad was a respected man in the community. She was his beautiful, charming wife. If she became the poor battered woman, people would change how they saw her. She'd be thrown sad sympathetic gazes, another statistic of a woman subject to domestic abuse.

And Simone? She'd had fruit thrown at her on stage. The last thing she needed was more humiliation. More people pointing and staring and shaking their heads. Her parents, our friends…they would stop seeing her as a cool, sparky musician. She'd just be that poor, sad girl. Poor, sad Simone who was taken advantage of.

I studied her, and saw history repeat itself in the form of another person. I saw the cycles of my life, spinning around, the people replacing one another. I substituted Zoe for Simone — another upbeat, chatty chum, only she was Zoe 2.0, the "upgraded" version, more advanced and more developed with far more problems. I substituted Meg for Karen. Meg was my dream girl; Karen was that dream come to life. I switched Lucy for Luke and Zoe's friends for Simone's friends and my awful father for my English teacher, the surrogate daddy in my life.

And my mum? My mum was irreplaceable. But maybe Aunt Colette gave me what my mum couldn't, despite trying desperately. She gave me security and stability. I didn't need to watch, agonising at the phone, wondering if I needed to dial 999 and have her rushed to A&E. I could be taken care of, not the one taking care.

I knew what I had to do.

But first, I had to help my friend.

"I'm going to take you to Matron."

She shook her head. "No, Anne, I won't go. She'll want to ask why."

"She can't disclose anything you don't want her to. She's the school nurse."

"I just want to stay here." She looked at me. "I just need to be alone."

"I don't want to leave you here. You might do something s-self-destructive."

"I just want to go to sleep and forget about all of this."
She lay down on her bed. "I'll be fine. Just please, leave me be."

So, I left her be. When I think back to that moment, I always wonder if there was any way I could have done something else. If I'd have stayed with her, or told Mr. Oseni, or done something — anything. But maybe there was nothing I could have done. Simone's mind was made up. She did the thing that made the most sense to her. I guess all she wanted was a way to stop the pain.

The screams rang from the girls' boarding house all the way into the main building. Key Stage 3 was eating dinner in the canteen when a girl came bursting into the hall. A little girl with blonde pigtails. She was yelling in such hysterics, the entire school could have heard her screams.

Mr. Mittles and two dinner ladies rushed towards her. "Arya," he said. "What's happened? What's the matter?"

The girl shook her head, as if a massive troll had been discovered in the girls' toilets like in the first *Harry Potter* movie. But this was real life, and there were no trolls. There were worse things.

"A girl…in the girls' toilets, up in the girls' boarding house…oh God!" She slapped her hand to her mouth, shaking her head, her pigtails swishing around. "She…she…OH GOD!" She was panicking horribly, as if she might pass out. More teachers and students had rushed towards her, trying to help her to calm down.

"She was lying there…on the floor…her wrists, they were bleeding…I don't think…she wasn't breathing…"

My worst fears became realised. I will never forget that date. Saturday, February 7th, 2015. Simone Van Pyre committed suicide by slitting her wrists with razor blades. She didn't live to see her fourteenth birthday.

At first, it barely registered with me. I was in a strange sort of trance. The world went dull and people transformed into shapes that faded into one another. I started to rise upwards, walking towards the girl as her screams echoed and the sounds of people around me slowed like musical electronic ambience. Someone pulled my arm. I burst into tears. Roger sank towards the floor. Steve fell with him, trying to comfort his friend. Melvin — peacemaker, level-headed, friendly Melvin — crumbled while trying to hold us all together. Karen flashed by. Her eyes locked with mine and she rushed to me, holding me so I wouldn't shatter into shards of human flesh and bone and blood.

Chapter Thirty-Three: Forward

Three weeks later.

Me, sitting in the therapist's office, talking to Henry about the recent events. My aunt thought it best for me to talk to a grief counsellor, but also that therapy might help me to get over everything that had happened.

Simone's death was a clear suicide. The scarring evidence of her past self-harm was slashed side-to-side on her arms, but the slices that took her life ran up her wrist. I once heard a crude joke about self-harm: *sideways is for attention, longways is for results.* I guess humour is an effective way to deal with pain.

She had been very drunk. According to the autopsy, her body had been in a paracletic state. She may not have realised what she'd been doing if she had blacked out. But I knew it was intentional, and it had been building up for a while. Probably years.

Cases of young people and mental illness had started to rise. People in the online sphere were trying to beat the stigma around teenagers who suffered from depression, anxiety, schizophrenia, and conditions like autism and ADHD. I've never been much of an internet person, even now, but I saw floods of news articles. Back in 2017, I read some article about an eighteen-year-old girl in Bletchfield murdering her boyfriend and classmate. No one ever suspects things in small towns.

There was a funeral. It was a small one. I went with my aunt and Zoe, even though I hadn't wanted to. The sight of Simone lying still with her black hair brushed neatly at the sides of her face felt unbearable. I half-expected her to jump out and thump me on the back with some brash statement.

There was also an assembly commemorating Simone, where they also discussed mental illness and suicidal ideation. Mr. Saydes talked about the rise of depression in young people and the overattachment to social media, as well as online bullying. A new school counsellor was appointed, as well as a 24-hour service hotline for people going through a crisis.

Olivia, Kim, Tasha, and Emma all changed their tunes. They kept a distance, and when they saw me, they looked solemn. It didn't last, of course, but the nasty glances and provocative murmurs lessened. They knew they were being watched anyway.

Karen and I started speaking again. While I was at Lakeland, we regained a friendship of sorts, but it was never what it was. She found new friends and a new girlfriend. There was some envy, but mostly, I was happy for her. I knew I'd never forget her — you never forget the sweet honey taste of first love, if you're lucky enough to find it.

Simone wasn't lucky. In a frenzied rage, I went to confront Toby about a week before I started therapy. He was standing out in the school gardens, smoking, and I had an urge to tear his head off his shoulders. He was taller, probably twice as strong as me, but I was willing to take the risk. Hell hath no fury like a woman scorned, as the saying goes.

I marched up to him and thrust my hands deep into his chest, knocking him slightly. He stumbled, utterly confused and confrontational. *"What the hell is your problem?"* he'd said, his cigarette — or joint — falling to the grass. I thrust my fists against his chest.

"Bastard...you b-bastard! Simone is dead and it's all your fault! You k-killed her! You ruined her life! You should be in prison!"

Luckily, Melvin had noticed I had run off and teamed up with Mr. Oseni to find me. They pulled me off the stunned and angry boy, who stared at us in confusion. Later, I received a WhatsApp message from Toby — I had no idea how he'd gotten my number, but he said he was sorry about what had happened to Simone and he'd had no idea she would hurt herself like that. I didn't know if he was being genuine, but I'd had to accept it. We both knew it wasn't his fault. It wasn't anybody's fault.

Not that that made it hurt any less. And what could I have done? I could have charged at him, beaten my fists against his broad chest and thrown insults at him, but it wouldn't have made a difference. It wouldn't have brought her back or changed what he had done to her. And he wouldn't have cared. Maybe he felt bad about her dying, or maybe it was something that bore no resemblance to his life. She was just some emotionally unstable young girl he'd had a brief sexual affair with.

At the funeral, I saw Simone's mum and dad. She had always spoken so poorly of them. They both looked middle-aged, her mother dressed in a black dress with a veil over her head, her father in a black suit with a balding head. Both said they had no idea their daughter was going through so much pain and they wished they had done more to support her. They had no idea who I was, or who any of Simone's friends were. Canel, Melvin, and Steve hadn't wanted to attend the funeral, but they came to the wake ceremony with their parents. Roger was there as well. I felt the sorriest for him. He never got to hold her in his arms and tell her how he felt.

"I should have been there," he told me, the two of us sitting on the stairs of Simone's enormous house in Kensington. "Maybe if I'd told her, she wouldn't have gone out with that dickhead Toby. Maybe she'd still be here."

"There was nothing either of us could have done. We both loved her, Roger. But we c-couldn't save her. People need to save themselves."

"But we can help."

"You can't help a person who doesn't want it. Simone was troubled. I can't imagine what was going through her head. But whatever it was, it g-got the better of her in the end. She decided she'd rather be somewhere else than here."

"Christ, that's morbid." He began to cry, and I put my arms around him.

Where did we go from there?

"I don't know how to move forward," I said to Henry, in that second session, after I had confined the main horrors of my life into the space of forty-five minutes. "Everyone keeps telling me to b-be strong and things will get better, and I want to believe them."

"Don't you believe things can get better?" His German accent was strong. "You've been through so much, especially for someone of your age. But the way you've handled it all is incredible. It shows you have a great strength of character, Anne." He smiled gently at me. "You should be very proud of yourself for the way you've handled all this."

I shook my head. "My aunt and uncle are t-taking me to see her...after this."

"Will you be okay?" he asked gently.

I stared at my hands, feeling the numbness in my body. "I guess it's about time."

Uncle Brian picked me up, surprising me with raspberry filled doughnuts. He winked at me, saying he wouldn't tell my aunt about them. We would be meeting her at the hospital.

I dozed in the car. Their family doctor had prescribed me with a low dosage of antidepressants for my panic attacks and "low mood." Maybe my aunt and uncle were worried I was going to hurt myself like Simone had. I just wanted the pain to go away.

The drive to Charing Cross was long and packed with traffic. I sat up and peered at my shaking palms. My uncle gazed at me, his expression calm and patient.

"Are you all right?" he asked. "We don't have to go in unless you're ready. It will be a bit of a shock."

"Let's just do it. I ha-have to see her."

We got out of the car and entered the hospital, walking through the turquoise and white spaces that smelled of disinfectant and sick people. The intensive care unit was on the eleventh floor of the main tower block. My uncle and I got the lift up, my heart hammering. We entered the unit and the room where she was lying. My aunt was standing outside...with my dad.

"What is *he* doing here?" I hissed. My uncle had his arm on my shoulder. "It's okay, Anne."

"I wanted to make peace with you," said my dad.

I glared at him. "P-Peace? It's *your* fault my mum is in that room right now. If you hadn't—"

"Anne," said my aunt, calmly but firmly. "Now isn't the time."

"Come on, let's go see your mother," urged my uncle. I scanned between the three of them, then walked into the room.

She was lying there, tubes attached to her and white bandages wrapped around her face and arms. Her curly black hair spilled either side of her face. Her arms were so thin, as if they would snap. I approached her. Her eyes were open, and she was gazing at me.

"Anne?" Her voice was breathy and light, like a little girl's. But it was her. I walked towards her, tears welling up my eyes. I took her hand in mine, gazing at my mother, the beautiful woman who had raised me and given birth to me and suffered horribly at the hands of a monster, yet managed to survive despite it all.

The door closed behind me. My uncle clearly wanted to give us some space. I sat on the little chair next to her, rubbing her hand with mine. She blinked, tears running down her face. I wanted to take off the bandages and see her face, but I knew that wasn't wise.

"Mum…I'm here now, Mum. Everything's going to be okay."

Epilogue

Mum's recovery was slow. I don't think she'll ever be the same after what happened. All the trauma associated with my dad and her life in Richmond combined with damage to her brain after he had hurt her created gaps in her memory. She still can't re-call much of the early years of her marriage.

There were a lot of tears and a lot of talk. The next few months were some of the hardest of my life. I ended up not returning to Lakeland until the following year, but I did my GCSEs early so I could go on to do my A Levels faster.

Mum came to live with Aunt Colette and Uncle Brian. I was touched at how hospitable they were. They had to be two of the most incredibly welcoming people I'd ever met. If it weren't for them, I don't know where I'd be today.

Despite everything, I wanted to keep going to Lakeland. It was a good school, and even though things had been tough, I preferred it over Copperwood. I took English, History and Psychology at A Level, achieving A's in all three of them. I'm currently at Royal Holloway University studying History and English. I liked the fact that the campus was on the outskirts of London, but still near enough the city. It was on the commuter belt, so getting the train up to Copperwood was no problem. The campus is surrounded by beautiful trees and parks, just like Lakeland.

I have a new girlfriend as well. We met during my first week at uni, and she's in my history classes. Her name is Natalia, and she's Polish. She's a lovely, sweet girl. There was an older girl I saw briefly during my A levels, but I was too focused on studying and reconnecting with my mum for it to really go anywhere.

I continued seeing Henry for about a year. I rarely stutter nowadays. My panic attacks stopped. I think they started to descend after Simone died, strangely enough. I still think about her sometimes. She's like a ghost that haunts me in my sleep, but she's a friendly ghost. I'm still on antidepressants, though. I was diagnosed with clinical depression last year, which isn't all that surprising.

My dad is another ghost. He passed away in late 2015. I was angry at him for a long time, but I made my peace with him. To say I've fully forgiven him for all the pain he caused would be a lie, but I've let go of a lot of my anger. It won't change what's happened. Life must go on despite terror attacks, missing children, and the world's chaos.

It's 2019, as I sit in my room, writing this. I don't know who I'm writing it for or what I'm going to do with it. My name is Anne Mason, and I'm eighteen years old. Things don't always happen the way we want them to, but in the end, life unfolds on its own terms. It has a way of surprising us — sometimes horribly, sometimes beautifully — but the wills of the universe will always triumph against the wills of humankind. All we can do is let things be and hope good things will come to us while we do our best.

[The End]

Author's Note

People always think that writers base stories on themselves. When I first read *Lolita* I was scratching my head thinking 'was Nabokov a paedophile?' Obviously he wasn't; he was a story-teller weaving fiction.

Anne is not based on me, but of course there are things in my life and other lives I have observed that seeped their way into the story's thread. I would like to stress that Anne's father is in no way like mine. My relationship with my dad has always been wonderful, and he is the greatest man I know. I have a wonderful relationship with my mum as well, who is also strong and loving.

I did not grow up in an abusive household, but I am aware that many across the world have. We're living in an age where single mothers and broken homes are on the rise, and many grow up barely knowing or talking to their fathers. I consider myself deeply lucky to have grown up not only with two parents who care for me, but as someone close to my dad.

This book covers a lot – domestic abuse, family, friendship, class, race, sexuality, growing up, mental illness. Above all, it is a book about finding yourself and your place, and about how the lives of us all intertwine with one another. Anne is a strong girl who goes through a lot and comes out of it well-adjusted despite it all. Young people are swamped with pressures of social media, a tough economy and rising mental illness, yet a lot of us are still able to turn out alright. Anne is three years younger than me, but I like to think that she goes on to be happy and successful in her life.

Simone is the character most like me; both musicians, both talkative, and both struggle with anxiety, depression and drinking problems. Thankfully I made it to recovery; Simone wasn't so lucky, but I wanted to show that for every person that comes out in one piece, there are those that don't make it. Her story is part of Anne's story and probably many of our stories because we all know someone who sadly doesn't make it through their pain.

The story of how and when this tale was executed is unusual. We'll have to travel back in time to the year 2006 – I was nine. This is taken from my diary at the time:

I saw her on Monday 23rd October 2006. Me, mummy and Ona were walking to the bus stop to go to Wood Green. We were near Stamford Hill Library, just a road away. I saw her; without an adult. Mummy and Ona paid no attention, but I kept on glancing at the calm, boring face. She wore all black except for her lovely earrings. She looked at least 10-12. She got on a bus and left afterwards.

This was my original blurb:

He couldn't cope with me. So I was shoved into Boarding School.

Hello. My name is Anne Wayleds. My only friend is my dead mum. My horrible dad actually KILLED her when I was 10. I'm 12 now. My dad shoved me into Lakeland Boarding School. I suppose it's ok, except for one big problem.

Karen.

Enjoy my story.

In my original idea, Karen was to be the main bully, but later she changed to become Anne's love interest.

How did I come up with this? I neither know nor remember. Two big influences were probably EastEnders and the many Jacqueline Wilson novels I read as a child. In *Vicky Angel*, the two main characters visit 'Lakelands Shopping Centre' at one point which is where I likely got the name from.

I tried to write this story as a child but realised quickly that it was too dense and mature for me to handle. So, I put it aside and didn't resume until 2015, when I was seventeen and in sixth form. I began to work on it for the next few years as well as other works of fiction, including *Every Last Thought* and *Psycho Girl*, both of which came to form my self-published novella collection *Every Last Psycho*, which I published in 2018 after having no luck with agents and publishing houses.

After publishing *Every Last Psycho*, I had a dystopian novella I worked on for several months, until I realised after an editorial assessment that it needed a lot more work than I had thought it did. As *Every Last Psycho* was YA, I decided to turn my attention back to that genre, so resumed Anne in late 2018. Most of what formed the final novel was written in 2016 and 2017, and my dear friend Bibsi read through it and made notes and edits.

I never finished a full draft of *Anne* before this year; I had about 55K words down and so decided I would finish it in early 2019, get it edited and sort the cover out like I had with *Every Last Psycho*, and publish.

My goals are to continue writing and to hopefully get myself a literary agent this year or next. It can all get pretty overwhelming, but for someone who is not yet twenty-two and has been dreaming of publishing books since she was five, it's a pretty emotionally rewarding journey.

Zarina Macha
London, 2019

Acknowledgements

I would like to thank my dear friend Bibsi, who read this one first. Your endless support and love are indescribable. My heart is always open to you.

Thank you to my parents, my sister, brother and Trish – great now I'm just repeating the same acknowledgments that were in *Every Last Psycho*. Eurgh, this is awkward. You know I love you, wouldn't be who I am without you, bring out the violins, etc etc. It's always good to have family, especially one that cares for you.

Also thanks to some wonderful humans I'm blessed to have known these past several years – Kinga, John, Steph, Alicia, Dienga, Mannie, Paloma, Rhasan and Deborah for your lovely support of my literary work, including this one. Friends should always support each other and build each other up. A big especial thanks to Kat – you're the best haha; thanks for editing the blurb, supporting me as a mate and as my personal marketing assistant! Let's thrive on this journey together.

Thank you to the brilliant bloggers and writers who have read and reviewed my stuff – Robert J. Fanshawe, Lloyd Dwaah, Petrina Binney, Christine Fritzen, MA Thomas, Lynn James and Steph Warren of the fabulous 'Bookshine and Readbows' blog in particular. Also thanks to all the other authors and bloggers I have been networking with online, especially on Facebook! I have a lot to learn about this self-publishing game, but with guidance from others I'm learning constantly.

Thank you to all the wonderful people at Global Fusion Music and Arts including Louisa Le Marchand, Gill Swan, Maggie Wood and everybody who has supported me and my family over the years and provided platforms for artistic expression.

Big thanks to Bethany Votaw for her beta read and suggestions which shaped my last draft. Cheers once again to the fabulous oliva pro design for another awesome (and affordable) cover. A major dollop of gratitude to the amazing word nerd Monica Black who polished up the manuscript and totally understood Anne's story.

But most of all, thank you reader. Seriously, without an audience, artists are just talking to the wall. It's nice to have something come out of my bedroom and into another human's hands. Dunno why that sounds wrong. ANYWAY. If you enjoyed this book, a quick review on Amazon and Goodreads would be a MASSIVE help, and if you could review any other independently published books you've enjoyed by other authors (one or two sentences is enough, guys and gals) then that would be fabulous. We all need to help one another out in this ever-growing world of entrepreneurial artistic spirit. Ok at this point I'm running out of things to say. Look, a cat with bright eyes.

(If I forgot to mention anyone please do not take it personally – this section is more bloody difficult to write than the actual book. Let it be known that I appreciate the support of every soul that ignites the fire within my creative work.)

To see more info about me and my stories, visit the links listed here:

Website: www.zarinamacha.co.uk
Blog: www.thezarinamachablog.co.uk
Facebook: www.facebook.com/zarinamachaauthor
Twitter: www.twitter.com/zarinamacha
Instagram: www.instagram.com/zarinamacha
Music: www.zarina.bandcamp.com/releases
Music blog: www.zaridoesmusic.co.uk

Email: info@zarinamacha.co.uk

Many thanks for reading and purchasing. It really does mean a lot.

Printed in Great Britain
by Amazon

43713095R00158